AUG - - 2017

Hello,
Sunshine

Hello, Sunshine

LEILA HOWLAND

HYPERION

Los Angeles   New York

First Hardcover Edition, July 2017
3 5 7 9 10 8 6 4 2
FAC-020093-17151
Printed in the United States of America

This book is set in Adobe Garamond Pro/Monotype
Designed by Torborg Davern

Library of Congress Cataloging-in-Publication Data
Names: Howland, Leila.
Title: Hello, sunshine / Leila Howland.
Description: First edition. • Los Angeles ; New York : Hyperion, 2017.
Summary: "When Becca Harrington is rejected from every college on her list, she
decides to move to L.A. with dreams of becoming a star, until reality sets in to often
hilarious and sometimes heartbreaking results"—Provided by publisher.
Identifiers: LCCN 2016027020 • ISBN 9781484725450 (hardback) •
ISBN 148472545X (hardcover)
Subjects: CYAC: Interpersonal relations—Fiction. Self-esteem—Fiction. Actors
and actresses—Fiction. Moving, Household—Fiction. Los Angeles (Calif.)—
Fiction. BISAC: JUVENILE FICTION / Performing Arts / General. JUVENILE
FICTION / Social Issues / Friendship. JUVENILE FICTION / Love & Romance.
Classification: LCC PZ7.H8465 Hel 2017 / DDC [Fic]—dc23
LC record available at https://lccn.loc.gov/2016027020

Reinforced binding
Visit www.hyperionteens.com

SUSTAINABLE FORESTRY INITIATIVE
Certified Sourcing
www.sfiprogram.org
SFI-00993

THIS LABEL APPLIES TO TEXT STOCK

For my mother, Phebe Jane,
who gave me roots and wings.

PROLOGUE

"OH MY GOD, we're almost there!"

Alex smirks at my enthusiasm as we see a sign for the exit we've been headed toward for two weeks. We've driven all the way from Boston in this rickety old Volvo, and the passenger seat has kind of started to feel like home. I can't believe our trip is almost over. My breath gets shallow and my heart accelerates. The dream that's been in the future since April—since I was a little kid, actually—is about to be the present.

I'm totally psyched, but as a clammy sweat breaks out on my forehead, I also feel queasy. It doesn't help that it's a hundred and twelve degrees outside, and this car's old air-conditioning system only gets the temperature down to the low nineties. I switch to a more upbeat playlist on the iPhone, unroll the passenger-side window of Alex's car, and let the hot, dry wind wash over me.

"Look out, LA! Here I come!" I shout out the window.

A guy in an old BMW makes a nasty gesture with his tongue.

"Ew!" I say, and I duck back inside the car and roll up the window. "Ew! Alex, that guy just went like this." I show him the tongue move and Alex laughs, waving it off.

"Forget about him, Becca," Alex says. "Stay focused. What's your number-one goal again?"

"Get an agent. I will not rest until I have one. If Brooke can do it, so can I."

"Bet your ass," Alex says, and switches lanes.

Brooke was my main acting competition in high school, and she got into Tisch, NYU's theater school. When I didn't get accepted anywhere she was such a dick about it. Everyone felt bad for me—Carter Academy has a 99.9 percent matriculation rate, after all—but Brooke took her pity to a new level. I almost barfed on the spot when I learned that she'd found an agent literally the day after she moved to New York for a summer Shakespeare seminar. She'd been discovered at a café near Washington Square Park, wherever that is. Within a week, she'd booked an in-flight safety video for Delta.

"Oh, I love this song." I turn up the volume to get Brooke and her perfect skin out of my mind. The latest girl-power song from my favorite pop princess blasts from the speakers. "I know you hate this jam, but I really need to sing it right now. Okay?"

"Go for it," Alex says, and turns up the volume even higher. He grins at me as I belt out the song off-key. When he smiles, lines from his eyes frame his cheeks—the result of a relentlessly happy childhood. He's had everything that money can buy and everything it can't, too. It was really no surprise when he got into Stanford early.

The car does that shaky thing it's been doing since Utah whenever we get up to seventy miles an hour. "Come on, Ruby, don't fail us now," Alex says.

I thought of the name Ruby when he bought the car from his next-door neighbor last year.

"What do you think, is Ruby actually going to make it all the way to Palo Alto?" Alex asked. After he drops me at my cousin's place, he'll be taking the scenic route up the coast.

"Oh yeah," I say. "She's a trouper."

"Easy, baby," Alex says to Ruby, who is rattling more than usual. Alex's jaw flexes as he signals and heads toward the exit. Even after two years of dating he can still make me melt. He has a strong jaw and the nose of a future leader. His eyes are the color of a lake on an overcast day, and his blond hair smells woodsy close to his neck. And don't even get me started on his body. He's a champion skier and has the legs and ass to show for it. Last night we had the most amazing time at a motel in Palm Springs. We couldn't get enough of each other. We barely slept. The people in the next room actually complained to the front desk, which we laughed about for the next hour, as quietly as possible, of course.

Alex turns on his indicator and takes the exit for Orange

Grove Boulevard. Vivian's exit. We're almost there. Oh my God. *We're almost there.*

"How hard can getting an agent actually be?" I ask. Alex opens his mouth to answer, but I stop him. "Famous last words, I know. I should probably learn how to wear eye makeup for on-camera auditions. I'm going to need some new looking-for-agent clothes, because everything I have feels a little too . . . I don't know . . . Boston." Alex seems nervous as the car slows, and we turn onto a wide boulevard lined with tall, evenly spaced palm trees. I know how he feels. I'm so nervous I can't seem to stop talking. "Can you believe how perfect last night was? That was the best night ever. We have to go back to Palm Springs!"

"Becca," Alex says. He bites his lip as he makes a left on to Bradford Street, Vivian's street.

"I don't want to say good-bye. I really, really don't want to," I say. I feel carsick actually, and a little untethered. We slow down in front of Vivian's complex.

Alex looks pale as he parallel parks, and yet, even with his pallid complexion, the sight of him nearly takes my breath away. I snap a picture, the last of the roll of film. Before we left, my mom gave me her old camera so that I could take pictures with actual film. It's nothing fancy, just a vintage-y point-and-shoot from when she was my age. I've spaced the twenty-four shots out over the course of our road trip.

"Why'd you do that?" he asks.

"You just look so cute when you parallel park, and I'm not going to get to see you do it again for a while," I say, and inhale sharply. I have a cramp, like I get when we do the mile run for gym class. I clutch my side.

"You okay?" he asks.

"I'm just freaking out a little. I can do this, right?"

"Of course you can," he says. He turns the engine off and faces me. I put my hand on his leg. "But . . . we need to say good-bye now."

"I know. Your orientation is tomorrow. At least we have the Jones concert in six weeks. How many days? I think it'll be easier if I think in terms of days—"

"Actually," he says, his face rearranging in an unfamiliar way, "I think we should take a beat."

"A what?" At first his words don't register. But then he tilts his head, looks me in the eye, and squeezes my hand. My heart drops straight through the floor of the car and lands with a sizzle on the hot tar. "Wait. You're breaking up with me?"

He inhales a definitive breath.

"Why?" I ask. My stomach turns over. For a second I think I might throw up.

"Everyone knows long distance doesn't work," he says.

"But we won't be *that* far apart. It's only an hour by plane. There are airfare deals all the time!"

"It's not just that. I want to make a fresh start, you know? It's a new chapter of my life, and I want to be able to throw myself into it. And so should you."

"Are you telling me this is for my own good or something?" I ask.

"We're going to be doing such different things. I think it'll be hard for us to relate. We're in different phases of our lives."

"I wouldn't call it a different *life phase*. Didn't we just graduate from the same high school?"

"Look," Alex says as he wipes sweat from his upper lip. "A part of me wishes that I could stay with you and cheer you on. . . ."

"You can!"

"But I'm going to be so involved in my own life at Stanford. And I deserve to be able to enjoy myself."

"You *deserve* it?" It sounds like a sentence he's been practicing. I feel a sharp stab in my chest as I wonder how long he's known he was going to do this. "How long have you been planning this? The whole trip?"

"I guess I've been thinking about it for a while. Hey, you deserve your freedom, too."

"I don't want any more freedom," I say. "I'm scared of all the freedom I have."

"You're going to be fine," he says.

"You don't really think I'm going to make it, do you?" I ask. I'm in so much pain that I'm on the verge of hyperventilating. My ears are buzzing.

"That's not true," he says without looking me in the eye. He pops the trunk and gets out of the car.

Vivian emerges from her condo wearing a preppy tunic, white jeans, and a huge grin. She waves from her door. I try to signal for her to go back inside until Alex and I can talk more—this is all happening so suddenly, can it even be real?—but she doesn't get it. I step out of the car, heart pounding even as my blood seems to slow. Alex hands me my suitcase and purse as Vivian walks toward us across an impossibly green lawn.

"Hey, girl!" Vivian calls.

"Hi," I say through a broken smile, and then I turn back to Alex and ask quietly, "What about last night?"

"It was great," he says as though this has nothing to do with anything.

I open my mouth to speak, but I can't think of what to say to this boy who I've loved for two years, who I thought loved me.

"Take care," he says.

Take care? What does that even mean?

Seconds before Vivian reaches us, he gives me a stiff hug and hops in the still-running car. I wait for Ruby to be out of sight, and then I turn to Vivian and burst into tears.

ONE

"REFRIGERATOR, what are you trying to tell me?" I ask. It's five days later. It's also 4 a.m. I've been listening to the refrigerator's cycle of whines and moans for hours now. Since other methods of quieting it have failed, I talk to it. My hand grazes the white door. "I can't help you unless you tell me what's wrong." It sputters. "Fine, be that way." I turn over, curling into a question mark on my sleeping bag. I'm lying on the kitchen floor in my Carter Academy T-shirt and granny panties I've had since eighth grade. I thought they'd be comforting, but they aren't.

I've been trying to fall asleep for five hours. I've breathed according to a pocket-size book about meditation, read the *People* magazine I bought near the bus stop in Pasadena, memorized half of a Shakespearean sonnet, and flipped the pillow to the cool side, but nothing has worked. I'd hoped that tonight's sleep would be long and deep and give me a new perspective in the morning, because right now the challenges ahead seem to await me like the pack of wolves that I imagine are prowling outside the door of this Hollywood apartment building. The building is named the Chateau Bronson. The only castle-y things about it are the majestic font on the building's sign and the odd drawbridge-inspired door.

At 4:17, I decide to get up and finish cleaning my new apartment. Maybe scrubbing this place until it gleams will get my spirits up. A single bird chirps somewhere outside. I kick myself out of the sleeping bag that still smells vaguely like a camping trip I took as part of the junior year science program, the one where Alex and I first kissed. Why does everything have to remind me of him? And why does it take five whole business days for 1-800-GET-A-BED to deliver a twin bed to a major US city?

I turn on the halogen lamp that I found on the sidewalk yesterday. It leans a little to the left, but it works. I almost took the mattress that was next to it—it looked brand-new, but in a flash I could see my mom's face grimacing in disgust, and I didn't touch it. I blink for a second against the light and look around at my new place. I'd shut the curtains, but I don't have any. I pull on my pajama bottoms, tie up my hair in a ponytail, and get to work.

The apartment is one room, about the size of my bedroom back home, with a wooden floor that's covered in a thick layer of brown paint. The kitchenette is off to the right. There's my friend the fridge, whining and pitched slightly forward, a mustard-yellow 1970s oven, and a small sink. It could be depressing, but the nook by the window has potential. I narrow my eyes and picture curtains, a bunch of wildflowers in a mason jar, a steaming cup of tea. I can fix this up, I think, instagramming it in my mind.

I open a kitchen cabinet that has a strange metal interior. I don't know what it's for, but I feel like Alex would, because he just knows stuff—like that the raised stones on the cobblestone streets in Beacon Hill were used by ladies to step into their horse-drawn carriages. Or that when people say something is "neither here nor there" they're quoting Shakespeare without knowing it.

My heart lurches at the thought of him up at Stanford, where he's probably started his classes. Did we really break up? How is it possible that just a week ago we were in Texas, dancing in a country bar, laughing and getting stepped on because we were the only ones who didn't know the moves? How have we not spoken since he dropped me at Vivian's? I feel a sharp pain in my gut, like a thumbtack is being stuck into a vital organ. What the hell happened?

I've gone over our conversation a hundred times at least, trying to remember every detail in order to make sense of it, and it doesn't add up. How does a person just cut another person off like that with no warning? Was he just having a pre-college freak-out? That's got to be it. He had a similar freak-out the summer after junior year, before he headed to Maine. He broke up with me saying that he wanted space, but called me the next day practically in tears and invited me up for the Fourth of July. This is probably just a more exaggerated version of that.

And anyway, he didn't actually say he wanted to break up. He said he wanted to "take a beat," which is a totally different thing. I was the one who said the words *break up*. He's obviously in denial. It's not possible that I can just be erased. Right? I'm not calling him first, though; there's no way. He's the one who messed up. I have to let him figure that out on his own.

Be present, I think, fishing up a bit of wisdom from the mini meditation book. Be where you are. I grab the cleaning spray and paper towels from the weird metal cabinet and open up all the windows. I lean out of one and inhale the predawn air, looking for the bird with the continuous, high-pitched chirp. The streetlights illuminate the treetops, telephone wires, other apartment buildings, and the sidewalk below. A subtle breeze washes over me. There is the faint smell of jasmine, which I only recognize because of the tea my mom drinks by the gallon back home.

A few streets over there's some kind of palace. The grand, gold-tipped turrets stand high above the dingy rooftops crawling with satellite dishes. What is that place? A temple? An embassy? A movie star's home?

I hold the windowsill and feel the grime like soft sand on my fingertips. I pull my hand away—it's gray. This place is so dirty. I'd better tackle the bathroom before I lose all my courage. It's like Mom always said: do the hardest homework first while you have the energy. I take in one more lungful of morning air and get down to business.

The bathroom looks like it hasn't been updated . . . ever. There's black mold in the corners of the shower, mysterious yellowy-brown spots on the ceiling, and an all-over film of filth. I admit it: for a moment I think about going back to Boston, but there's no chance in hell. I'm not going back east until I prove that everyone is wrong to feel sorry for me for not getting accepted into college. It was all so unfair. I was suspended for skipping school to go to a secret daytime concert at Cambridge Comics. A bunch of us did it, but I was the only one who got caught, and I wouldn't name names. It turns out that one black mark on my school record was enough for college admissions people to put me in the reject pile. It makes me so mad to think about it. I'm not leaving this place without a victory.

I can do this, I tell myself as I spray the bathroom mirror and wipe it down. I already am doing this. I smile at my reflection. Even though Mom didn't want me to go, even though she wants me to do something practical and résumé-building, or as she puts it "creative *and* practical," I can't help but think that on some level, if she could see me right now with this adventurous spirit flickering behind my tired eyes, she'd be proud.

"So can I ask your advice about something?" I ask Mom a few minutes later on FaceTime. I'm still in the bathroom cleaning, but I hold the phone close to my face so that she can't get a good look at my surroundings until I've had some time to explain. She's going to be pissed. I was thinking I would wait until the just-right moment to tell her, but the state of this bathroom is an emergency. I've doused the tub with several blasts of All-Natural Multipurpose Cleaner but can't make any headway with the stains.

"Sure, honey. What is it?" Mom blinks back at me from our kitchen, where I watch her pour hot water into a mug. "Wait, what time is it there?"

"Four thirty, I think."

She almost chokes on her tea. "What are you doing up?"

"I never went to sleep."

"Why?" Mom asks. I drop the soaked paper towel in a grocery bag, which I'm using as the trash, and head into the main room. The faintest light is seeping into the sky. If I had a comfy sofa, I'd flop on it. Instead, I sit back down on my sleeping bag and lean against the wall. Noticing the background for the first time, Mom asks, "Where are you?"

"Before you freak out, I want you to know that I'm safe," I say.

"Jesus. Where's Vivian?" Mom asks, trying to see behind me.

"Probably at her place in Pasadena?" I say, and I brace myself.

I was supposed to stay with Vivian until I got a job to support my acting dreams in LA. Mom was hoping for some sort of 9-to-5 office-job-with-potential, even though I explained I needed something more flexible for auditions, like waitressing. But Pasadena felt almost worse than Boston, where my failure followed me like a stinky fart. Vivian's condo complex was full of what she calls "young professionals," but what I call "middle-aged squares." There were literally no sidewalks within a two-mile radius, so I couldn't go anywhere except the condo complex gym, and she made her point of view on my situation abundantly clear. ("Acting is a total waste of time. Hardly anyone makes it. You're just going to wake up when you're my age and realize that you're five years behind everyone else! Quit now and focus on getting your shit together.")

"You've lost me, Becca," Mom says, her brow pinched with concern.

"I'm not exactly at Vivian's anymore," I say, gritting my teeth.

"What?" Mom yells. "Becca Harrington, where are you?"

"I couldn't stay there. Vivian's energy was really getting me down. She's not a feminist, Mom. She told me I needed to get married on 'the right side of twenty-five.' Can you believe it?"

"I want answers," Mom says in her sternest voice.

"I found a place in Hollywood. It's a studio in a vintage building. It's cute. See?" I pull the phone back to give her a narrow view of my place.

"No, no, no. This was not our deal. Our deal was that you were supposed to find a job before you left Vivian's—if you left Vivian's at all."

"I'll find some sort of way to pay my rent. Bartending or babysitting or something."

"Babysitting?" The vein in Mom's right temple pops out.

"How is that going to look on your college applications? Don't you know how important this year is?"

"I'm going to put my *acting* work on my applications," I say, regretting this phone call with my entire being. "That's the whole point of being here!"

"We agreed that you'd find something résumé-building to do out there *while* you auditioned. You can do two things at once, you know. We had a plan—"

"I never agreed to that part of the plan, remember? The only thing I officially agreed to was reapplying to college, and that I'd come home after a year if I didn't get in anywhere. That's what we shook on." She sighs. "It's just one year, Mom. If I'm going to do this, I have to really do it, you know? I can't hide out in a condo in Pasadena."

Mom closes her eyes and takes a deep breath.

"Where is this apartment?" she asks. She looks as tired as I feel. Mom had me when she was only twenty. I was the result of a one-night stand she had on Martha's Vineyard. My dad, some guy who could speak French fluently and who had awesome cheekbones, was never in the picture. This was right after her sophomore year of college, so she's much younger than my friends' moms. Her dream was to be a marine biologist. She'd just declared her major when she learned I was on the way. She promises me that she doesn't regret a single moment of my existence, but I know being a pharmaceutical sales rep was not what she had in mind for herself. I swear, sometimes she could pass for a teenager, especially when she does stuff like sit on the floor in bookstores. But right now, she looks older than her age, and I don't like it.

"I'm near the Hollywood Hills. That's where the movie stars live." I say. "See?" I hold the phone so that she can see the Hollywood sign in the distance. I have to hang out the window a bit and twist my body to the left to get a view of the whole thing, but it's worth it for the inspiration.

"That *is* kind of cool," Mom says, her voice a little softer now. I turn the phone back to face me and see in her eyes that light I've been waiting for. "But is this neighborhood safe?"

"Would movie stars live somewhere unsafe?" I ask, glancing at the sidewalk below. A skinny guy talks to himself as he searches through garbage cans. I smile back at Mom, and she raises an eyebrow. She's not exactly buying this pitch. "It's really cute, Mom. There are cafés and a used bookstore and a supermarket all within walking distance. You'd love it."

"You know you can always come home, right?"

"I know."

We stare at each other for a second. She's sensing something's off. I can tell by the way she's searching my eyes. I study the floor.

"What does Alex think of all this?" she asks.

Damn! She's good.

"Actually, we're . . . taking a beat," I say, and hold my breath.

"A what? A *beep*?"

"A *beat*. Like a rest. As in . . . not permanent," I say.

"That doesn't sound good, Becca," Mom says. "Are you

okay?" I nod, still holding my breath. "I want to talk to you about this, but I'm already running late. Why didn't you call me earlier?"

"Because I'm fine and he's just having a panic attack. Please, trust me, okay?"

"I'm trying," she says, lines gathering in the corners of her eyes as she squints. "I'm trying. Bye, sweetie. And remember you can always come home."

"Wait, wait, Mom! What about the advice?"

"Oh yeah. What is it?"

"The bathroom is a little . . . nasty. I need to know how to get rid of mold and rust." Her eyes widen in horror. "Mom, deep breath. It's fine, really. It just needs some freshening up. Please."

"What have you been using?" she asks.

I hold up the All-Natural Multipurpose Cleaner.

"You need bleach," she says, shaking her head. "And Lime Out for the rust." Then she tells me how to put a rag on the end of the broom to get the corners of the shower. "And please wear gloves."

"Should I really use stuff that toxic?" I ask.

"You know what's toxic? Mold. Call me tonight. I love you, Becca."

"Love you, too," I say. "Mom?" I'm waiting for her to tell me that she loves me to the sky, to which I always reply "and back." It's our thing. But it's too late. She's already hung up.

TWO

ONCE THE SUN RISES, I throw on some clean clothes, deciding there's nothing more civilized than fresh, well-fitting underwear, and head to the supermarket to get my toxic cleaning supplies and some food. A cool breeze rustles the palm fronds high above me, though I can feel heat coiled in the air. Bright, tropical-looking flowers peek at me from slightly dilapidated front yards. I reach Franklin Avenue and am surprised by the number of cars rushing by. It's not even 6 a.m. yet. Where is everyone going?

I stop by a supermarket called the Mayfair Market and pick up yogurt, a bagel, soap, Lime Out, and bleach, and then search for shower curtains. They don't sell them here, so I'm going to have to make my own. I'll get a real one later, but the need for a shower *now* is intense. I feel a little kick of pride at my ingenuity as I throw duct tape and extra-large, heavy-duty garbage bags into the cart.

I spot a copy of *Backstage*, the trade magazine for actors, in the checkout lane. For a moment my hunger and discomfort disappear. The lead to my first job might be inside this magazine. Slightly breathless, I open to the casting section. The first notice calls for four "adorable actresses" who must be "comfortable with love scenes." After noting where aspiring ingénues should send their headshots it says in bold: "Nudity required. No pay."

Ugh.

"Miss, are you okay?" the cashier asks.

"Yes," I say, debating whether to buy the magazine. It's just one ad, I tell myself. I toss the *Backstage* on the conveyor belt. "I'm fine."

When I get back to the Chateau Bronson, I put my cleaning supplies and groceries away and then head all the way up the stairs with my untoasted, unadorned bagel. The landlord said something about a rooftop terrace. I push the door open and almost laugh. This is hardly a "terrace." It's just a regular roof, the uneven surface covered in a gray, sandpaper-like material. There are a couple of scattered, rusty beach chairs. Still, the light is a cool blue-yellow and there's a nice breeze. I see a bunch of tall buildings in the distance, and I'm trying to figure out what it is—Santa Monica? Downtown?—when a voice startles me.

"Sometimes you can see the ocean."

"Huh?" I relax when I see the guy who's sitting in a beach chair with a computer on his lap. He looks about my age, maybe a little older. He has a soft smile and bright eyes. His hair is cropped close and neat. An open collar displays his long neck and a peek of clavicle. Even though he's sitting down, I can tell he's not too tall, which I like. I already feel too short most of the time.

"Sorry," he says. "I didn't mean to scare you. I came up here to see if I could find some writing inspiration. I'm Raj Singh."

"I'm Becca Harrington," I say.

"Did you just move in?" he asks, and stands up.

"Yesterday," I say. I was right. He isn't too tall. In fact, he might be one of those rare guys short enough for me to kiss without having to stand on my tiptoes. I hope that thought travels to Alex. I hope it zips up the 5 Freeway all the way to Palo Alto and bites him like a horsefly.

"Welcome to the Chateau." He makes a goofy gesture, bowing like he's lord of a great castle, and I have to laugh. He's suddenly serious again, and I worry that I've embarrassed him. "It's kind of smoggy today. But on a clear day after it rains, you really can see all the way to the ocean." I squint, but a stripe of brownish haze rests along the horizon, blocking the view. "Raymond Chandler used to live across the street." I'm not totally sure who Raymond Chandler is, but from the way Raj said his name I know I'm supposed to. "But who knows. They say he lived everywhere. Pretty much any historical building you go to, Raymond Chandler lived there."

"The guy got around, I guess. Hey, what's that place?" I ask, pointing to the golden turrets.

"Oh, that's the Scientology Centre. Stay away. You don't want to mess with them," Raj says. "Did you move here by yourself?"

"Yeah," I say. And even though seconds ago I wished my thoughts would sting Alex, I miss him in a punched-in-the-gut way.

"That's really brave," he says.

"Thanks." But I don't feel brave, just alone. Alex literally left me on the curb, Vivian thinks I'm a nut, and if I'm honest with Mom about how I feel, she might actually convince me to go home. *Don't cry,* I tell myself. *Hold it in.*

"You okay?" Raj asks.

"I'm just really tired. I didn't sleep much last night."

"Maybe you could sleep now?" Raj asks.

"I think I'll try," I say.

"Hey, I'm in number seven if you need anything."

"Thanks," I say, and I head back down to my apartment, more exhausted than I've ever been in my whole life.

Despite my grand plans and new supplies, I can't imagine cleaning the shower right now. I put on flip-flops, make my duct-tape-and-garbage-bag shower curtain, and take a hot shower without touching anything but the faucet handles. Then I climb back into my sleeping bag, throw a T-shirt over my eyes to keep out the light, and after twenty-four hours of being painfully awake, I finally fall asleep.

THREE

THE CALIFORNIA SUN wakes me up after only three hours. I squeeze my eyes shut and bury my head in my arms. I had that dream about Alex again, the one I've had several nights in a row. We're at a costume party and he pretends he doesn't know me, even when I take off my elaborate feathery mask. My mouth is dry, my jaw hurts, and I'm sweating through my T-shirt. I unzip the sleeping bag and stretch out on top of it, hoping I can get at least another hour, but it's no use.

The apartment is wide-awake, flooded with buttery mid-morning sunshine. Outside birds are singing, a truck beeps as it backs up, a leaf blower roars, and someone coaches her dog to go potty in baby talk. The *Backstage* lays disheveled and exposed next to me like a one-night stand, the kind I've only seen in movies. I push it aside, sit up, and rub my eyes.

The day in front of me seems gaping and enormous. I think about my friends—and of course Alex—starting college. They probably have orientations and class schedules and planned-out days. They're decorating dorm rooms and becoming instant best friends with their roommates. I wish someone would orient me, but I'm going to have to do it myself. Mom once told me that happiness can be as simple as creating goals. The important thing is to keep them realistic and achievable. I grab my notebook, prop myself against the wall, and start my list.

1. Get an agent!
2. Get curtains.
3. Get a pillow.
4. Buy pots and pans.
5. Get a kitchen table, bed, and a dresser.
6. Go to the grocery store and get ingredients for healthy meals.
7. Learn how to apply subtle yet effective eye makeup.
8. Get a job to make $$$!
9. Get a friend. (Friends?)
10. Get a new style, new wardrobe, etc.
11. Become a working actress!

The list veers so quickly out of the realm of the realistically achievable that I feel nauseous, but before I can stop myself I have to add one more thing.

8.	Get a job to make $ $ $!
9.	Get a friend. (Friends?)
10.	Get a new style, new wardrobe, etc.
11.	Become a working actress!
12.	Get Alex back

My autonomic nervous system is about to accelerate into full panic when there's a knock at my door. I tense up and lean forward. Who is it? The Scientologists? The landlord? Raj? The knocker knocks again, this time a little more firmly. I leap to my feet and pull on my jeans. Maybe it's 1-800-GET-A-BED, running ahead of schedule.

"Hello?" I ask from behind the safety of the locked door.

"Hi," a girl's voice answers.

With the chain still fastened, I open the door a crack and peek outside. Standing there is a girl with brown eyes as big as a cartoon princess's. Her dark hair falls around her shoulders in loose, fresh-from-the-beach curls. She's wearing a short white dress and cowboy boots.

"I'm Marisol," she says. "I live in number nine. I need some help."

"I'm Becca," I say, unlocking the chain and opening the door. "What's wrong?"

"You are not going to believe this shit, but I just locked myself out of my apartment. And literally seconds later, I started my period. I have an audition in exactly twenty-eight minutes in . . . Wait for it." She holds up her hand and purses her lips. "Culver City."

"Oh my God," I say, though I have no idea where Culver City is.

"I know, right? I have about five more seconds before I ruin my dress and ten seconds until I'm officially late. If I could have a tampon and use your bathroom, I will love you for life."

"Oh, sure. Come on in," I say, feeling a little self-conscious as I gesture for her to enter. "It's a little, um, rustic. I just moved in."

"Girl, is that where you sleep?" she asks, pointing to my sleeping bag with one hand as she holds her dress away from herself with the other.

"Kind of," I say. "I just got here yesterday." I dig through my suitcase until I find the crushed box of tampons that's traveled with me all the way from Boston. "I didn't exactly sleep last night. It's more . . . where I lie down." Marisol throws her head back in a genuine laugh, and I feel myself relax. "Take as many as you need." I present her with a fistful of tampons. "Take them all!"

"I only need a couple," she says, plucking two from the bunch. She tiptoes over my strewn belongings to the bathroom. The air she's passed through buzzes with energy and the scent of hair product. She's going to be my friend. I can just feel it.

"Dude," she says as she shuts the door. "This shower situation is hard-core. The garbage bag and the duct tape . . . ?"

"I only brought one suitcase," I say, wondering if she thinks I'm some kind of psycho. Seconds later, I hear her running the water and wish I'd bought hand soap at the Mayfair instead of just the bar of travel-size Dove. At least there's toilet paper, I think, even if it is painfully cheap. Literally. "And I don't have a car, so I just had to grab what I could from the Mayfair and make the best of it."

"No car?" she asks, emerging from the bathroom and flicking the excess water from her hands. I shake my head no. Some mixture of surprise and horror darts across her face before she assumes a neutral expression and says, "That's probably for the best since there's no parking here at the Chateau Bronson." She casts her eyes around the apartment. "But somehow, someway, you need to make an Ikea run stat. I'd take you myself, but I won't be back until tonight."

"That's okay. I can take the bus."

"How are you going to get the stuff back?"

"A cab?"

"That will cost a fortune! Just wait. I can do it on Friday if you want. I'm free." She glances in the vanity mirror, scrunches her hair, and swipes on orange lipstick. If I wore that color, people would think I'd lost my mind, but Marisol looks chic as she smiles in the mirror.

"What's your audition for?"

"Dog food," she says, swinging her purse over her shoulder and heading for the door. "That's right, I'm getting all dolled up for one line in a dog food commercial. Just what my grandma dreamed of when she swam here from Cuba."

"Your grandma swam from Cuba?"

"I'm teasing," Marisol said. "She had a raft. Anyway, knock on my door tomorrow. I'll show you my place."

"You bet," I say, blushing because I sound just like my mom. I watch Marisol skip down the stairs to her own little rhythm. I go back inside the apartment, pick up my list, and put a faint but hopeful check next to number nine.

	7.	Learn how to apply subtle yet effective eye makeup.
	8.	Get a job to make $$$!
✓	9.	Get a friend. (Friends?)
	10.	Get a new style, new wardrobe, etc.
	11.	Become a working actress!

After Marisol's exit, my apartment swells with emptiness. Seeing the place through someone else's eyes makes me realize how much I have to do to make it livable. I take in the wooden floor, which seems to have acquired another layer of dust in just a few hours, the sleeping bag, the suitcase and rumpled clothes, the open *Backstage*, the paper shopping bag/trash can from the Mayfair, and of course, the refrigerator. I snap a few pictures with my phone. I left the camera that my mom gave me on the front seat of Alex's car. As soon as he calls I'm going to ask him to send it. But I couldn't post those pictures online anyway, and right now that's what I want to do. I'll need to capture the "before" of this place so my mom and my forty-nine followers on Instagram can truly appreciate the "after."

The despair of the apartment catches up with me, and I remember the day I found out I'd been rejected from Juilliard. I'd been holding out hope for my last possibility. It was the only school I hadn't heard from yet. The letter was late, which I knew was sometimes a good sign. I'd been waiting all day for the mail to arrive and was distracting myself by applying a homemade beauty mask. I watched the clock on the microwave turn to 3:00 p.m. as the avocado-and-cucumber mixture stiffened uncomfortably on my cheeks. Mom was upstairs doing laundry. She'd worked the weekend and had the day off. I was beginning to think the mailman had forgotten us until I heard the sound of the next-door neighbor's dogs barking. I peeked out the window and there he was, coming up the driveway, his bag possibly containing the key to my future. I froze, my heart pounding in my teeth. Seconds later a thick bundle dropped through the mail slot and landed on the kitchen floor.

I knelt down and tossed the *Pennysaver*, the bills, and the triplicate copies of the Pottery Barn catalog aside. There it was. The envelope I'd been waiting for, with the return address printed in the distinctive navy-blue font. My fingers were shaking as I ripped it open and pulled out the letter.

We regret to inform . . . Unfortunately . . . Highly competitive . . . Record number . . . Talented pool . . . Wish you luck . . .

A glop of mask dropped onto the paper, and a scream, high and pure, escaped my lungs.

"Becca?" Mom called from upstairs. "Are you okay?"

I sank to the tile floor. Mom's footsteps pounded down the stairs as I sat up and reached for an Easter-themed dish towel.

"Jesus H. Christ, what is on your face?" Mom asked.

"A mask," I said, and handed her the letter. I felt my face crumble again as I wiped the goop from it. "I'm not going to Juilliard."

Mom put a hand to her heart and let out one of her quiet, breathy gasps. "I'm so sorry. I'm so, so sorry."

My mother's sympathetic voice unleashed another wave of tears, and she pulled me in for a hug even though she was wearing an ivory-colored sweater. We sat like that, hugging, Mom stroking my back in even circles until I finally caught my breath.

"It's official," I said. "I didn't get into college."

"How did this happen?" Mom asked quietly. Then she pursed her lips and, sitting across from me, wiped the places I'd missed: my hairline, my nose, my jaw. She was focused and calm, but I could see her mind working like the gears of a clock.

"Mom?" She steadied my chin with her hand and wiped my eyebrows. "Say something."

"I'm just . . ."

"Just what? Say it."

"I'm not sure what we're going to do."

I wanted comfort and reassurance. I wanted her to tell me this was going to be fine, that it was perfectly normal or that we were going to turn it all around. I wanted her to say, "In five years, will you even remember this?" like she had that time Brooke Ashworth was cast as Ophelia when I knew I'd done a better job in the audition, or when I'd gotten a C on the chemistry final.

"What now?" I asked. "Mom?"

"I don't know," she said as if I weren't her baby or her little girl, but a full-blown adult. Just like her. "I really don't know."

The whining fridge brings me back to the moment. I'm suddenly ravenous. Luckily, I bought that container of yogurt early this morning. The only problem is that I don't have a spoon. I fashion the lid of the yogurt container into a scooping mechanism that looks promising. With no chairs, I sit on the floor under the window and try to eat, but it's not working. I wash my hands with the travel-size Dove, abandon the yogurt lid, and use my fingers to eat it over the sink. I'm an animal, I think, a human-animal. I'm glad that no one can see me until I notice that a lady in the apartment across the street, an old woman in a bathrobe, is watching me. She tilts her head in what I think is curiosity.

"I don't have a spoon," I say aloud even though I know she can't hear me. I look at her and shrug in an exaggerated way. She shuts her curtains. Raj told me he lived in number seven if I needed anything. Well, I think to myself as I wipe the yogurt off my face, I do need something. A fucking spoon.

"Hi!" I say when he opens the door, a coffee mug in hand. I could be wrong, but his eyes light up a little when they see me. "Come on in," he says. "Becky, right?"

"Becca," I say, stepping inside. "I'm actually wondering if I could borrow a spoon?"

His apartment is spare and well organized. It has the same basic setup as mine, but actually looks like someone's home. A neat someone's home. His bed is made with crisp, folded corners. No clothes on the floor. No piles of papers. I bet I could open any drawer or cupboard at random and everything inside of it would be lined up, purposefully arranged, just so. There are several bookshelves, one dedicated entirely to titles about movies, and another filled with books about everything, from architecture to American history to classic literature. One corner of the room, with a large L-shaped desk and a huge, pristine desktop computer, is clearly what he uses as his office.

"Your place is really nice," I say.

"Thanks," he says.

I smell fresh coffee, and my mouth begins to water. My hunger had hardly been satiated by the yogurt. I have to stop myself from running toward the scent.

"You, ah, want some coffee?" he asks, one corner of his mouth turning up in a grin.

"Was I that obvious?" I pull my hair back into a ponytail and tie it with the elastic that's been around my wrist all night, leaving a red indentation.

"Let's just say that you look like you could use some coffee. I only made enough for one, but I can brew another pot," Raj says, leading me to the kitchen nook, where two chairs are tucked under a little table. He hands me a plate with a warm piece of buttered toast on it.

"Thanks," I say, and take a seat at his kitchen table. I eat the delicious toast in four bites as he scoops coffee into the filter. There are three screenwriting books on the table, all of them marked with color-coded Post-its. "So, you're a screenwriter?"

"I'm more of a director, but I write some, too. And there's this screenwriting competition at my school that's coming up. The winner gets a hundred-thousand-dollar grant to make a movie."

"A hundred thousand dollars? Wow."

"I know. And I have this idea that I think is promising, and I really want to win, but there's not a lot of time."

"When's the deadline?"

"December first," Raj says. "Coming right up."

"That's ages away," I say, thinking of my own promised college deadlines. "You can totally make that."

"It takes a while to construct a really good screenplay. It's all in the planning," he says.

"What do you have to plan?" I ask. I know a lot about putting on a play because I've been in so many, but I guess I've never thought that much about what goes into making a movie. They just seem to tumble into the world fully formed, though of course I realize that's not how it works. "Do you outline, like a term paper?"

"Definitely. But I'm nowhere near the outlining phase." He takes in my confused expression. "I'd like to have a logline by the end of the day and a beat sheet by the end of the week."

I don't really know what any of these things are, but I nod as if I do.

"You'll do it," I say. "I believe in you."

"Thanks," he says. The coffee pot sputters, indicating it's ready. He smiles as he pours me a mug. "Anyway, how was that nap?"

"I don't have a bed yet, so I was on the floor . . . so, not great."

"No bed? No spoon?"

"No nothing," I say. As he hands me the coffee, I feel for the briefest second like I might cry. I bring it to my lips and after a few sips, the hot liquid seems to zip through my veins. I've never been a coffee drinker, but I become one in this moment. "Oh my God. This is so good! This is like the best coffee I've ever had."

He smiles again, this time with his whole face.

"What?" I ask.

"You're just very enthusiastic. Where are you from?"

"Boston," I say as he butters more toast and hands me another piece. I devour it. He laughs. "What now?"

"Nothing," he says, smiling and shaking his head.

"Do you know how to get to Ikea?" I ask.

"In Burbank?"

"I guess?"

"Take Western to Los Feliz to the Five."

"Can I do that on a bus?"

"You're going to take a bus to Burbank?"

"Is that so crazy?" I ask. "I could take a cab back."

"A bus from Hollywood to Burbank?" he says, topping off my coffee. "Actually. Yes. It's crazy. You need a car."

"That's what everyone keeps saying, but there have to be people who live here without a car. I mean, what am I supposed to do? I can't buy a car until I get a job. And I can't get a job until I stop living like a human-animal. And I can't stop living like a human-animal until I get some furniture and a spoon. But I can't get furniture until I get a car. But I don't drive. So that puts me back at the beginning."

"It really is a vicious cycle, isn't it?" Raj says.

"Yes, it is," I say. "I used a sweatshirt stuffed inside another sweatshirt as a pillow last night."

"Tell you what. I don't have to be at work until four. I'll take you to Ikea."

"Really? You'd do that for me?"

"For the most enthusiastic human-animal I've ever met? Sure," he says, grabbing his keys off a hook.

"What about your logline?"

He hesitates. "Eh, I'll do it tonight."

"Are you sure?"

"Yes, but we have to leave now so we can beat the traffic home. Can you do that?"

"Let me check," I say, and scroll through an imaginary calendar in my mind. "What do you know? I'm free."

FOUR

RAJ'S DENTED WHITE COROLLA is parked five blocks away, uphill—the closest parking spot he could find last night—on a narrow street that feels like a totally different neighborhood. The homes are enormous, with big gates surrounding the front yards and driveways with expensive cars parked in them. And the hill is so steep that Raj and I are both breathing pretty heavily by the time he spots his car. When he points it out, I realize that I'm about to do what I've been cautioned not to do since kindergarten—get in a car with a near stranger. In fact, he's basically at the exact position on the stranger spectrum to make him a likely predator. Someone I know but not that well.

It's fine, I tell myself, remembering that at no point has

he made me feel uncomfortable. But still, as he's unlocking the door, I snap a picture of his license plate and text it to my mom—just in case, on the *very, very* off chance, he kidnaps me. There is nothing about Raj that would indicate he is dangerous, but I've read enough shared statuses on Facebook warning us young women to always be careful to take precaution. At least if I disappear, Mom will have a clue.

"Everything cool?" Raj asks as I scan the inside of his car for chloroform and rags.

"Oh yeah," I say.

He laughs a little, releases the parking break, does a sixteen-point turn on the narrow road, and we head down the hill.

"Where do you work?" I ask.

"Hotel Uno. Downtown. Very hip," Raj says.

"Cool," I say.

I realize pretty quickly how ridiculous it would have been for me to take the bus. Getting around LA is nothing like getting around Boston, where everything feels pretty close together and a ride on the T gets you where you need to be without too many scenery changes.

This is a completely different experience. Raj and I travel past a huge park with a mountain and a zoo inside of it; drive down a wide boulevard flanked by enormous pastel apartment buildings with names like the Villa Pacifica, Fountain Manor, and Tropical Estates; hop on a freeway that I swear has ten lanes; and get stuck in standstill traffic for a solid fifteen minutes before narrowly avoiding death by collision with a cement mixer, until we exit to a land of strip malls.

"I think it might have taken me half the day to figure out how to get here using public transportation," I say.

"So we have two hours here," Raj says, as we pull into a parking spot. The sun is a force. I'm sweating within seconds of emerging from the car.

"Is it just me, or is it ten degrees hotter than when we left?" I ask.

"It's definitely hotter. Always is. We're in the valley now."

We step into the cool of the store, and I lead us to the frozen yogurt, ordering us each a cone.

"So, we're in a different ecosystem?"

"A different microclimate," Raj says, blushing for a second. "I wanted to be a meteorologist in fifth grade."

"Aw, really?" I was so silly to think he'd kidnap me! The woman behind the counter hands me two cones.

"Well, here's a treat from the north," I say. The frozen yogurt is sweet and pleasing after the hot and windy drive. "A taste of Sweden." We eat in silence for an awkward minute.

"Okay," I say, as I pop the last of the frozen yogurt cone in my mouth. I pull my list out of my pocket. Chair. Table. Nightstand. Curtains. Shower curtain. Silverware. Plates. Bowls. Pots. Pans. Towels. Trash can. Laundry basket. Sheets. Blanket. Pillow.

"So I've got a budget of two hundred and fifty dollars." I'm going through the four thousand dollars I brought with me—years of babysitting earnings, my summer as a camp counselor, birthday money, and a little extra help from Mom—much faster than I expected. I'm already down to twenty-five hundred. The expenses included first month's rent and a security deposit for my apartment, but still. I only got here a few days ago and I'm almost halfway through my entire savings.

"Two hundred and fifty bucks? To furnish your whole apartment?" Raj asks.

"The next thing on my to-do list is to get a job," I say. "But I can't—"

"I know. The vicious cycle," he says, yanking a cart free from the shopping cart snake. "It's okay. Let's do this. We'll start with the kitchen. The most important room in the house."

"Or corner of the studio apartment," I say, heading toward a display of colorful teakettles.

An hour and a half later, when the cart is fully loaded with the least expensive, most essential household items for one person to survive in this world, and after finding ourselves in a maze of lighting fixtures and bathroom accessories and rugs we couldn't seem to escape, Raj and I take a break in a staged living room. He sits on a sofa and I recline in an armchair, both of us exhausted in that shop-till-you-drop way. We stare at an un-plugged-in TV screen.

"I can't believe we made it out of there alive," I say, putting my feet up on the ottoman. "I was beginning to think we were trapped with those laundry baskets for the rest of our lives."

"It was all you," Raj says. "You were the one who took the left by the rugs. How did we not notice that door before?"

"The way out was in front of us the whole time, but we refused to see it," I say.

"Classic human-animal behavior," Raj says, and I laugh, relaxing back into the chair. "Have you heard about the Ikea effect?" I shake my head no. "It's the idea that something actually means more to you if you build it, or I guess assemble it yourself. So if you buy a table and put it together, you'll value it more than if someone just gives you the table. Someone at Harvard Business School came up with it."

"Makes sense," I say.

"I'm sorry, but I have to ask. How old are you?" Raj rests an arm on the back of the sofa.

"Eighteen," I say. "Just turned."

I stroke the soft blue blanket artfully displayed on the arm of the chair. I wish I could afford it. It reminds me of the blanket that lies folded at the bottom of Alex's bed. But it's $39.99. Out of my budget. I smooth it over my lap. It's so comfortable in this fake living room. I'm the most comfortable I've been since I arrived in California. Part of me wishes that I could just move in here, to the fractured home spaces of this Ikea store, where the beds are soft and the food is warm and cheap. Would they really notice me, curling up in one of the bunk beds at night?

"There's got to be a story here," Raj says. "You didn't want to go to college?"

"I'm taking a year off to give acting a try." This is not entirely a lie, even though the knot in my gut reminds me that it's not really the truth either. There's no reason my new LA friends need to know about my epic failure. Besides, everyone else comes to Los Angeles to start fresh. "I figured, what better time than now. You're only eighteen once, right?"

"That's bold," Raj says. "Insanely bold." He tilts his head and studies me. "But I get it, I think. You seem like an actress."

"Really?" I ask, not sure if this is a good thing or a bad thing. An Ikea employee restocks a throw pillow display nearby, intruding on the illusion that Raj and I are relaxing in my modern and brightly decorated living room.

"No, no," Raj says. "I just mean that . . ." He pauses, regarding me with an open expression as he searches for the right words. Our eyes meet in a moment of unexpected intimacy. "You're very expressive. That's all."

"Thanks," I say, looking away. "What about you? How old are you?"

"I'm twenty-one," Raj says. "I'm a senior at the California Film School."

"What's your style like? I mean, as a director."

"I'm still figuring it out, I guess." His cheeks flush. It's official. He's a blusher. "Of course I love Hitchcock. Do you?"

"I've actually never seen one of his movies."

"No way! I'll have to show you one sometime. If I weren't working tonight, I'd show you one as soon as we got back. God, which one should I start with?"

"Can I just say that you two are so cute," a mom says as she enters our fake living room. There's a tiny, sleeping baby strapped to her chest in some elaborate wrap. "It looks like you live here together. Are they paying you to sit here?"

"Nope. We do it for free," Raj says.

"You're an adorable couple," she stage-whispers.

"We're not together," I say, surprising myself with the speed of my reaction. I see something—hurt? embarrassment?—flash across Raj's face. The truth is that I can't imagine being anyone's girlfriend but Alex's. Not yet.

"Oh," the lady says and makes an *oops* face. "Sorry," she adds before heading toward the dining room display.

"Aaaannnyway," Raj says.

I stare at the carpet. I feel the cozy spell of the staged living room break. It's my fault. I couldn't seem to help it, though. It's like my heart has an electric fence around it.

"Let's get going," Raj says. "I gotta get back."

"You're the best for helping me today," I say with a little too much enthusiasm. "I don't know what I would have done without you."

"No problem," he says, but there's heaviness in the air between us.

My phone rings and I'm grateful for the distraction. "It's my mom. I'd better get this." I answer. "Hi, Mom. I'm actually at Ikea right now, so I can't—"

"Why did you text me that license plate? Whose white car is that? Are you in some kind of trouble?" she asks with the kind of speaking-loud-but-not-yelling volume exclusive to mothers. I hope Raj doesn't hear her.

"You texted your mom my license plate?" he asks.

"I didn't know if you were going to kidnap me," I say with a shrug.

"Do I look like a criminal?" he asks.

"Oh my God, no!"

"Honey, who are you talking to? Are you okay?" Mom asks through the phone.

"Yes, I'm fine, Mom. I'm just at Ikea. I promise I'm okay." I turn to Raj and whisper, "I barely knew you when I got in your car!"

"I look like a criminal," he says, and walks a little taller. "That's kind of awesome."

After we return to the Chateau, Raj helps me carry the stuff up to my apartment. He has to get to his job.

"So, are you a waiter at this downtown hotel?" I ask as we navigate the stairs with my overflowing bright blue reusable bags.

"Bartender," he says. "I kind of hate it. My cousin Brandon is the manager. He's a douche bag, but the money's green."

"I bet you're a good bartender," I say as we put the stuff inside my apartment. "You're clearly very service oriented."

"Yeah, well." He laughs a little. "You're on your own for the assembling part. Unless you want to wait until tomorrow?"

"I can do this," I say.

"Okay. I'll go get my tool kit and drill for you."

"You have a drill?" I ask as he walks down the hall and disappears into his apartment.

When he returns and hands the drill to me, I hold it as if it's a loaded gun. "I've never used it. But good luck to you," Raj says.

"The Ikea effect," I say.

"Exactly. So, what's your plan?" he asks. He folds his arms and leans against the door frame.

"I think I'm going to start with the table . . ." I say.

"No, I mean the big plan. You're giving yourself one year to become an actress, so what's your plan?"

"Oh, I'm going to get an agent," I say, thinking of my list. "I'm going to get one tomorrow."

"Tomorrow?" His face brightens. "Do you have a meeting?"

I nod. I don't have an official meeting, but I know that if I try hard enough, I can make something happen by tomorrow.

"Good for you. I'm impressed." He lingers for a moment. "And stop by the bar later if you want. Hotel Uno."

"I'm only eighteen," I say.

"That's a problem." Raj smiles. "Unless you know the bartender."

As soon as he leaves, I open my notebook and put a check next to numbers two through five.

	1.	Get an agent!
√	2.	Get curtains.
√	3.	Get a pillow.
√	4.	Buy pots and pans.
√	5.	Get a kitchen table, bed, and a dresser.
	6.	Go to the grocery store and get ingredients for healthy meals.
	7	Learn how to apply subtle yet effective eye makeup

Mom was right. Checking off my notebook goals is satisfying.

That afternoon, I tackle the things that need to be assembled first. I'm able to jump onto someone's unprotected Wi-Fi network called SAFARISOGOODY. Even though the signal cuts in and out, I watch YouTube tutorials by someone named Helpful Dan who guides me as I put the table and chairs together in under an hour. I had originally only wanted to get one chair so that I could also afford the soft blue blanket, but Raj convinced me the second chair was the priority.

"You need a minimum of two chairs," he said. "You have to think positive about your social life. You're at least going to want the option of eating with another person."

I open the curtain package to realize that not only are the

panels way too long, I have no fixtures to hang them with. The lesson of the day seems to be that in order to be a successful person in this world, I have to think of the beginning, middle, and end of my ideas. I can't just wake up and expect there to be breakfast. I have to buy not only the food, but also be prepared with a spoon. I can't just "go to Ikea." I need to think about how to get there and bring the stuff back. I can't just toss a package of colorful curtains in my shopping cart and think that as soon as I unwrap them in my apartment they will somehow hang themselves. Without my mom here prompting me to think these things through ("How are you going to hang those, Becca? Will they need to be hemmed?"), and without Alex, who somehow knows how to do just about everything (even if he'd never used a drill, he would figure it out and have built a working boat by the end of the day), I'm finding myself either needing to be bailed out by the kindness of strangers, or stranded midway through my missions, realizing I've skipped some vital steps in the process.

And of course, as I hold the curtains up just to see what they'd look like if I had thought everything through, I realize that I'm starving. Again. Even after the $3.99 lunch at Ikea.

I wonder why I'm so hungry all the time. It's as if the taking in of new landscapes and information is burning twice the calories. I make another half-starved trip to the Mayfair. When I get there, I take a deep breath and remember the lesson of the day: think things through. After all, I'm not the spoonless girl of this morning. I've got brand-new cookware, a colander, a chopping board, and a full set of cutlery. I buy what a smart woman on a budget would buy. Beans and rice. Tofu dogs. A head of lettuce. Spaghetti and sauce. Maybe I'll be a vegetarian like Raj, I think, who chose the pasta over the meatballs today. I add a couple of bananas to my cart. I buy mac and cheese and frozen peas for old times' sake, a loaf of whole wheat bread, some peanut butter and jelly, three apples, and a large container of yogurt, which is more cost-effective than the single servings.

I carry the heavy bags down the block, putting them on the curb to push the "walk" button. I check Instagram while I wait for the light to change. I'm bombarded with pictures of college life: a fountain at Georgetown, selfies with roommates, the insanely cute Boston College crew team in the cafeteria. The traffic rushes past me on Franklin Avenue, coughing exhaust in my face. I catch glimpses of the people in their cars. The girl eating a salad in her BMW, the guy head-banging in the beat-up van, the gardeners with a truck full of equipment. They seem to belong here as much as the letters of the Hollywood sign. I take another glance at the photo of Brooke curling her hair (#auditions #psyched #blessed). My throat feels like it's full of cotton balls.

After the letter from Juilliard, I experienced a full week of post-rejection crying—like breaking down in math to the embarrassment of Mr. Stebbins, weeping quietly through French class (the unflappable Madame Laurent ignoring me), and faking period pains in gym class so I could sob in the locker room. Mom let me stay home from school on Thursday and Friday. I got a new haircut on Saturday morning and spent the weekend giving myself pep talks in Mom's full-length mirror. I steeled myself on Sunday night. On Monday, with my shoulders back, my head held high, and a big smile on my face, I told my classmates my plans. "I'm moving to LA to be an actress."

A bunch of kids were impressed, but Brooke tilted her head, pouted, and said, "Aw, my heart really goes out to you. Sounds so tough."

She'd seen my pulsing jugular and gone for it. As I sucked in my breath, I felt tears welling. I hated myself for feeling so much—always and all the time. As I stood to clear my lunch tray, I heard her remark that NYU was in the best neighborhood in New York. I hid in the science wing. Alex found me and wrapped me in his arms. I breathed into the soft cotton of his oxford shirt.

"You're going to make it," he said. "I know you are. You'll leave all these idiots in the dust." He was so confident and sure that I believed in myself all over again.

If he believed in me so much then, he must still. That doesn't just go away. Love doesn't turn off like a faucet. Otherwise it couldn't have been love. And if I know anything, it's that Alex and I were in love.

I'm going to make it, I tell myself.

After I cross the street, I take a selfie with the Hollywood sign in the distance and post it. A breeze is blowing my hair across my face, and I can see myself as that person. *Did you hear about Becca?* people will say as they look at this picture. *She's this very cool, very independent LA actress. She lives near the Hollywood Hills. Her building is full of artists and filmmakers. Oh, and she's a vegetarian now. Her skin is, like, luminous.*

When I get home two guys from 1-800-GET-A-BED have just arrived. Yes! They're early! I let them into the apartment. They set up the frame and stack the box spring and mattress on top. I give them water using my new Ikea cups. Then I unload the groceries and feel a sense of satisfaction at the sight of the stocked refrigerator. I proudly check off number six.

✓	3.	Get a pillow.
✓	4.	Buy pots and pans.
✓	5.	Get a kitchen table, bed, and a dresser.
✓	6.	Go to the grocery store and get ingredients for healthy meals.
	7.	Learn how to apply subtle yet effective eye makeup.
	8.	Get a job to make $ $ $!

Standing on my tiptoes on a chair, I hang the curtains with thumbtacks. Curtain fixtures will just have to wait. I use the ties that came in the package to gather them in the middle. Sure, there's an extra foot of material on the ground, but the way the white cotton pools on the floor actually looks kind of romantic. I unpack my suitcase. I sweep the floor clean. I plug in the lamp. I place it on the bedside table that I found in the AS IS department. I try the sisal rug in three different spots, finally settling on the area under the windows. Then I make the bed and lie down.

I have a place now. It still needs so much stuff. It needs

pictures on the wall and a sofa with some colorful pillows. But it's mine. My little corner of the world.

It's not until later that I realize that the soft blue blanket, the one I had wanted but been unable to afford, is at the bottom of one of the giant Ikea bags. Raj must have bought it for me. He must've put it in the bag without me noticing. I wrap myself in it. I close my eyes and the first thing that comes to mind is the Leaping Dolphin Inn, this little place off of Highway 1, which is at the exact midpoint between Palo Alto and LA. It's right on the beach. Alex and I were supposed to meet up there every two weeks. We'd even studied the website and decided that we were going to stay in room 2 every time. According to the pictures, room 2 has it's own patio, a fireplace, and views of the sunset that would melt even the coldest heart.

FIVE

THERE'S NO BIG SIGN for Mathis Allen Artists on the outside of this Beverly Hills office building. It's not until I locate the intercom system inside the entryway that I see a small plaque with the talent agency's name on it. I take a deep breath and press the intercom button.

You got this, I tell myself.

I slept a blissful ten hours last night in my single bed and woke up ready to tackle my most important goal, and number one on my list.

	1.	Get an agent!
✓	2.	Get curtains.
✓	3	Get a pillow

I took a shower, put on my favorite jeans, my cutest top, and a pair of flats. I couldn't blow-dry my hair because I didn't bring a hair dryer with me, but I towel dried it roughly to add some volume. I own barely any makeup, but I did the best I could with some lip gloss and mascara. Then I searched online for "best talent agencies in Los Angeles," read a little about what seemed like the consensus for the top ten, and narrowed the list down to five.

From what I read, Mathis Allen Artists seems like a great option. It's a medium-size agency with clients who range from recent graduates to pretty famous. A little more investigation turned up an interview in *Backstage* with a young agent there named Aaron, who aside from coming across like a really nice guy, said he was actively looking to build his list and loved nothing more than the thrill of discovering emergent talent. That's me, I thought. Emerging talent! And here I am at eight thirty, most likely the first hopeful actress of the day to knock on their door. I review the confident-but-not-pushy line I came up with on the bus ride: "Hi, there, my name is Becca. I'm new in town and would love just a minute of your time to see if we might be a match."

To my surprise, the buzzer sounds. I push the door open and make my way to suite 213. And I thought I might have trouble making it past the entrance. Maybe this is going to be easier than I thought!

"Thank God you're here!" a pretty receptionist says as I walk into the lobby, which is decorated with mid-century furniture and contemporary art. I thought I looked put-together today, but in this context and in comparison to the receptionist, who can't be much older than me, I feel like some kind of adult orphan. In her oversize blazer and statement necklace, this chick has got casual elegance down to a science. Her eyes are expertly lined, her hair professionally blown out, and her teeth—oh my God, her teeth—are so white they almost glow.

"Hi," I say. I'm about to launch into my rehearsed line when she cuts me off.

"I'm Daisy. Thank you so much for coming right away." It's pretty clear that she's mistaken me for someone else, but she doesn't give me an opening to explain. "Okay, so Miranda just dropped off Max even though Todd says it's her day. This divorce is getting messier by the minute. And poor Max is losing his mind. Like, in general, but also today. Our intern, Marley, is entertaining him in the copy room, but he's already jammed the machine twice. I'm hoping you can take him to the park and just run him around—he had gluten by accident and it's been HELL. . . ."

"Um, I'm not—"

"There's also a nine a.m. class at the Kid's Gym, which you could make if you hurry," she says, glancing at the clock. "They have a membership there. Let me just grab Max and the two of you can get going—"

"I'm not who you think I am," I blurt before she can pivot down the hallway to which she's been gesturing.

"Huh?" Daisy asks.

"I'm hoping to meet with Aaron Danielson," I say.

"You're not the babysitter?" she asks. I shake my head no. She covers her face with her hands and takes a deep breath. "You're here for the meeting? Oh my God. I'm so sorry. No one is ever early to these things. Are you a new client?"

"Actually, I'm not a client. YET! My name is Becca, and I'm new in town—"

"Wait. Hold on." Daisy's face falls. "You just came in . . . off the street?"

"Technically, yeah, but I wouldn't put it like that," I say with a laugh, trying to hold on to my courage. "See, I read about this agency online, and I think Aaron and I would be a great match. I've just turned eighteen and I have a monologue prepared."

"I'm sorry. I don't have time for this," Daisy says, looking as if I'm causing her physical pain. "The agents have a meeting in twenty minutes, and I need to set up and find the babysitter who was supposed to be you. And where the fuck are the caterers?"

"I can babysit," I offer, thinking that maybe this will be my in. I can see that Daisy is actually considering this when a girl in a UCLA sweatshirt appears in the doorway.

"I'm Olivia from Sitters at Your Service," she says.

"Oh, thank God you're here!" Daisy says.

"So . . ." I feel the opportunity slipping away from me. "Would it be okay if I just waited here in the lobby for Aaron? Or I can come back after the meeting?"

"This better be the caterer," Daisy says as the phone rings. She hops behind the desk. "Mathis Allen Agency." Relief floods her face. "Yes, come right up!" She hangs up the phone and sighs. "Phew! Olivia, Max is in the back to the right. Can you grab him and take him to the park around the corner?" Olivia nods and heads down a hallway.

"How about me?" I ask, and smile at Daisy expectantly.

"Oh, there's no way I can just schedule a meeting with Aaron for you." I'm about to protest when she cuts me off. "I'll tell you what. I don't normally do this, but I'll take your headshot and keep it on file. How does that sound?"

"I don't have a headshot," I say. "Yet."

"Wow, you are green!" She laughs loudly and it catches me so off guard that I almost cry. "I'm sorry, but it's time for you to go, okay?"

"Okay," I say. It takes all of my strength to smile as I walk out the door. My stomach grumbles as I pass the caterers with baskets of sweet-smelling pastries and steaming carafes of coffee.

I stop at a juicery called Feeling Fine on the first floor of the office building before I tackle the next agency. I could certainly use a little extra help feeling fine. Daisy's cackle is still echoing in my ears. I pick out a bottle of green juice called Your Best Self and head to the cashier, who with her perfect complexion and shining flaxen hair looks like she probably drinks Your Best Self by the gallon.

"That'll be ten fifty," she says.

"Excuse me?" I ask. She can't possibly be telling me that this single serving of juice costs more than the cutlery set I just bought.

"Ten dollars and fifty cents," she says, her nose ring glinting in the light.

"I didn't realize that's what juice went for these days," I say.

"Yeah," she says. "It's all organic, locally sourced, and fresh pressed."

"That's nice," I say. "I'll just put this back."

"I got it," says a voice behind me.

I turn and see a pleasant-looking guy in a nice suit holding his own bottle of Your Best Self. His smile is genuine and a little goofy.

"Wait, really?" I ask, confused.

"That is so sweet," the cashier says. "I love it."

"I really can't accept—" I start, wondering if he's going to want something in exchange, but before I can finish my sentence, he's swiped his card.

"Too late," he says.

"Uh, thanks," I say.

"You look like you could use someone doing something nice for you today," he says.

"I do?"

"Let me guess. You just moved here?"

"A week ago," I say.

"Knew it. You have that look about you," he says, though not in a way that makes me feel bad about it. "Welcome to LA."

"Thank you so much," I say, feeling a little off-balance from this wave of niceness coming so quickly on the heels of Daisy's laughter.

"Ain't no thing. And chin up," he says, shaking his juice. "It'll happen."

"What'll happen?" I ask as he walks toward the door.

"Whatever it is you're waiting for," he calls over his shoulder. And then he disappears around the corner.

"That was, like, beautiful," the cashier says, a hand on her heart.

"Yeah," I say. "It really was."

And just like that, my courage is back. I feel like a better version of myself before I even take a sip of the juice.

I stop by the other places on my list, but I don't have any luck. Three of the agencies are in office buildings with guards in the lobby. They won't let me up without an appointment. I ask if there's any way they can make an exception, because don't they want to help give a hopeful young actress her shot, but the first two don't even crack a smile. I feel as small as a flea. The security guard at the third agency says, "Aren't you a little young to be wandering around by yourself? Shouldn't you be in school?"

"I'm eighteen," I say. He wiggles his eyebrows in a way that makes me really uneasy.

The last agency has a plaque that reads HEADSHOTS HERE, with an arrow pointing to a mail slot. After I've stopped by all the agencies on my list, I catch the bus east. I'm actually looking forward to seeing the Chateau Bronson—a place I'm absolutely sure I'm allowed inside.

When I get back to the apartment, there's a note tucked under my door. It's a hand-drawn invitation to dinner from Marisol. She's written her number at the bottom and the letters RSVP.

Can't wait for dinner, I text.

Marisol: Yay! Be here at 7.

Me: Do you think you could help me with my résumé?

Marisol: Most definitely! Bring your laptop!

I definitely wasn't premature in checking off number nine—at least not the first half.

✓ 6.	Go to the grocery store and get ingredients for healthy meals.	
7.	Learn how to apply subtle yet effective eye makeup.	
8.	Get a job to make $ $ $!	
✓ 9.	Get a friend. (Friends?)	
10.	Get a new style, new wardrobe, etc.	
11.	Become a working actress!	

"Hello?" I knock on her door. I hear country music playing inside, which is a surprise. There's nothing about her that says country to me.

"It's unlocked," she calls. "Come on in."

As soon as I walk into her apartment, my Mac under my arm, I can tell that Marisol has real style. Like, *magazine* style. Instead of my bare-bones setup, her place looks like the inside of Anthropologie, only more original. The walls are an unexpected shade of gray, and the floors are painted white. A shaggy cream-colored rug adds coziness. An artful stack of books sits on a sleek glass coffee table. Her jewelry is organized in little boxes on a tea cart. Instead of posters, real art hangs on the walls. An iron-frame bed with a batik bedspread adds a splash of bohemia to the refinement. Where did she get all this stuff? Not Ikea.

"I love your place," I say. "It's gorgeous."

"Oh, thanks," she says, emerging from the kitchen area in a kimono, gold slippers, and giant earrings. She sings along to the feisty country music. I'm too swept up in her performance to feel bad about the fact that I'm wearing a boring Old Navy T-shirt and jeans.

"You have a nice voice," I say when the song is over.

"I just love Loretta Lynn," she says. "Do you like her?"

"I don't know her music."

"Let me educate you." She gestures for me to take a seat on a butterfly chair with a cowhide cover. If someone else said this, it might come off as patronizing, but with Marisol it feels more like an invitation.

She turns up the volume on her speakers as I take a seat, pours white wine into juice glasses, and dances a little as she pulls a couple of frozen potpies from the freezer. She unwraps the plastic covering and puts them in the oven. I had lots of friends at the beginning of high school, but after I got serious with Alex, I kind of drifted out of the bigger cliques and into our party of two. Alex became both my boyfriend and my best friend. But I realize now that deep down I've always wanted a friend like this—wild and free. I don't think I've ever met someone who can pull off orange lipstick, a kimono, and a penchant for country music all at once.

"Ah! This is beautiful," I say, spotting her headshot on the coffee table. I lean forward and pick it up to study it. She looks gorgeous, relaxed but professional. It perfectly captures Marisol—her quirky charm and her soulful beauty. "I need a headshot! Did a friend take this picture?"

"Uh, no," she says, turning the music down. "That's a professional shot."

"But some people take their own headshots, right?" I ask hopefully.

"I guess so. I mean, I've heard of it. But I wouldn't. You're all the way out here. You don't want to waste your time with something that looks homemade. You know what I mean?" She reads the back of the potpie box and sets the timer on the microwave.

"How much did it cost?" I ask.

"A thousand," she says with a shrug and bites her lip.

"Dollars?" I almost spit out my wine. "Whoa. That's my rent."

"But that included everything," she says, and sits on the sofa. "Hair and makeup and all the digital images."

"Still," I say.

"Anyway, that's why we're going to make you two résumés: an acting résumé and a bread-and-butter job résumé. I bet you'd do well as a waitress."

"I've never waitressed before in my life," I say, placing the headshot on the table with great care and opening my laptop. "And I've never acted professionally either."

"Doesn't matter. We'll just make some shit up and you'll be fine."

"You mean lie?" I ask.

"Trust me." Marisol tucks her feet under her. "You need to make shit up. Everyone lies. And by the way, you're too cute for someone to actually check your references."

"I am?" I ask.

"Hell, yeah," she says. "With those freckles? Are you kidding me? And people pay for cheekbones like yours."

"Oh." I smile and touch my face. "So, do you have an agent?" I ask.

"I'm freelancing with a commercial agent, but she doesn't send me out very much," she says, exhaling in a pouty, French sort of way.

"How'd you get her?"

"I was in this weird acting class for a little while in West Hollywood, and one of my scene partners gave me a reference after we worked together on a bunch of stuff. I sent the agent my headshot, and a few days later I had an audition," she says as she tops off our juice glasses.

"That was nice," I say. I feel very grown-up drinking wine on a random night. I hardly ever drank back in Massachusetts, and when I did, it was only sips of beer. But here I am on a Wednesday, sipping white wine like the ladies in Mom's book club. I spot a camera on her bookshelf. "Hey, is that a real Polaroid camera?" I ask.

"Yeah," she says, grabbing it up. "It's called a Joy Cam. My boss, Agnes, gave it to me because she said it no longer 'brought her joy.' She even gave me a whole box of film to go with it, but I don't really use it." She snaps a picture of me and the film comes out, a black square in a white frame. She places it on the coffee table. "That's going to be cute. Hey, can I do your makeup?"

"Sure," I say, grinning. Her instant familiarity takes me by surprise. I've heard about friendship-at-first-sight, but it's never happened to me before.

"Okay." She licks her lips. "Sit on the sofa; the light is better there."

As she skips to the bathroom, I move to the tufted velvet sofa. Her attention is like a ray of sunlight. I feel a part of myself coming to life—something tender and green shooting up through a crack in the sidewalk.

She returns from the bathroom with what looks like a professional toolbox of makeup.

"What do you do for money?" I ask as she pushes the coffee table out of the way, pulls up a stool, and sits across from me. She studies my face. "Are you a waitress?"

"I'm a personal assistant," she says. She selects a giant fan brush and dusts it with powder. Then she taps the brush on her wrist to remove the excess.

"To a movie star?" I ask. The makeup brush is light and gentle on my skin. As she tilts my chin, I realize I haven't been touched since I arrived in California.

"Nope. To a rich housewife," she says, leaning back to consider her next move. "I mean, she thinks she's an actress, but

she's just playing at it." Marisol sighs. "I'm part of the sad cha-
rade. Hey, how do you feel about a really smoky eye?"

"Great," I say.

"Let's go violet." She taps her lip with one finger as she
selects a tube of mascara. "I'm going to bring the drama out of
you, okay?"

"Sounds fun," I say. She smiles as she leans in. She opens
an eye-shadow palette and rubs a tiny brush over a dark green
color.

"Close your eyes," she says.

I do, and I can smell the wine on her breath as she covers my
eyelids. "How long have you been living here?" I ask.

"At the Chateau Bronson? Just a month." When she adds
mascara she says, "Oh, this is going to look so good on you."

"Did you go to college?" I ask.

"I went to University of Miami, but I dropped out and
moved here."

I'm a little taken aback by how casually she says this. Why is
it that getting into college feels so easy to everyone else?

"Why'd you drop out?" I ask as she does my lower lashes.

"I want to be an artist, not a student. Artists don't need
school," she says.

"You're so right," I say and open my eyes. We exchange a
meaningful smile.

"Hey, do you have a boyfriend?" she asks.

"Yeah. I mean, yes and no. We've been together for two
years, but we just broke up."

"Did you break up with him or did he break up with you?"

"Technically, he broke up with me. He's just up at Stanford."

"Fancy."

"Yeah. He's insanely smart."

"Not if he broke up with you," she says, and even though she's trying to be nice, I flinch. She rubs her hands together. "Okay, your eyes are almost done. I just need to add a final touch."

"The thing is that we *just* broke up. And the only reason is because he was going to college and I wasn't and blah, blah, blah, but I don't know. We've been together since junior year. He's just an hour away by plane. I'm pretty sure this isn't a permanent thing."

"But why do you want to be with someone who, even for a second, decided he didn't want to be with you?" she asks as she searches for something in her makeup kit. I feel the wind knocked out of me for a second—I hadn't thought about it like that.

"He's just going through something," I say. "We're really close. I doubt it's over for real."

"Whatever you do, don't look at his social media, okay? That's a recipe for heartache and depression," she says. And I know she's right. Checking up on him is the worst thing I can do. I promise myself I won't do it, and then I nod, now officially on the verge of tears. "I'm sorry," she says, pausing to look me in the eye. "Obviously you know the situation and I don't. I'm just protective of my friends."

"How about you?" I ask, dying to change the subject. "Are you with anyone?"

"Nope. I'm single and loving it," she says with a grin. She pulls out a little tub of cream and unscrews the top. The stench makes me cough.

"What's that?" I ask, wincing.

"Pig placenta," Marisol says, scooping up some with her finger.

"Ew! I don't want that on my face."

"Why?"

"*Why?* It's pig placenta! Is that even legal?"

"Not sure." She bites her lip. "I got it at this place near Koreatown. It's what all the movie stars use. My boss is obsessed."

"It smells like poop."

"Maybe. But it's going to make me beautiful." She dabs it around her eyes. "I'm going to walk down the street and people are going be like, Who is that fine-looking baby-faced bitch?"

We both laugh. Then she stands back and looks at me. She places her hands in front of her chest in prayer position. "Okay. I may have been a touch heavy-handed with the eye shadow."

"Let me see," I say. She holds up a mirror.

"I look like a prostitute!" I exclaim, and she shrieks with delight.

"A very expensive escort," she says.

"An expensive escort who wears Old Navy," I say. And we laugh again—louder this time.

"Look at this," Marisol says, picking up the Polaroid picture of me sitting cross-legged on her sofa. She hands it to me and calls it adorable, but to me, I look a little lost.

The oven timer goes off.

"Oh, our potpies!" she says and leaps up. Her dangly earrings make a clinking noise as she sashays into the kitchen. I love her so much.

SIX

"HERE'S YOUR DRILL," I say to Raj a few days later when I knock on his door, and amazingly enough, he answers it— wearing a fedora. Alex would never wear a fedora—he thinks they're for douche bag hipsters—but I think Raj looks elegant. He can definitely pull it off. I've tried to return his drill several times, but he must have the busiest schedule because he's never home. Today I figured I'd try to get him first thing in the morning. I know from our rooftop encounter that he's an early riser.

It's not like I've been around a lot either. I've spent the past few mornings searching for agents and hitting up restaurants in the afternoon. I know I need a headshot, but it couldn't hurt to try to literally get in the door. My theory is that if the agents have actually met me, then when I send my picture, I'll be following up rather than just taking a shot in the dark. I figure this way my headshot will have a better chance of not landing in the trash. I've stopped by eight more agencies but only made it in the door of Liz Harper Agency, which specializes in child actors. Many teen roles are played by adult actors who look really young. The receptionist took a snapshot of me but was very firm about how I should not call them. Still, it made my week.

I've been taking the same approach to getting a restaurant job—going door-to-door wearing my best smile, a fake résumé in hand.

"Did you use the drill?" Raj asks. He's got his backpack on and is clearly on his way out. He puts the drill on the entryway table, steps into the hall, and locks the door behind him.

"I did," I say.

"Then you're the first," he says. "How was it?"

"Well, it works! I'd been using thumbtacks, but the curtains kept falling, so I took the bus to Target and bought actual curtain rods and brackets—and get this, a stud finder."

"Why do you need a stud finder? I live right down the hall," he says, and then instantly blushes. "That was the worst, stupidest joke in the world."

"No, it's funny," I say, giggling.

"Please, can you please forget that I ever said that? Just continue your story."

"Well, it took a few tries to find the studs in the walls, and yes, the rods are a little crooked, but hey, I did it."

"I'm impressed," Raj says as we walk down the hall, pausing

in front of the door to my apartment. "Do you want to walk with me to class? It's just up the road."

"Sure," I say. "Let me just put on some shoes and lock up."

"This is a huge improvement," he says when we step into my apartment. He admires the curtains and gives them a little tug. "And those curtains aren't going anywhere. Not with those brackets."

"Nope, they are *drilled* into the studs!" I say, slipping into my sandals. I see him notice the blue blanket, which is tangled with the sheets on my bed. I've slept with it every night, either wrapped inside it or clutching it. "And oh my God, thank you so much for the blanket. I love it. It's the softest thing I've ever owned."

"No worries," Raj says, as I lock the door behind me.

"It was so nice of you to get it for me," I say.

"I figured you deserve it," Raj says. "Moving out to LA all by yourself."

"That's really sweet," I say, but I have to look away. I deserve it? I can't help but wonder would he feel the same way if he knew that I'd been rejected from every single college I applied to. That I was the only one in my class who was rejected on such a massive scale? Would he say that if he knew that I broke my mom's heart by moving out here instead of doing something practical and working twenty-four seven on college applications?

"So I got a job," I say, as we step outside and head toward the hills. It's September, but it doesn't feel like any September I've ever known. The air is hot and as dry as newspaper on the verge of catching fire. The light is so bright it feels like the sun is under a magnifying glass. I notice for the first time that there's a lemon tree in our next-door neighbor's unkempt front yard, and that its branches are heavy with fruit. I've never seen lemons anywhere except the grocery store. I actually wonder for a second if they're edible.

"Congrats!" Raj says. "Where?"

"Rocky's in Los Feliz."

"I bet you can make a lot of money there," he says as we turn down Franklin Avenue, which is blissfully shady. "Los Feliz is a cool neighborhood."

It *is* cool. There's a little movie theater, a taco stand, a bunch of restaurants and coffee shops. There are vintage clothing boutiques, an art supply store, and a supercool, bright bookstore with a tree growing in the middle of it. There's a library, a post office, and a yoga studio. And it's only a mile and a half from the Chateau Bronson. Almost walking distance, but not quite.

Rocky's is right in the middle of it all. It has a 1950s diner feel to it with miniature jukeboxes on each table. On my third day of looking for a job, a tired-looking manager named Gloria agreed to give me a shot without even glancing at my fake résumé.

"We need someone for brunch," she'd said, as a strong girl wiped tables at the back of the restaurant. "The first shift is on Sunday. It's a double. Can you handle it?"

"Yes," I said without hesitation.

"We'll see how you do," Gloria said. "You'll start training Wednesday. If it works, we'll give you more shifts, but I'm not guaranteeing anything. Okay?"

"Okay," I said, thinking I'm not guaranteeing anything either, then I rushed home and jumped for joy after checking number eight off my list.

✓	6.	Go to the grocery store and get ingredients for healthy meals.
	7.	Learn how to apply subtle yet effective eye makeup.
✓	8.	Get a job to make $ $ $!
✓	9.	Get a friend. (Friends?)
	10.	Get a new style, new wardrobe, etc.
	11.	

"When do you start?" Raj asks. At the crosswalk, he uses the side of his fist to tap the button that activates the walk signal. We're back in the sun, and I can feel sweat beading on my forehead.

"I'm training tomorrow," I say. The traffic is paused, and I'm about to dart across the street when Raj reaches for my hand and pulls me back to the curb.

"Careful," he says, his hand wrapped around my wrist. "People drive like psychos on this street."

"Thanks."

He smiles shyly. When he lets go of my wrist, it tingles.

"Now I just need to get headshots," I say as the walk signal lights up and we cross the wide avenue.

"I can take them for you," he says, "I mean, if you want."

"Really?" His strides are quick and purposeful, and I skip-jog to catch up.

"Sure," he says when we reach the other side. "I *am* a director, you know. I can take pretty good pictures."

"That would be so great, because there's no way I can afford professional ones."

"We can go to Griffith Park," Raj says.

"Where's that again?" I ask.

His face breaks into a warm smile. "It's right here." He gestures up the hill. "Remember we drove by it on our way to Ikea?"

"Oh, yeah." I hope I start to understand this geography soon.

"We'll get a really natural look there."

"That'd be awesome," I say. The sidewalk is on an incline. We're both sweating by the time we reach the gate of California Film School. "When can we do it?"

"How about Monday?" Raj asks. "I think you're getting a sunburn." He takes off his fedora and puts it on my head.

"Thanks," I say, surprised. "What about you?"

"I'm fine," he says. "I'll be inside all day."

"Perfect," I say.

"See ya," Raj says. I watch him open a gate and walk onto campus.

He has a place where he belongs, I think—an actual gate to walk through and close behind him. For a moment, I want to follow him inside—just to be enclosed somewhere instead of so exposed. College is like training wheels for adulthood. You live away from your parents, make decisions about your own life, but in a place that keeps you safe if you change your mind or lose your footing. As I turn back down Franklin Avenue, I feel thrust out in the world too soon. I've been knocked off of my tricycle and been handed a bike, but there are no training wheels for me. I've just got to hop on and learn how to ride.

I might not have a school to attend, but I do have a mission, I tell myself as I, the lone pedestrian, walk along the cracked sidewalk, past a gas station. I'm here to be an actress. Even though my path is not mapped out with a curriculum or guided by professors, I know where I want to go. The traffic is getting thicker and the sun is getting hotter, but for the first time since I arrived, I'm relieved the whole day is in front of me. There's something great about knowing I've got a job and not having actually started yet. I decide that I'm going to finally stop in Word of Mouth, the used bookstore/record store near the Mayfair.

I'm the first customer of the day, arriving just as a clerk with dreadlocks and a hippie skirt unlocks the door, a mug of coffee in her hand. She nods hello and puts on a jazz record while I search the section labeled *drama*. There are tons of old books about acting, some of them dating back to the early 2000s or even earlier, but the one that catches my eye is a newer-looking book simply called *Making It in Hollywood!* The cover is an illustration of a girl who could be me, holding a suitcase and gazing up at the Hollywood sign.

On the back is a picture of the author, Suzi Simpson. She grins up at me from her headshot. She has red hair and a genuine smile. She reminds me of one of my favorite teachers, Ms. Bishop, and I feel just by looking at her that she's my ally. Like on a tough day she'd make me cookies and be straight with me. I flip to the table of contents and every chapter heading excites me, especially the first several.

"Welcome to Hollywood"

"Great Expectations"

"The Dreaded Day Job"

"Your Body Is Your Instrument—Taking Care of You"

"Help! I Need Headshots"

"Getting an Agent (Or How to Deal Until You Do)"

Perfect. I check the copyright. The book is six years old, but I buy it anyway.

After I leave the bookstore, I stop at the Mayfair for groceries. Now that I have a job, I don't have to be quite so frugal, and, as Suzi Simpson says, I need to take care of my body, so I buy sliced turkey, apples, grapes, Cheerios, organic milk, English muffins, and a package of mint Milano cookies. It's gotten hotter as the morning has gone on, and by the time I get back to the Chateau, I'm sweating through my shirt. I'm unlocking the front door with my groceries balanced on my hip, when I hear someone humming to himself behind me. I turn and see a guy who looks about forty on his way up the steps. He must live here, too.

"You're new," he says, taking a quick step up so that he can hold the door for me.

"Yeah," I say. "I'm Becca."

"Let me carry that for you, Becca," he says, taking my groceries. "I'm Nathan. You can't be from here. You're too sweet."

"I'm not. I'm from Boston," I say. He gestures for me to go up the stairs ahead of him. "Where are you from?"

"The rotten apple!"

"New York?"

"You got it. Now, I can't help but notice that you have a very nice rear end," he says as I stop in front of my apartment. I laugh nervously. "Hey, would you like to nibble on some raw fish with me this Friday?"

"I have a boyfriend," I say, as I grab my groceries. "And I hate sushi. But thanks!"

He's openly staring at my butt now. I put my groceries down, fumble with my lock until at last I get the door open. I walk briskly into my apartment, covering my "rear end" with my hands. As the door shuts behind me I hear him say, "Oh fucky, fucky, fucky!"

Fucky? What? Who says *fucky?*

Should I have not talked to him at all? Should I have just flipped him the bird when he held the door open for me, and then sprinted up the stairs? I lock my door and sit on my bed, trying to decide if that was funny or scary or both.

I'm about to open my new book when I get a text from Mom.

Mom: Hi, honey. How's it going?

I debate telling her about Oh Fucky, but it will only scare her.

Me: It's great. I have my bed now. And my apartment is looking cute.

Mom: When do you start at the diner?

Me: On Sunday.

Mom: So proud of you for getting a job, sweetie. Look, I know it's only September, but it's not too early to think about those applications! Just a friendly reminder!

Me: The deadlines aren't until January 1.

Mom: Not if you want to apply early.

Me: Okay, Mom.

Mom: Love you to the sky.

Me: And back.

SEVEN

"GO GET THEM!" says Gloria in a harsh whisper.

"What? No! I can't."

The two customers left at Rocky's don't notice this tense exchange next to the elaborately old-school cash register. I wish they would. I wish they'd stand up for me, but they're not paying attention. They're busy enjoying their own conversations. My apron's stiff with ketchup and maple syrup, and my knees are tingling with fatigue. It's almost the end of my first real day of waitressing, and I'm afraid I might pass out from exhaustion.

I trained on Wednesday, Thursday, and Friday, shadowing a waiter named Manuel. I was scheduled to train for two days, but Manuel suggested I extend my studies to include a third. He's a true gentleman, introducing me to the rest of the staff as though

I were a dignitary. "Peanut," he said to a rough-looking cook. "This is our newest server, Becca." Peanut just grunted in return. Manuel is also the embodiment of patience and calm. With him by my side, talking me through every order, my training days were easy and kind of fun. I was okay even when he treated me like a toddler.

"Good girl!" he said when I successfully punched an order into the computer in less than ten minutes. "Way to go!" he said when I finally managed to carry two plates of cheeseburgers at a time. (The other waiters can all carry four.) I didn't mind. I needed the extra encouragement. I wouldn't have minded if he coached me through the rest of my day, saying things like, "You can do it!" when I opened a bank account or, "Keep trying!" when I got lost looking for a CVS.

But I'm a mess without Manuel. I can't keep the orders straight or deliver the food fast enough. I keep forgetting to ask how people want their burgers cooked or if they want fries or a salad, which means I have to go back to the table and apologize and ask them to clarify. Of course, the salad answer begs the dressing question. And there's the appetizer thing. You need to punch a special button on the computer if someone orders appetizers. If you don't hit that button, all the food comes at once. People hate that. People hate it so much that they yell. I had no idea how sensitive people can be about their fucking appetizers. Also, I only trained for two to three hours at a time, but today I got here at 7:00 a.m. and now it's almost 10:00 p.m. I sat down only once to scarf a turkey burger.

And now . . . this disaster.

Gloria looks at me sternly. Her haircut reminds me of my strict fourth-grade teacher. "You heard me. Don't just stand there, go get them!" She points at the street, to the four guys who walked out on their check.

"But they're huge." The unpaid check for eighty-three dollars is trembling in my hand.

"If they don't pay for it, you will."

Gloria makes a harsh gesture toward the door. I cannot pay eighty-three bucks for random strangers' food, so I open it. The wind could just blow me away, and I want it to when I see the guys sauntering down Vermont toward Sunset. They are pale, too pale, like they live in a basement. They have skateboards under their arms. They are skinny but also look weirdly strong. I don't think I can do this. I don't think that I can confront these guys and ask them for the money they owe me. But then I wonder if I'm being judgmental. They could be playwrights or producers for all I know. I jog toward them, my heart flapping. When I'm a half a block away, I downshift to a speed walk.

"Excuse me! Excuse me but you forgot to pay your bill." They keep walking. I know they can hear me. "You forgot to pay your bill," I say. The smallest one turns around to face me. He smiles in a way I don't understand. "It's eighty-three dollars. Here." I hand him the check with a shaking hand. He bends down so that he's looking me right in the eye.

"Caw! Caw!" he says, flapping his arms like a prehistoric bird of prey.

I scream, pivot, and race up Vermont Avenue. I can hear him laughing. Where are the police? Where are the helpful people of the world? I turn my head around to make sure that they're not following me, and sprint across the street. I open the heavy glass door of the restaurant and run inside. The last remaining customers have left, and Chantal, my fellow waitress, is laughing so hard she can barely breathe.

"You're going to get all the tables next Sunday, now that I know how fast you can move," she says, wiping her eyes.

Gloria is straight-faced and jowly as she counts her money, expertly flipping the bills so that they all face the same way. "Because I'm in a good mood we'll let it go this time. But don't let it happen again. Polish the dessert station, tip out the busboys, and you can go."

You. Can. Go. The words fall on my ears like *not guilty* from a jury.

Chantal and I wipe down the dessert display, take off our aprons, tip out the bussers, and get our purses from behind the bar. Gloria locks the restaurant behind us as we leave. Chantal takes a cigarette from her purse and walks to her new-looking truck, toting a plastic bag full of food. I'm debating whether I should walk or take the bus, when I see Chantal waving me toward her, away from the glass door. Is she going to offer me a ride?

"Here," she says, taking out a plastic container with a slice of banana cream pie in it. "I was going to eat it, but I'm giving it to you instead. The first night at a new place always sucks."

"Thanks, that's super sweet of you!"

"Don't get too excited," she says, stepping backward. "I'm not always this nice. See ya tomorrow."

I speed walk back to the apartment in the half-dark of the light-polluted evening, gripping the container of pie. The late September winds they call Santa Anas are blowing strong and warm. The smell of fire is in the distance. The palm trees brush above me like brooms sweeping the sky. I'm hoping that Marisol or Raj will want to share the pie with me, and I can tell them about the guys I chased. But when I knock on their doors no one answers.

As soon as I get into my room, I pull off my jeans and Rocky's Café T-shirt. I put on an old sweatshirt that I haven't worn yet, so it still smells like home. The money I earned today, two hundred and fifteen dollars, goes in my desk drawer, and I head up to the roof with the slice of pie. One faint star hangs above. I take a bite and wait to stop shaking.

"I can't believe I'm in a city," I say to Raj when we've made our way to the top of Mount Hollywood in Griffith Park for my photo shoot. My legs are throbbing from yesterday's double shift, but I try not to think about it as I take in the scenery around me. The pine, sycamore, and oak trees; the dry scraggly brush; the bright September sky; the smell of eucalyptus and sunbaked dirt; the feel of sunlight filtered through branches; and the back-and-forth song of birds. It's hard to believe that this park, which has to be at least one hundred times bigger than Boston's Public Garden, is right in the middle of LA and that we live so close that we can walk to it. "This is practically the wilderness, right?"

"That might be an exaggeration," Raj says as he looks through the photos he's taken so far. I watch his expression to see how he feels about the pictures, but I can't tell what he's thinking.

"Excuse me, but we saw signs warning us about rattlesnakes and mountain lions. To me that means wilderness," I say.

"Maybe 'urban wilderness,'" Raj says as a traffic helicopter hammers above us.

"Yeah. That sounds about right."

I was glad we didn't see any snakes or mountain lions. Squirrels and birds were our only wildlife sightings. We passed a few other people on our way up Mount Hollywood—hikers, a woman walking two giant German shepherds, a group of high school kids hanging out by a picnic table, and a couple on horseback (horseback!)—but mostly it seemed like we had the park to ourselves.

The wide, dusty trail curved along ridges, offering views of a mountain range that Raj said was the San Gabriel Mountains. He also pointed out downtown and Santa Monica. After a half hour or so and several steep inclines, we arrived at a large, round building that Raj said is an incredible observatory. He shot a bunch of pics around the exterior and then continued on to the top, which took us another twenty-five minutes. By the time we reached the peak of Mount Hollywood, my heart was pounding in my chest and I could feel the color in my cheeks. Marisol had insisted I bring makeup, but I read in Suzi Simpson's book that the most important thing about headshots is that they look like you, and I never wear makeup. Besides, Raj kept telling me that I looked great in the natural light.

I wonder if he was just saying that to help me relax, because there were some seriously awkward moments. Even though I knew this was what I was signing up for, it was just plain weird to have someone taking my picture constantly as I hiked up a mountain. Raj kept saying, "Just pretend I'm not here," but that's actually a really tall order. How can I not be aware of the guy following me with a camera? I realize that this is the essence of film acting, but it's got to be less weird if it's not your neighbor behind the camera.

During a break, Raj leans against a big rock, grimacing as he scrolls through the pictures.

"Any good ones?" I ask.

"Well, you're really cute," Raj says. "There's no doubt about that." He smiles as he looks at one picture, and I feel myself blush. "But something's missing."

"What do you mean?" I ask, joining him by the rock to look over his shoulder at the viewfinder.

"I feel like you have a wall up. Do you see what I mean?" Raj says, showing me some examples. In the shots where I'm making eye contact with the camera, I see that I'm a little removed.

They look like pictures for Facebook, not headshots. "I think you need to open up a little and . . . how do I say this? . . . reveal something."

"Okay," I say. The muscles on the back of my neck tense. "You're a director, can you . . . direct me?"

"Sure," Raj says, standing up. "Let's try some shots by that bench."

I walk over to the bench, sit down, and smile, feeling even more self-conscious than before I knew I was inadvertently putting up a wall.

"Just close your eyes and breathe," Raj says. I take a few deep breaths. Then I open my eyes, look up at him, and smile. He snaps a picture. "Let's try that again." We do, but clearly I'm not letting my guard down enough. In fact, the harder I try, the tenser I feel. "Okay, I have an idea," Raj says. "Think—without thinking too hard—about a moment when you felt really happy. Get really specific. Where were you? Who was with you? What were you doing?"

What comes to mind immediately is Maine, the day before Alex and I set off on our road trip. We were on the ferry to the little island where his family has a summer home. It wasn't raining, but it was misting. There was supposed to be a send-off party for us with his whole family and all of his cousins, before we drove across country together. I picture Alex, one arm wrapped around me, as he leaned in to kiss my cheek. And suddenly I can feel his skin—my hand on his. I remember thinking that we fit together like pieces of a jigsaw puzzle. I remember feeling lucky, even though I hadn't been accepted to college, because I already knew where I belonged. I remember that my fingers were chilly, and then he took my hands in his and blew on them. I remember the smell of his damp wool sweater. And that's what does it. That's what sends up a wave of emotion from my gut so forceful it hits me like a fist. Raj is clicking his camera, but I cover my face and turn away.

"You okay?" Raj asks.

I nod, but I can't speak. If I do, the tears will surely start. And once they start, I'm not sure they'll ever stop. I walk away and face the San Gabriels. I hold my breath until I feel the wave subsiding.

"Hey, are you okay?" Raj asks again.

"Yup," I call back, and I hold up my hand as if to say, *One minute.* I don't turn around until I'm one hundred percent positive that I won't cry.

"Do you see what I mean about shooting headshots outside?" Marisol asks later that night as the three of us eat Thai food and look over the pictures in Raj's apartment. I promised Raj I would buy him dinner for all of his help, and Marisol didn't have any cash on her, so I bought enough for all three of us. There are no less than eight Thai restaurants within a two-mile radius of the Chateau. "There are too many factors to consider," she says as she slurps her spicy shrimp soup. "Not to mention hair and makeup."

"Yeah, but you can't beat the setting," Raj says as he pops a spring roll into his mouth. "Or the natural light."

"These are amazing shots," I say, clicking on a picture of myself leaning against a curved wall of the observatory. "Couldn't I use this one?"

"It's a beautiful picture, but it's too serious for you," Marisol says. "If you were in your forties and hoping to play a divorced mom, I'd say go for it. But you're eighteen and comedic, I think. People aren't going to know what to do with you with that shot."

"So we need a close-up of Becca smiling," Raj says, quickly clicking through the one hundred and ten pictures he took.

After a container of pad Thai, two sides of chicken skewers, some fried tofu, and a fistful of fortune cookies, we narrow it down to three good pictures. Even if I do seem somewhat removed in them, and despite the fact that I could use some mascara and some concealer, they are at least a good representation of me.

Marisol sighs. "As brilliant as you are, Raj, I just don't think they look like headshots."

"But they're shots of my head," I say.

Raj laughs. "She has a point. I'd call her in for one of my films without a doubt."

"I'm afraid that if you use them, you're going to look like you don't know what you're doing," Marisol says. "No one will take you seriously with those shots."

"Whaaaat? Come on, now." Raj's voice has a defensive edge.

"Relax," Marisol says. "Let me show you what I mean."

Marisol shows us the online portfolio of her headshot photographer, and I see that she's right. The actors look perfectly groomed and flawless. They look, well, like actors.

"Okay, okay, we get the point," Raj says after we've seen enough doe-eyed ingénues to sink the *Titanic*.

"I've come all this way, the least I can do is get a headshot that looks real," I say.

"I'm sorry, boo," Marisol says. "I'm just telling you the truth."

"The sad truth," Raj says. He gives my shoulder a squeeze. "Our pictures are much cooler."

"It's okay," I say. "Friends are honest, right? But I don't know how I'm going to do it. I don't have a thousand dollars just, you know, lying around."

"That's why God made credit cards," Marisol says, and smiles.

EIGHT

MARISOL'S PHOTOGRAPHER IS booked until Christmas. So I research headshot photographers online and meet with my three favorites. I hire Theresa Vasquez because she accepts credit cards and the people in her pictures look engaged, like they're listening to a story with a luminous vulnerability or a charming, restrained enthusiasm. I scroll through the pictures on her site. The last one is a picture of a lady angling for school principal and judge parts. "I'll allow it, Counselor, but you're on thin ice," her expression says.

"Bring five of your favorite outfits. You want to feel like yourself because you need to look like yourself," Theresa says when we schedule. "And bring lots of textures. I love texture." I choose a blousy top that has metallic threads running through it, a tank top with lace trim, a T-shirt with a scoop neck, a retro denim jacket, a sundress, a chunky cardigan, and my favorite jeans.

The morning of my shoot, I wake up early, leaving plenty of time to take a shower, wash and dry my hair, pick up a coffee at Starbucks, and get the bus downtown without any stress. I'm making my way to the bus stop on Hollywood Boulevard, an Ikea bag with my outfits in one hand and my latte in the other, when a Honda Civic pulls up next to me.

"Becca?"

It's Oh Fucky!

"Hi," I say, wishing I'd never told him my name.

"Can I offer you a lift?" he asks.

"No, thank you," I say, continuing to walk. He drives slowly next to me. I feel like I should be scared, but I'm not. I just want him to go away.

"Do you like avocado?" he asks.

"Um, yes?"

"I knew it. Women love avocados. Now, I know you don't like sushi, but I can make an avocado filled with itty-bitty shrimp that will blow your mind. What do you say? A bottle of red. Avocado and prawns. Chocolate. My place or yours— wherever you feel more comfortable. We'll light some scented candles? Maybe take a bubble bath?"

"No, no, no thank you. I don't think my boyfriend will like that."

"Oh fucky!" He hits the accelerator and drives off.

Ew! A bubble bath? Itty-bitty shrimp? I feel gross just knowing that Oh Fucky's been planning this evening for us. And he lives right upstairs! I try to shake off the encounter so none of its weird residue interferes with my shoot. My shoot!

Theresa picks through my clothes and pulls out the cardigan, holding it with her thumb and forefinger. "Okay, this could work." She drops it on a chaise lounge. "If you were fifty." I feel my throat close a little, the way it does before I cry. She picks up the tank top, checks the label, and runs her fingers over the lace trim. "I'd hate for you to look cheap." She tosses it on top of the cardigan. My breath gets shallow as she picks up the sundress and frowns, then does the same with the jean jacket. She considers the T-shirt. "We'll start with this."

She's just being honest, I tell myself. This is why I'm paying a professional. She knows what works and what doesn't.

Her friend Adele walks in from the kitchen and sets up a stool. I'm paying an additional hundred dollars for her to do my makeup. It's nothing like when Marisol did my makeup. She applies it without tenderness.

"Um, do you think the lipstick's a little dark?" I say when I look in the mirror. She gives me a condescending look, shakes her head, and touches up her own face with a sponge.

I sit in a chair and smile. Theresa takes a few shots. She lowers the camera away from her face. I wonder if I'm putting up the wall that Raj mentioned again.

"Do you smoke?" she asks, wrinkling her nose.

"No," I say. "I mean, I did once. I was really stressed-out."

"I can tell," she says. Jesus. Wait. I did it once. Don't all the movie stars smoke for, like, years? "And what kind of stress can you have at your age?"

"Seriously," Adele says, pressing powder to her forehead. They laugh.

"Kind of a lot," I say. I'm paying this lady a thousand dollars for an hour and a half of her time, the least she can do is not laugh at me outright. After I leave, fine. Have a laugh at my expense—my very great expense, actually. But now? In the middle of my shoot?

She takes a few more shots.

"How old do you think I am?" She puts her hands on her hips. I know I have to aim low—like ten years low.

"Um, twenty-eight?"

"Forty-three." She smiles.

"Wow."

"Doesn't she look fantastic?" Adele asks. The way she says it sounds like *funtastic*.

"Want to know how I do it?"

"Sure." *No. I want you to focus on me and take my headshots.* I'm talking about a thousand dollars that I don't have, that I'm putting on a new credit card.

"I'm a vegan. I get ten hours of sleep a night. I do yoga every day. I drink four glasses of water before breakfast. No sugar. No caffeine. No alcohol. And certainly, no cigarettes." Well, she's definitely not *fun*tastic. Up close I think her skin looks a little too moist. I think she might need to take her moisturizing routine down just a half step so she doesn't glisten with quite as much aggression. She stands back and assesses me. "Okay, babe. You're stiffer than a corpse. We need to loosen you up," Theresa says. "What kind of music do you like?"

"I don't know," I say, afraid I'll have the wrong answer.

She frowns, puts on a hip-hop mix, and takes what feels like a million pictures. Half the time I'm in the scoop neck T-shirt. The other half I'm wearing one of Theresa's kurta shirts. We try to do something with a scarf, but it doesn't work. We seem to reach the same point I did with Raj. I'm guarded, but in this environment, I don't know how not to be.

"Okay, here's the deal," Theresa says. "Pretend like I'm your best friend." I sigh. This is going to be a stretch. "Imagine you're about to tell me something funny, something that you know will make me laugh." Immediately Oh Fucky and his gross date suggestion comes to mind.

"I can see you've got something," Theresa says, softening. "Perfect. Can you tell me the story?"

"So there's this guy in my building . . ." I start.

"Yeah?" Theresa says. I can see a smile forming behind her camera. "Go on."

I tell her the story, imagining that she's Marisol, and as I go on about the avocado and the scented candles, Theresa laughs and shoots away.

"I think we got it," she says, biting her lower lip.

A week later, I return to her studio, where we go over the pictures. In some of them I look like I'm in a yearbook trying to appear casually popular. In others, I have a deer-in-the-headlights, glazed, nobody's-home look. And then there are the I-could-eat-you-with-my-enthusiasm shots that were taken when I was imagining she was Marisol. All the pictures I like, in which I think I look good, Theresa tells me look nothing like me.

"This is the one," she says, pointing to a shot I skipped over.

"I look like an elf."

"But you're connecting with the camera." This makes me think of what Raj said, about how I have a wall up. Still, I can't help but notice she's not arguing with my elf assessment. "And your smile's not too big. It's natural. You can see your collarbones. That's a good thing. Shows you're thin." She looks at me with narrow eyes. "How do you stay so thin?"

"I don't know."

"Be careful. You almost look prepubescent." Gee, it's hard to win around here. Last week I was prematurely aging due to a single cigarette. She points to the image. "This is the one. See how alive your eyes are? The way you're looking up at the camera?"

"But do you think I look pretty?"

She sucks air in through her teeth. "I wouldn't worry about that too, too much."

"Why?" The whole point of these pictures is to look as good as you possibly can. Everyone knows that actors and actresses are supposed to be beautiful.

"You're a character actress," she says. My heart drops a little. A character actress is one who plays a supporting role—someone unusual or eccentric. "What? Did you think you were a Leading Lady type?"

"No, no. Not at all. No," I say. I guess I hadn't thought about my looks beyond believing that I'm appealing and maybe even pretty. I certainly never thought of myself as weird-looking.

"Do you mind if I ask what type you thought you were?"

"I don't know," I say, answering honestly. A Leading Lady type in Hollywood is someone indisputably beautiful. Maybe a tiny part of myself hoped I was a lead and indisputably beautiful, and just hadn't realized it yet, but another more realistic part of myself knew it wasn't true. I guess, if I were a great beauty, I'd know it by now. Theresa is smiling at me as she awaits my response. "I guess I thought I was a Girl Next Door," I say. A Girl Next Door type would be someone with a sweet, normal sort of prettiness. Not expected to be a great beauty, the Girl Next Door can nevertheless be a love interest and score a big part.

"No, no, no. You're a character. Trust me. I've been in this business a long time," she says, as she scrolls through my pictures.

I unnecessarily push my hair behind my ears and guzzle my sparkling water. A character actress, especially one as young as I am, is relegated to a lesser role like the *really* kooky best friend, or a slightly bonkers camp counselor, maybe the member of a cult, or a teenage mom living in dire straits. Even female high school "nerds" are played by the Girl Next Door types.

"I haven't upset you, have I?" she asks. I study my jeans. "I think you're taking this the wrong way. Lots of nice-looking girls are characters." She points to another one of my shots. "Hey, in this one, you look like you could be the Girl Next Door's sister."

"Oh," I say. "Okay." The part of Girl Next Door's sister doesn't sound so bad, but it certainly isn't the stuff that dreams are made of. It isn't why I moved to LA with nothing but a broken heart and a few suitcases.

"This is totally your shot," Theresa says, tapping her computer screen. "You can send this one out for more serious roles. The other one is a better commercial shot." She downloads the files onto a memory stick, hands it to me, and smiles, sending her glossy crow's-feet down her cheeks. "You have the files now. You're on your way. Don't worry. You're going to make it. I know you are. Just stay positive and drink a lot of water. And please, don't forget to leave a review on Yelp. It'd really help me out."

❦

As I'm unlocking the door to the Chateau, I run into Marisol, who is on her way to an audition. Her hair looks like it's been professionally styled, and her barely there makeup gives her a polished yet fresh appearance. She's definitely a Girl Next Door, if not a Leading Lady. I feel a stab of jealousy, but before it sinks in or starts to ache, Marisol embraces me. She smells like soap and laundry and kindness.

"I have a plan for us for tonight," she says. "We're going to this cemetery where they screen movies. Tonight it's *Edward*

Scissorhands. How fun is that? We can bring a picnic and blankets, and it's totally free."

"I'll make some pasta," I say.

"Perfect," Marisol says. "I'll bring the blankets and swing by around five. Love ya!" She blows me a kiss.

"Love ya, too!" I say, and blow a kiss back.

When I get back to my apartment, I download the pictures immediately. A few minutes later I get a text from Mom with a picture of her at our favorite restaurant attached. The sight of her face on my screen after being away from her for a whole month makes my breath catch in my throat.

Mom: Hi, sweetie. Did you pick out a good headshot?

Me: Yes, I think we got some OK ones. I have a
     commercial one and a serious one, too.

Mom: Send them to me!!

Me: Here.

I send the pics and she writes back right away.

Mom: Becca, you are GORGEOUS! How is that my
     baby?

Me: Thanks, Mom.

Mom: I miss you like crazy.

Me: Me too, Mom.

Mom: You're my brave girl.

Me: Do you think you can come visit?

Mom: I've been thinking the same thing. Unless of
     course you want to come home?

Me: You come here!

Mom: OK. Christmas?

Me: Yes, come out at Christmas!

Mom: I'll start looking at tickets. Now, I hate to
ask . . .

Me: I haven't started!

Mom: BECCA. I want you to get your college list in
order. Tomorrow is October 1!

Me: OK.

Mom: You'll have a list in a week?

Me: Yes.

Mom: You'll get online now?

Me: Yes.

Mom: Promise?

Me: Promise.

Mom: Love you to the sky.

Me: And back.

I open up my laptop and, of course, the first school I look at is Juilliard. How could they not want me? I would so fit in with these people with their dramatic expressions, in their leotards and Shakespeare costumes! Ugh, I was born to spend the day in a leotard! I have to get off the website before I start to get angry. I take a deep breath and review the application. Of course, I'm going to have to get two letters of recommendation. Do I ask the same people I asked last year? Or do I ask new people because obviously the ones I asked didn't do me much good?

I look at the Stanford website next. There's no way I'd get in. Ever. I imagine Alex among the Spanish-style buildings. It's been five weeks since we've seen each other. Where is he? I scan the pictures as if he might actually appear in one. I look at my phone and consider calling him. All it would take is one push of the button. It's so weird that the number that I've called so many times in the past is off-limits now. At least it is, if I stick to my guns and make *him* call *me* after such a big fuckup. But why hasn't he reached out? How long is this "beat" going to last? Looking at the Stanford website is turning into an exercise in torture.

I decide to check out Raj's school, California Film School—a place with no personal pain associated with it. The website looks nothing like the others. It's different because of the angle of the pictures of the campus, the way the students all appear to be in motion, the totally un-academic font, and the neon color palette. Here, the goal is total authenticity, I read. And my heart starts to race.

The school calls itself a laboratory for storytelling and asks its students to set themselves apart by diving deep within, while at the same time building personal relationships to create a community of artists. And the classes look so cool: Screenwriting for Animators, Finding Your Story, Visual Personal Essay, Real World Survival Skills. There are even acting classes like Scene Study, Improvisation, Advanced Acting, and Clowning. Clowning? That actually sounds kind of fun.

I click on the "apply" button and scan the requirements. No SAT—that's a relief. (But then, does that mean it's not a real school? How come I haven't heard of it until now?) I read on. I'll also need two letters of recommendation, which should be written by someone who understands my artistic voice. In addition, students must submit a screenplay, a film, or video. Finally there's a choice between an essay and a collage. Either one should express where you've been, where you are, where you're looking to go.

A collage. I haven't made one of those since middle school.

Hmm, I think, and make myself a cup of coffee. Hmm.

"I think he likes you," Marisol says quietly, nodding at Raj. We're spreading one of Marisol's blankets on a patch of grass as Raj chats with a classmate about ten feet away from us. We're in the Hollywood Forever Cemetery, where every hipster in Los Angeles has congregated to see the classic *Edward Scissorhands*. Raj seems to know half of the people here. On our walk into the cemetery, he stopped to talk with at least five people who are either friends from work, his regular customers, or people he goes to school with. I'd asked Raj to join us at the last minute, and he said yes without even thinking, and even offered to pick up samosas from his favorite Indian restaurant. I don't know what a samosa is, but he's promised me that I'm going to love them.

"Raj is supercool," I say, sitting down on the blanket and unpacking our picnic food.

"And cute," Marisol says. "In that doesn't-see-the-sun-much-and-drinks-too-much-coffee filmmaker kind of way."

"But I'm still in love with Alex," I say.

She raises her eyebrows. I spray cheese on a cracker and hand it to her. Marisol brought spray cheese and Ritz crackers to our picnic, saying it was the only cheese she could afford.

"What?" I say, in response to her look. "I can't help it."

"When was the last time you talked to him?" Marisol asks, munching on the cracker. "This is delicious, by the way."

"Five weeks ago," I say, spraying cheese on a cracker for myself. She's right—the spray cheese is so bad that it's good.

"I don't mean to be harsh, but don't you think he would have called by now if you were going to get back together?"

"A month is nothing in the grand scheme of things," I say. "Not when you've been together for two years. And by the way, yes, that's harsh."

Mom said that if I was patient, she was sure he would come back to me. She told me the important thing was not to chase him. Men are like rubber bands, she'd said, quoting some dating self-help book. Give him lots of room and he'll snap right back.

"I think you should call him," Marisol says.

"Really?" I ask, excited by the possibility.

"Why not?" Marisol says.

"Shouldn't I let him come to me?"

"What are you, some damsel in distress? Hell, no. You are a modern woman. If you want to talk to him, call his ass."

"Maybe you're right," I say, imagining how incredible it

would be to pick up the phone and hear his voice. Maybe he's feeling the same way I am, but he's scared to make himself vulnerable. "I think I will."

"Do it," Marisol says, helping herself to more spray cheese. "Right now, you're just reading tea leaves. But if you call him, you'll at least get some answers." A breeze sends picnic plates and napkins flying and people jump up to chase after them. "If you're looking for a *new* boyfriend, though, Raj would make a good one. You can tell he's really sweet, you know?"

"Do *you* like him?" I ask.

"Just as a friend. And anyway, like I could get him to look at me if you're nearby."

Could this be true? When I'm with her, I'm hardly ever thinking about my looks. But if I do, I feel plain in comparison. Is she just being nice? I wonder as she pushes my hair behind my ears. And yet, right now, she's regarding me like I'm the most interesting, adorable creature on earth.

"You'd look awesome with a topknot," she says.

"Really?"

"I'm all about playing up those cheekbones." She nudges me. "Oh, he's coming."

As images begin to flicker on the giant inflatable screen, Raj saunters toward us with his bag of samosas, striking a lean silhouette, which for some reason reminds me of a cowboy.

And just like that, I have an idea. I turn to Marisol. "Hey, can I borrow your Polaroid for a little while?"

"The Joy Cam? You bet," she says. "And take the film, too."

NINE

"HOLD STEADY," Marisol says as she applies a final swoop of blush. We're in her apartment, and various outfits are splayed all over the available surfaces. We settled on a chambray shirt-dress, flats, and a bold cuff bracelet. She's blow-dried my hair and done my makeup so that I look polished and put together, but in a way that's just right for an eighteen-year-old. I have my first actual appointment with an agent today, and I want to look absolutely perfect.

"There," she says, stepping back so that I can see myself in her full-length, freestanding mirror. She stands behind me, her hands on her hips. We look like such a pair.

"Don't move," I say. I grab the Polaroid and take a picture of our reflection.

"What are you doing with all these pictures?" she asks.

"Making a collage," I say, blowing on the undeveloped picture. As it comes into focus I have to admit to myself that I look good. I smile at my friend. "I think you nailed it."

"I had a lot to work with," she says. She scrunches my hair to add a bit of messiness and hands me a container of organic coconut water. "Now drink up. Hydration is your best friend."

"No, you are," I say. She actually blushes. "Wish me luck."

Suzi Simpson says that when you're searching for an agent you should let everyone know that you're looking. "You never know who has the perfect connection. Don't be embarrassed, hon! That's not going to get you anywhere. Go ahead, ask your second cousin who works in corporate law, your pals from the coffee shop, and don't forget the folks at your day job."

I found out on Tuesday while we were setting up for breakfast that Chantal has a cousin, Athena, who's an assistant-on-the-rise at one of the most reputable agencies in town: the Talent Commune. It was one of the first agencies I went to, the one with the creepy security guard in the building's lobby.

"Do you think she might meet with me?" I asked as I wiped fingerprints off the jukeboxes.

"I dunno," Chantal said, setting the tables at her usual rapid speed. "She thinks she's better than me because she went to USC and I didn't go to college—at least not yet."

"Me either, Chantal."

"Really?" She paused her setup and looked at me as if reconsidering her original assessment. "Go figure. You look like such a perfect little 'college girl.'"

"Well, I'm not." I shrugged.

"Anyway, now that she has this job, her head is so fat I'm surprised that she can fit into her brand-new MINI."

"Is it a convertible?" I asked with a smile.

"It is!" Chantal hooted with laughter. "That's how she does it! Good one, Shrimpy." She's been calling me this on occasion and even worse, she's also said, "Don't fall in" every time I take a bathroom break. I tolerate these little abuses because it's the only way to get along with Chantal, and getting along with Chantal is critical to making it through the day at the diner.

"Do you think you could find out if your cousin might possibly schedule an informational interview with me?" I asked. Suzi Simpson suggests the term "informational interview" as a way of putting agents at ease. She says that it's a "softer" way of requesting a meeting.

"Okay, I'll do it. I'll text her," Chantal said. "But I'm not making any promises."

Mid-shift, Chantal grabbed me by the arm and said, "Smile, Shrimpy!" Before I could respond, she'd snapped a picture of me with a Coke in one hand and a plate of fries in the other.

"What are you doing?" I asked as I bumped open the kitchen door with my hip.

"Athena wants a pic." Chantal stared at her phone as she texted.

"Oh my God, you're sending that to your cousin?" I delivered the Coke and fries to table ten and returned to Chantal.

"You could've at least warned me! I have a professional headshot, you know!"

"I don't have time for your professional headshot. Table nine is being a pain in the ass. They're all, 'Can I have the chicken salad, but without the chicken?'" Her eyebrows raised as she read a message on her phone. "She'll meet with you. How's Friday?"

"Holy shit! She said yes?" I gasped and jumped up and down. "Are you serious?"

"Hey," Gloria said, bursting into the kitchen. "Would you two Chatty Cathys get your butts out on the floor? I just sat a table of six."

"Of course," I said, masking my joy for Gloria's sake.

"I'm picking up food," Chantal said defensively.

"You're texting on the job. I can get new waitresses like this, you know," Gloria said, and snapped her fingers briskly. As soon as she was gone, Chantal and I gave her the finger.

"Friday at two. Take it or leave it," Chantal said as Peanut lined up her plates on the counter.

"Friday's perfect!" I told her, smiling so big that it hurt.

"Careful, plates are hot," Peanut said.

"I am so grateful. So, so, so grateful!" I opened my arms to hug her, but she'd given me the hand.

"Don't," she said. "You'll make me drop something. Follow me with their sides?"

"Anything, Chantal." I grabbed the platters of greasy onion rings and fries. "Anything for you!"

"Remember us when you're famous," Peanut said, as Chantal kicked open the out door and we'd headed back into the fray.

❀

Now Friday is actually here. My first agent meeting! I'm really looking forward to crossing my number-one goal off of my list today. My mouth goes dry at the thought, and I guzzle the coconut water.

"You're going to kill it," Marisol says, unbuttoning yet another button at the top of the dress I'm wearing. "Better."

"Too much?" I ask, glancing down.

"Please, this is LA."

There's a knock at the door.

"Taxi service here. Are you ready?" Raj asks. Marisol opens the door. Raj takes me in. "Whoa. You look amazing."

"Raj!" I say, surprised to see him. "Are you seriously going to give me a ride?"

"There's no way you're taking the bus to a meeting at the Talent Commune," he says.

"It's a special occasion, so I was going to grab an Uber . . ." I say.

"What if you get an idiot driver who takes Melrose?" Raj asks, waving me into the hallway.

"Or even worse, Fountain," Marisol says.

"No, you can't leave this in the hands of a ride-sharing service." Raj tosses his keys and catches them. "I'll take you."

"That's so nice." As Raj and I head out the door, I feel so

taken care of. I am definitely going to cross number nine off my list—boldly now—the tentative *s*, too.

"Break a leg," Marisol says, and gives my hand a squeeze. "This afternoon I'll take you to the hotel pool I've been crashing and you'll tell me all about it."

Raj drops me off in front of the building on Sunset Boulevard. "I'd wait for you at the Coffee Bean, but I have to get to work," he says.

"Thank you for the ride," I say, and lean over to hug him.

"Remember, you're interviewing her, too. A bad agent is worse than no agent. Not that I'd know, but that's what I've heard."

The same creepy security guard is in the building lobby. I can tell he's trying to place me, but I don't give him a chance.

"I have a meeting with Athena Jordan at the Talent Commune," I say in a tone of voice that makes it clear there'll be no suggestive glances today. He locates my name on a list and asks for an ID, which I hand over without making eye contact. I don't acknowledge him when he lets me through the turnstile.

What a difference having an appointment makes! Not only does the receptionist welcome me, she actually smiles and offers me a choice of water, tea, or coffee.

"Water would be lovely," I say. "Is it around the corner?"

"Oh, I'll get it for you," she says with a little laugh. "Sparkling or flat?"

"Flat, please," I say, taking a seat on the white leather sofa. If Athena becomes my agent, I will always remember this white leather sofa, I think. A moment later, the receptionist hands me a real glass of ice-cold water and a cocktail napkin with the Talent Commune logo on it.

"You must be Becca," Athena says when she arrives a minute later in the agency lobby. She looks like an older, taller, better-groomed, better-dressed version of Chantal.

"Yes," I say, standing up to shake her extended hand.

"Come with me," she says, gesturing down a hallway. "To the smallest office in the world." I follow her with my water, because I don't know what else I'm supposed to do with it.

Athena's office is small, tiny even, but there's a window with a view of the Sunset Strip. She sits at her desk and I sit across from her, still holding my water. It seems presumptuous of me to place it on her desk, where there's so little room. We chat for a few minutes about Chantal and waitressing and Boston, which she visited once when she was twelve.

"Here's my headshot," I say, removing it from the folder in my bag.

"Let's have a look," she says. I hand it to her. "Cute shot."

"Thanks," I say.

"So, you don't really have any training," Athena says as she looks over my résumé.

"I just got here. As soon as I find the right class I'm going to enroll."

"But you can play super young, so that's good."

"I'm totally willing to go out for young roles, tween roles even."

Her phone rings. "Hi, can I call you back in one sec? I'm just finishing something up." My heart sinks. Finishing up? I've only been here for five minutes. Athena hangs up and smiles at me, hands folded on her desk. "I love that you're so new in town. I love that you haven't made the rounds yet."

"Thanks," I say. Okay, this is better. This is more like it. "I'm definitely a fresh face! I've only met about twenty people total in all of LA, not counting the restaurant customers, of course."

"And I like your attitude," Athena says. "You have a great vibe. Casting is going to love that."

"I can't wait to meet them," I say.

"You can definitely give me a call when you get into SAG," she says, pushing her card across the desk.

"Oh," I say, picking it up. "How do I do that? I have the rest of the day off, so if you tell me where to go . . ."

"OMG, you are so cute," Athena says. She checks her watch. "You have to get into the Guild to get a SAG card, and that's . . . kind of a whole Catch-Twenty-Two thing."

"What do you mean?" I ask.

"Basically, in order to get into the Guild, you have to get hired in a speaking role for a SAG production, but you can't go out for those roles unless you have your SAG card. It's totally annoying."

"Sounds kind of . . . impossible," I say.

"It is, but it isn't," Athena says, waving away my concern. We smile at each other awkwardly, and then she opens her office door and I follow her down the hallway in awkward silence, my full glass of water still in hand. When we arrive at the agency's entrance she smiles again and says, "Don't look so worried. You'll figure it out. And when you do, you have my card."

"Thank you so much for meeting me," I say. I hold up the glass of water. "Should I . . . ?"

"I'll take that," Athena says.

As I ride the elevator to the first floor, I wonder how our meeting is already over. It feels like it barely even happened. I'm dreading getting my ID back from the security guard, but he's so engrossed in conversation with a guy about the LA Dodgers that this time it's he who hardly acknowledges me.

"Name?" he asks without looking up.

"Becca Harrington," I say. He pulls out my ID and slides it across the counter as he launches into a speech about what makes a good pitcher. As I place my ID in my pocket, the guy who he's talking to says, "Hey, it's you!"

I look up and see the man who bought me juice after my first disastrous non-meeting. "Hi!" I say.

"You know, it's only been what—a week or so?—and you don't look like you're from out of town anymore."

"I'm working on it," I say, wondering what it is about me that has changed. There's something about him—his sparkling eyes and boundless energy—that gives me a lift.

"Fast learner," he says, and checks his watch. "Great catching up with you, Joe." He nods at the security guard and then turns back to me and winks. "I'd buy you another juice, but I don't think you need it anymore."

"Thanks," I say. "And thanks again for the first one. It really did make me feel better."

And then he's off, jogging toward the elevator bank, calling, "Hold the door!"

TEN

WHEN I GET BACK to the Chateau Bronson, I review my list. I officially check off number nine.

√	6.	Go to the grocery store and get ingredients for healthy meals.
	7.	Learn how to apply subtle yet effective eye makeup.
√	8.	Get a job to make $ $ $!
√	9.	Get a friend. (Friends?)
	10.	Get a new style, new wardrobe, etc.
	11.	Become a working actress!

Raj and Marisol feel like really solid friends. Then I make a note next to number one:

	1.	Get an agent!	~~Met with Athena at Talent Commune.~~ Follow up on SAG.
✓	2.	Get curtains.	
✓	3.	~~Get a pillow~~	

It's not what I wanted exactly, but once I write it down, I realize that it's *something*. It's progress.

I stare at number twelve:

✓	1.	~~Get a friend. (friends?)~~
	10.	Get a new style, new wardrobe, etc.
	11.	Become a working actress!
	12.	♡ Get Alex back. ♡

Without thinking about it too much, I decide to call him. Marisol is right. I'm not a damsel in distress. I'm a modern girl. If I want to call him, I should. It's not as if my mom has had the best luck with men, anyway. She broke up with her last boyfriend almost four years ago now. What am I waiting for?

"Becca?" Alex says. I hear in those two syllables excitement, sweetness, and joy. Maybe he misses me just as much as I miss him, but has been too embarrassed about the way he acted to call me.

"Hi," I say, very aware of the sound of my voice, which is too perky and higher than normal. "What's up?"

What I really want to say, of course, is what happened? What are you thinking? Where have you been? Meet me right now at the Leaping Dolphin Inn. We will talk and you will tell me how sorry you are and you will hold me so tight and make this better. But for some reason, even though, except for my mom, there is no one I know as well as Alex, and no one who knows me as well as he does, I can't find those words. Something inside tells me to hold back. I'm not used to holding back. I don't want to, but I can't seem to let go and speak my mind.

"Becca, wow. It's great to hear your voice," he says.

"It's great to hear yours," I say, melting into the moment I've been longing for. I feel the wonderful relief of talking to someone who is deeply familiar. Because as great as Marisol and Raj are, nothing can replace the bond of first love. I say his full name in my mind, Alexander William Goddard, and collapse on my bed. "How are you? How is everything?"

"It's awesome and beautiful here. The classes are amazing, my roommate is this kid from New York City who's, like, the smartest guy I've ever met, and, oh, hold on—"

I hear some shuffling in the background. Alex's muffled voice. I smile up at the ceiling and wonder, Has this already become a funny story? If we get back together, and this moment is crystallized and clarified by hindsight, will we hold it up like a special Christmas tree ornament: the moment we knew we were still in love?

"How's Ruby?" I ask.

"Ugh. Ruby died," he says.

"What? That's so sad!" I say.

"Not really," he says matter-of-factly. "I sold her for parts. It was time for an upgrade."

"How can you say that?" I ask. I feel a shift in energy that's both subtle and incredibly clear. Ruby: the car I named, the one we made out in at stoplights all across the country, the metal beast that carried us safely to California. Lovely, quirky, one-of-a-kind Ruby. "You just discarded her like a hunk of junk?" I'm trying to sound casual and funny, but I can feel the edge in my voice.

"So many things went wrong as soon as I got here. She was on her last legs. Or . . . wheels."

"What about my camera?" I ask, swallowing even though my throat is dry. Could all of our memories have vanished along with the Volvo?

"Oh, yeah. No, I got it. I took it out. It's here somewhere."

"Did you get the pictures printed?" I ask, verbalizing what I suppose has been my secret wish all along—that he would discover the film, get it developed, and remember us. Remember me. Those photos are evidence of our love.

"No. Wait. Was I supposed to?"

"Oh," I say, feeling disappointment like a sandbag on my chest. "No. That's—"

"I'll FedEx it to you when I find it."

"Okay. Good." My heart hammers. "Aren't you going to ask about LA?"

"How is it?"

"It's so great," I say, forcing enthusiasm into my voice. "I have really good friends. And I'm waitressing and it's so crazy. I got my headshots. And today I actually had a meeting with an agent."

"I'm happy for you." There's an awkward silence. I feel like I'm scaling a wall of ice. This conversation started out so well, but now I can't get a foothold.

"Um. I kind of have to go. Is there something you need?"

"Not really. Do you know what you're going to be for Halloween?" I ask. I'm grasping at straws, I know, but this all feels so slippery. I'm afraid that when we hang up, he'll disappear forever.

"Halloween?"

It's October, so it's totally legit for me to ask. "Remember when we went as a shark and a lifeguard?"

"This isn't a great time for me, Becca. I can't really talk."

"Alex. Wait. I don't know. I just feel like . . . Like. Ugh. I don't know." I cover my eyes. I'm shivering. "I guess the thing is . . . The thing is that . . . I miss you."

"Yeah?"

"Yeah. I mean yes. Yes." I lie back on the bed, phone held tight, straining for his response, gauging his breath.

"Thanks," he says. He mutters something under his breath.

"Is someone with you right now?" I swing my legs off the bed, put my feet on the floor, and stand up like a jack-in-the-box released. "Are you dating someone already?"

"I don't think now is the time—"

"Alex, are you with someone?" I actually feel like I'm going to throw up.

"Kind of."

"But it's only been a few weeks! That's nothing." My breath is rapid and shallow. My body is going into some kind of shock. How can I just be dropped like that? It dawns on me that I was actually left on the side of the road, traded in like Ruby.

"Are you sure you want to argue about this?"

"Yeah. I am. I don't think it's healthy for you. I don't think you've processed your emotions. And I think you might be headed straight for a midlife crisis to be totally honest with you."

"A midlife crisis?" He laughs.

"I'm being serious!"

"Okay, well . . . I'm sorry that you feel that way."

"Why are you being like this?" I ask.

"Like what?"

"So polite and distant and weird."

"I apologize. I have to go, Becca."

"Don't say my name like that."

"Like what?"

"Like that." *Flat*, I think. *Devoid of emotion. As if I'm just an actress knocking on your door without a headshot or résumé.*

"Look. I've got—"

"I know. You gotta go. So do I." I turn the phone off and slide down the wall, my face in crying position. The floor feels like it's dropping away from me, and that I might fall straight through the apartment below, through the hot center of the earth, all the way to China. Did that conversation really happen? I feel warm and gross like I'm getting the flu. There's a knock on the door. My hand is still clutching the phone. A drop of sweat rolls down my rib cage.

"Hello?" Marisol asks, opening the door. I guess I'd forgotten to lock it, which is a really scary thought considering Oh Fucky is right upstairs.

"Hi," I say, heaving a breath.

"Are you okay? I was taking out my trash and heard you yelling in here."

"Not really. I just called Alex, and he's *dating* someone."

"Oh, boo. I'm so sorry."

"I thought he loved me," I say. "He said he did, like, last month. Can people's feelings really change that quickly? Can love just disappear?"

"I don't know," she says.

"He was talking to me like I was a nobody," I say to her.

"You're not a nobody," she says. "You're my best friend in Los Angeles."

Marisol holds me while I cry. She lets me cry a good long while. And then she pours me a glass of water. As I drink the cloudy tap water from my Ikea cup, she brushes my hair with her fingers.

"So, more important, how did it go with the agent?" she asks.

"She told me to come back when I had my SAG card. But how am I going to get my SAG card if I don't have an agent?" As

I explain it to her, all of my previous hopefulness seems to fall away. "Do you have a SAG card?"

"Yeah, I got mine because of my boss. Her husband's a producer, and he gave me a really small role in one of his films so I could get in."

"That was so nice of him!" I say. "You're so lucky."

"It was my plan all along. It's why I took the job," Marisol says. "There are other ways to get a SAG card. You can be an extra on a SAG production—you can apply to Central Casting and see how that goes. But it'd be better if someone just hired you. Central Casting is pretty demoralizing."

"It's all so demoralizing. This sucks."

"Here's what you need to do—apply to every playhouse, every production company, get a body of work together. You want someone who wants to work with you."

"What do you mean?" I ask.

"I guess I mean that an agent who really wanted to work with you wouldn't have given you the SAG runaround," Marisol says.

"So even if I do go crazy trying to get my SAG card, she might not want to work with me?"

"I'm just being honest," Marisol says with a shrug.

"I know," I say. "That's why I love you."

"I love you, too." A mischievous grin spreads across her lips. "I saw something in the hall that I think will make you feel better."

"Really?" I ask, wondering what she could have seen in our dirty, disgusting carpeted hallway that could change anything.

She scampers to my door, opens it, and comes back holding out a fake rose.

"What's that?" I ask as she hands it to me. It's made of a shiny, synthetic fabric.

"I saw the guy with the big teeth drop this in front of your door."

"Oh Fucky?" I ask. She makes a face. "That's, like, his catchphrase." She bursts into laughter. "He's so freaky!"

"He's a hard-core Scientologist," she says.

As she says this, the rose shape comes apart in my hand, quickly revealing itself to be a pair of panties. Marisol covers her mouth. I can see from her eyes that she's laughing.

"Stop laughing. This isn't funny. It's gross and scary." For a minute I'm seriously pissed at her. She turns away, her back shaking with laughter. "Marisol!"

"I'm sorry, it's just . . . I can't."

"What if he tries to abduct me or something?"

"He's a Scientologist, not an alien. All you have to do is tell him that you're super into therapy and he'll leave you alone."

"Really?"

"Yeah. It would be literally against his religion to associate with you."

"Oh, well, then, do you want these?" I throw them at her and they land on her sock. She shrieks and tries to kick the panties off, but the cheap fabric sticks. As she gets more frantic, I laugh. She picks them up and flings them across the room. I dive for them before they reach my pillow and toss them out the window, but they blow right back in, and Marisol falls on the bed in giggles. I throw them out again, and together, laughing, we watch them fall to the sidewalk below like a bright, exotic bird that's forgotten how to fly.

After Marisol and I visit "her pool" and before I go to bed, I text Mom. I know it's late there, but she never goes to bed before midnight.

Me: Hi, Mom. I talked to Alex today.

Mom: Really? He called?

Me: No, I called him.

Mom: Uh-oh.

Me: He has a new girlfriend.

Mom: Sweetheart, are you OK?

Me: Not sure. Actually, no.

Mom: He's adjusting to college. I think he'll be back.

Me: Does love just go away? Or does that mean it wasn't love to begin with?

Mom: That's a big question, honey. I don't know if I have the answer.

Me: Everything hurts.

Mom: I know. Do you want to come home?

Me: Mom!

Mom: Sorry. I just miss you so much.

Me: Did you find a ticket for Christmas?

Mom: Yes. I'm coming out December 23. I hope
there's room in that apartment for me.

Me: Yay! I'll get an air mattress.

ELEVEN

"MY NAME IS THOMAS. I'm an independent filmmaker with Vagabond Productions and you sent me your headshot."

I'm walking to work, my cell phone held tightly to my ear. I remember sending my headshot to this production company. To get my mind off of Alex, who I've decided is in complete and total emotional denial, I've been doing exhaustive research and sending my headshot to every production company in Los Angeles, just as Suzi Simpson recommended in her book. ("I know you've got a good brain because you bought this book. Go ahead and use it, kiddo! Research the production companies. Get their addresses. Be a bloodhound!") Suzi Simpson also advises her readers to use other people's doubts as fuel to work even harder. Alex has certainly given me that. Once I'm famous, once Alex sees how talented I am, he will regret treating me the way that he did on the phone.

I know from my research that Vagabond Productions formed in 2012 to make political films. Last year, they produced a small film called *Clotilde* that won several awards at festivals. I hadn't exactly heard of the festivals where it won awards, but I was still impressed. It was reviewed by the *LA Times*, and one of the actors went on to get a part in an HBO drama. I started reading the reviews and found myself swept up in the film's purpose, which was to expose our internalized racism. In my cover letter I said their work was courageous, ambitious, and necessary. Let Alex play his stupid guitar within the ivory tower of Stanford. While he's paying insane amounts of money to hide from the world, I'm out in the city, among artists like the director on the other end of the phone.

"We're auditioning for a new film and we'd like to see your work," Thomas says.

"Oh, I'd love to. *Clotilde* sounded amazing. I was moved by the reviews alone."

"Thank you. You're the only one who wrote a letter with your headshot. A very well-written letter, I might add. It made a big difference that you were familiar with our work. I probably wouldn't have called you otherwise, as it seems you haven't started your training in earnest."

"I'm going to start taking classes soon," I say. Once I win the lottery.

I really would love to take classes. I've even called a few

studios around town ("around town" is an expression I picked up from Suzi Simpson). But they all cost way more than I can afford. I'm not sure how I'm supposed to pay for them and all of my living expenses. November's rent nearly wiped me out completely.

I have five minutes to get to work, which is three minutes less than I need to get there on time. But I pick up my pace when it dawns on me that my headshots and cover letters are working. Just like Suzi Simpson promised, action equals results. I pause at the curb and then dart across the street, hoping I don't get a jaywalking ticket.

Thomas continues. "Let me tell you a little bit about the project. It's titled *Hamlet Lives*."

Ohh, Shakespeare!

He tells me that its purpose is to bring art to the people with the hope of sparking political action. "Art has become cake for the elite, but it should be bread for the masses. If people see actors transforming themselves, they feel that they have the power to transform their own lives, and maybe even their government." Even when diluted through a cell phone, Thomas's voice is full and rich—and vaguely British. His natural speech pattern has a strong rhythm. "And where are the everyday people every day?"

"Um, every . . . where?" I round a corner onto Vermont, breathless as I pass a man whose stride is twice as long as my own.

"Yes, but how do everyday people get everywhere every day?"

"Every . . . which way?"

"The Metro," he says.

"In LA?"

"Touché," he says, and laughs. "We can't shoot an inspiring, modern *Hamlet* in someone's Kia Soul, can we?"

"I guess not," I say.

Thomas explains that this abridged version of *Hamlet* will be shot entirely on the red Metro line using the latest iPhone. All rehearsals, filming, and meetings will happen on the subway. The only compensation for the actors will be an unlimited monthly bus pass.

"You'd be amazed at the industry attention our last film received," Thomas says. "My lead from *Clotilde* is now—"

"On that show about the prison guard, I know!"

"Becca, do you want to be a Vagabond?"

"Yes, I do." I don't know how I'll pay my rent if I have to miss waitressing shifts, but if I get the part, I'll find a way, as Suzi Simpson says. ("We actors are a scrappy bunch!") In about six heartbeats, I come up with a plan. As soon as I get the shooting schedule, I'll trade shifts with someone. And if that doesn't work, well, now that I have some experience, I might be able to get a different waitressing job. And the job won't hurt as much, because I'll have this secret, private, other life that has nothing to do with waitressing. I'll be a working actress.

"Great," Thomas says. "You'll be auditioning for Ophelia."

"Awesome." Ophelia is a lead—hardly a character part. In your face, Theresa!

"It's a group audition, so there'll be a couple of other Ophelias there as well. Meet me tomorrow at three at the Hollywood and Vine Metro station. I'll be wearing a brown derby, just like the famous old Hollywood club. I'll be providing you with sides then."

"Perfect." I've learned that sides are a few pages of a script that are used in an audition. We say our good-byes just as I reach the restaurant. I stand outside the frosted-glass door and glance at my watch. I'm already one minute late, but I don't care because I have my first LA audition. An old lady passes me, wheeling a personal shopping cart. She smiles at me, craning her neck to maintain eye contact, and I realize that she's reflecting my own expression—I'm emanating happiness.

I take a minute to enjoy the moment before I enter restaurant hell. I text Marisol.

Me: I have an audition for an indie film!

Marisol: Yaaaaaaay!

A crisp breeze wraps around me. People say that there are no seasons in LA, but that's not true. The trees are turning red and gold. The sky appears to have been swept of all atmospheric dust; it's the cleanest shade of blue. The city seems like it's getting its act together, almost like a secretary is organizing it. Fewer people are wearing flip-flops. Even the homeless man who hangs out on the corner of Vermont and Franklin is more motivated. He usually mutters nonsense in circles, but now he's walking back and forth in front of the library with a mantra: "I've got to get back to Dallas. I've got to get back to Dallas."

I take a deep breath and open the glass door, fully prepared for Gloria to bitch me out. Instead, I enter some alternate version of the restaurant. The energy of the place actually matches the decor. The music is twice as loud as it usually is. Chantal is dancing near one of the jukeboxes with a can of whipped cream in her hand. Marvin is lip-synching into a broom. An open beer sits on the cash register.

"Guess who's not coming in tonight," Chantal says, and dances over to me.

"No! No? Really?" I start jumping up and down. Chantal nods. "Where is she?"

"She called in sick." I join Chantal in her dance of joy.

"Oh, this is a good day," I say. "This is a great day."

"Tell me about it," she says. "My boyfriend and I had sex twice this morning, and I got off both times." Then she sprays whipped cream from the can into her mouth. She points the nozzle at my face. "Want some?"

"Oh, no thanks."

"Yes, you do," Chantal taunts me, grabbing my T-shirt.

"No, no, Chantal! Stop!" I try to squirm away, but she's a lot stronger.

Peanut emerges from the swinging kitchen doors chanting, "Girl fight! Girl fight! Girl fight!" This would usually gross me out, but I can't stop laughing long enough to be disgusted or mad or to fight off Chantal as she backs me into a booth. Her face shows both a wild glee and seriousness of purpose as she points the nozzle at my mouth and says, "Open up, white girl!"

TWELVE

"SWEET PARKING SPOT!" I say when I see Raj's Corolla parked right outside the door of our apartment building. He's offered to give me a ride to my audition. I told him there was no need to, but he insisted, saying that he's totally invested in my career at this point. "The idea that you might be late to an audition because of public transportation gives me too much anxiety," Raj told me. "And besides, I need to get out of the apartment and clear my mind. I'm totally stuck with my screenplay."

Now, Raj rushes forward to open the door for me.

"This is the first time since I've lived here that I've actually gotten this spot. I almost don't want to leave it," he says.

I climb inside, and he shuts the door. As he walks to the

other side of the car, Oh Fucky emerges from the Chateau in workout gear. I immediately slump down in the seat. After the rose panties, I'm dreading seeing him more than ever, but it's too late. He catches my eye and waves enthusiastically. I nod a curt hello, hoping he'll pick up on my icy vibe. As soon as Raj gets in the car, Oh Fucky's face falls. I realize he must think we're together, and I hope that this cools his interest in me. But as he drops to the sidewalk and starts doing push-ups, clapping between each one, I wonder if instead it's activated his competitive streak.

"Tell me about your screenplay," I say, turning and focusing on Raj. It's hard to ignore Oh Fucky's loud grunts as he does his push-ups, but I do my best.

"It's a psychological thriller," Raj says, as he pulls away, thankfully leaving Oh Fucky and his strenuous push-ups behind us. "It takes place in an old hotel that used to be a sanatorium."

"Great idea," I say.

"Thanks. I've been thinking about it for a while. So this young couple checks in, but they can't seem to leave. Every time they escape, the scene resets itself. They're stuck inside the hotel until they figure out why it's holding them there."

"It sounds like you got this," I say as we cruise down Hollywood Boulevard. No traffic so far. "That's totally creepy."

"But how is this not going to be repetitive?" Raj asks, turning to me with panic at our first stoplight. "I'm starting to think it's a shitty idea."

"No!" I practically scream. "No, no, no!"

"Is that just your natural enthusiasm talking, or do you really mean it?"

"I mean it. It's meant to be repetitive. That's the whole concept."

"But how do I keep it from being boring?" Raj asks. The light turns green, and he steps on the gas, navigating around a minivan.

"Hmmm. Tell me more about the story," I say. We slow down as we hit our first bump of traffic.

"This couple has to try all kinds of different tactics, of course, but it still feels like there's not enough tension."

"What if one character knows the scene is resetting itself, but the other character doesn't, and the girl keeps trying to explain it to him, but the guy just thinks she's acting crazy."

"That's interesting," Raj says, his eyes lighting up. "So she has to convince him of this weird reality before the scene resets itself."

"Exactly," I say.

"I like it," Raj says. He smiles at me; all signs of panic are gone.

"Sometimes you have to lead with enthusiasm," I say. "And let the answers follow."

"Wise human-animal," he says, and tosses me his iPhone. "Pick out a tune. Something fun."

"You got it," I say, and select an old favorite of Mom's. Stevie

Wonder's "Signed, Sealed, Delivered I'm Yours." He cranks it up, and we both sing along. I can honestly say that there's nowhere else I'd rather be.

The Hollywood and Vine station is packed. I make my way to the man I've identified as Thomas—an attractive, sturdy-looking guy who, as promised, is wearing a brown derby. He's also donned a vest that evokes the Romantic era, and a pocket watch actually peeks out of one his pockets. His old-fashioned getup makes him seem like he isn't a serious person, but I try not to be disappointed. At least he's neat and well groomed, and when he shakes my hand, he smells like soap. He winks at me as he speaks into his cell phone in Russian. "Dah, dah, dah."

I read that I'm supposed to dress appropriately and neutrally for auditions. So I chose jeans, a white T-shirt, my ballet-style sweater, and zebra flats.

There are two other girls in Thomas's orbit who I assume are the other Ophelias. One of them looks like she's still in high school. I shouldn't talk because Theresa said I looked like I could be eleven. This girl is wearing a shirt with a plunging neckline and a miniskirt. She has blond ringlets, big blue eyes, and a look of constant, unprovoked amazement.

Another woman is in her late thirties. In her pilling sweater and faded black pants, she looks like an office worker who's been slowly deteriorating under fluorescent lights. I feel a pang of tenderness for her as I notice that her under-eye concealer has gathered unfortunately in her crow's-feet. She's holding her résumé in her hand. I see that she went to Juilliard. My Juilliard! As she sighs and shifts position, she flips it over, allowing me to study her headshot. She looks ten years younger in her picture than she does in real life.

Your headshot needs to look like you, I want to say. Didn't they teach you that at Juilliard? Theresa certainly made that clear to me, and Suzi Simpson mentions that on, like, page twelve. Thomas ends his call and gives us his full attention, which is as intense as floodlights. It physically hurts to meet his gaze.

"Okay!" He rubs his hands together and motions for us to gather closer. "You'll have to excuse me. That was the Moscow Art Theatre. I have a gig there this spring." Pocket watch or no, the Moscow Art Theatre is a big deal. "Who knows, maybe we'll take this film to Moscow." He claps my arm as if he can read my thoughts. I would love to go to Moscow.

"Let's get started, shall we?"

He hands us our sides and gives us a few minutes to look through them. The three Ophelias scatter to various benches and read over the material. It's the famous "get thee to a nunnery scene," in which her father, Polonius, and Hamlet's uncle and stepfather, Claudius, hide behind a curtain to eavesdrop on Hamlet and Ophelia. Everyone, including Ophelia, thinks that Hamlet is in love with her. Hamlet denies ever having loved her with very simple language. His line is, "I loved you not." It doesn't feel so different from Alex hopping in his car and driving off. I know that there's a difference—Hamlet's being ruthless, and Alex was just failing to be kind. But either way, it sucks to be told you're not loved. I can feel Ophelia's reply, "I was the more deceived," in my gut.

Stupid, stupid Alex. I take a deep breath and try to cleanse my thoughts of him. He will be so sorry when he reads about this film.

A casual observer might think that we actresses are crazy as we prepare to audition. Juilliard is pleading to a Metro map, and the blond chick is gesturing wildly, weeping real tears. I'm sure I look no saner as I continue to take deep, relaxing yoga breaths, occasionally opening one eye to make sure they haven't left without me.

"Come on, Ophelias. Let's make art!" Thomas cups his hands around his mouth, projecting his voice over the sound of a train grinding to a halt. The other actresses and I exchange nervous glances as we step aboard.

"Folks, the bard said that all the world's a stage, and I'm going to take him at his word. Welcome to the theater—or should I say the soundstage."

Thomas's voice is booming and tinged with that faint British accent. With the exception of four teenaged boys in school uniform and a half dozen people in matching "I Love Jesus" T-shirts, our spectators are a tired, downtrodden-looking crowd. Talk about a captive audience. A homeless woman cries, "Bravo! Bravo!" and bangs her heels against the bench. She's eating a jar of chunky applesauce with a stainless steel spoon.

"This is the last thing I need," mutters a tired medical professional in Betty Boop scrubs.

"I hope we don't piss them off," the blonde says as her eyes flit to an angry-looking dude in a bandanna.

Thomas explains to our audience that they're witnessing a different kind of filmmaking. If they feel moved to participate, they should. I have to bite back a smile as I imagine Marisol sitting next to me. Thomas gives a brief, entertaining lecture on the history of revolutionary theater that, to my surprise, garners applause. He explains to us, and to everyone riding in our car, that the actors will freeze when the train stops in the stations. We'll unfreeze and resume acting as soon as the train starts to move again.

We each take a turn performing the scene with Thomas as Hamlet. The crowd shifts at every stop, but people accept us as a group of actors within seconds of entering our car, and in general seem happy to be part of an audience. The Jesus Lovers are watching us with open, beaming faces, giving rounds of applause after each audition. I can hear them whispering to one another, "Oh, she's really good," or "That one's going to be famous," or "I think the guy's the best."

I'm the last one to perform the scene, and thankfully I only have to freeze once. Thomas is responsive and fun to act with. When we complete the scene, I feel exhilarated, my nervousness transformed to a simpler form of energy—happiness.

"That. Was. Great," Thomas says, looking me in the eye.

"Thanks." People do seem engrossed.

"Okay, so we'll have callbacks right now. I'm going to call back Becca and Sandra."

"Everyone except me?" Juilliard asks. Thomas nods.

"Thanks a lot." Juilliard stands by the door radiating annoyance until we reach the next stop, where she exits with a huff.

"This next scene is Ophelia's final scene, where she comes on singing and she's gone mad." He turns to the crowd. "Or in today's parlance, cray cray." They laugh. He hands us sides and continues. "I'd really like you to go first this time, Becca. And I think you should try it in the nude."

The audience engages. Torsos lean in. Legs cross. Necks crane. Eyes widen. The woman in Betty Boop scrubs covers her mouth.

"Excuse me?" I ask. This has to be a joke.

"I said I'd like this scene performed nude."

"Take it off, baby!" says the homeless woman.

"Um, is this legal?" I ask.

"Art isn't supposed to be legal. It's meant to push the envelope," Thomas says. "Actors in Myanmar risk their lives for their art, you know. I'm hardly asking for that."

I wonder for a split second if I'm uptight. Marisol said something the other day about me being "so East Coast." And then there's the wall I had up when Raj was taking my headshot. And it's not as if this guy doesn't have a proven track record. Am I really more in line with the conservative Christians than with the Moscow Art Theatre?

"Is it that you're feeling shy? About your body?" Thomas asks.

"Uh . . ."

"That's exactly how Ophelia feels."

I grip the subway pole.

"You're a feminist, right?"

I nod with narrowed eyes, so suspicious of where this is going.

"As a feminist, I'm sure you know that people have a completely messed-up view of the female form. They think it's meant to be perfect, but that's a lie. We need to expose that lie."

I look at the boys in their school uniforms, grinning in their braces. One of them lifts his eyebrows at me.

"No way," I say. "This is bullshit."

"What a wimp," says a random lady in a business suit.

"You go, girl," shouts the lady in Betty Boop scrubs.

"I don't see how exposing myself has anything to do with *Hamlet*."

"Amen," says the leader of the Jesus Lovers. I can't help but notice that a few of his flock look disappointed.

Thomas shakes his head. "I don't know how you expect to be an actress if you're not willing to take risks and reveal yourself."

"Sellout!" The homeless woman flings applesauce at me. It hits the pole and then slides in clumps toward my fingers. She laughs. I let go just as the train lurches to a halt. I jump out as soon as the doors open and stumble onto the platform, barely believing what just happened.

"Excuse me," I say to a hipster in stonewashed jeans waiting for a train headed in the opposite direction. "Where am I? What part of town is this?"

"You're downtown," he says. "Um, are you okay?"

"Yeah," I say. "Kind of. I just had a really weird experience."

"Right on," the guy says, nodding with understanding. I'm dying to tell Marisol and Raj about what just happened.

"Do you know where Hotel Uno is?" I ask the hipster. "Is it close?"

"Totally," he says, and gives me some simple directions. "That place is rad."

Downtown feels like another country, or at least a different city. In my neighborhood, opulent sunshine, tall palm trees, pink bougainvillea, and yellow hibiscus plants distract from the tree roots splitting the sidewalks, the furniture left out with the trash, the thump of the bass from the banged-up SUVs headed for the freeway. But here the grit isn't mitigated. The tall buildings keep the bright sky at a hazy distance. Design spaces, wine bars, yoga studios, and upscale lofts alternate with run-down movie theaters, churches, and five-dollar clothing stores. A blank-eyed homeless man who seems beyond despair, beyond life, passes me with a zombie's stagger at the same time as a young dude with a yoga mat under one arm and a green juice in his other hand glides across the street. His beauty is so thorough and pure that he seems like a form of genetic perfection that could will itself into another—a prized racehorse, for example. A woman rides past me on an old-fashioned bicycle wearing a dress, flip-flops, and no helmet.

I don't know who I thought would stop me, but I feel like I've gotten away with something when I get to the top of the Hotel Uno. As I step out to the rooftop bar, the city seems to stretch before me like a languorous sunbather, ending at the barely visible distant smudge of ocean. Up here, above the fray, the sun is closer. A hazy, golden warmth reflects off every surface: the pool; the curved white chairs; the winglike stretches of canvas providing shade; the blackish sunglass lenses on the still, collected faces of customers. Raj wasn't kidding when he said this place was cool.

Even though it's 1 p.m. in the middle of the workweek, there are plenty of people. Everyone looks what Marisol would call "fashion forward" in angular dresses and high-rise jeans. The men are in fedoras. The swimmers wear tiny bikinis or one-pieces with daring cutouts. A woman lounging by the pool and sipping a cocktail is topless, and no one seems to think anything of it. To my left is a yoga class with six lean students, led by a shirtless man with a tight, muscular torso and very baggy pants. They silently lean into Warrior II. Remixed old-school R&B permeates the mellow scene, playing from invisible speakers somewhere above me. Or are they below me? I can't tell. The music is just in the air.

I guess this is what a Tuesday afternoon in Los Angeles looks and feels like. I check the weather back home on my iPhone. If I were back in Boston right now, it'd be 4 p.m., fifty degrees, and drizzling. My former classmates are probably stuck in some academic building, listening to a lecture on something that's probably good for them, but which they don't even know if they care about, like literary theory or the Spanish conditional. Alex, who's either in extreme emotional denial or has become a callous asshole in a matter of months, is squirreled away in his precious little ivory tower, meeting snobs and brats.

I'm living life, I think. I'm going to crazy, hilarious auditions, and meeting my friends on a rooftop in Los Angeles. I'm looking at the fucking ocean. The next time I come here, I'm definitely bringing my bathing suit.

"Is Raj here?" I ask a bartender who is so beautiful that I can't believe she's not famous. Her glowing skin must contain multitudes of vitamins. She has to be an actress—and definitely a Leading Lady type. In the face of her beauty, I understand what Theresa meant when she said I was a character.

"He's going to be here any minute," she says with a disarming sweetness as she muddles mint and lime in a silver cup. "He has his film theory class today. Oh, no, that's Wednesdays. You know what? I think he had to shoot something for his web series class. Yes, that's it. He really wants to do well in that." A smile plays on her lips as she adds ice and rum to the lime mixture. "He's such a nerd."

"I know," I say as she shakes the drink and strains it into a tall glass.

"I'm Sierra," she says, wiping her hand on a bar towel before extending it.

"Becca," I say, and shake her delicate and chilled hand.

"Can I get you anything?" she asks.

"A Coke," I say.

"You're a friend of Raj?"

"Yes, and his neighbor," I say as she puts the Coke on the counter. I reach for my wallet, but she waves me away as she hands me the glass.

"Forget it. Any friend of Raj's is a friend of mine. He's such a love. Which reminds me, I need to see if he can cover for me tomorrow. I have an audition." I knew it. An actress.

"What's your audition for?"

"*Murder Two*," she says as if it's no big deal to be auditioning for the most watched crime show in the country. "My agent thinks I'm perfect for it, so here's hoping." She puts her phone on the bar. "Oh, here he comes."

"Becca!" Raj's eyes light up when he sees me.

"Hi!" I say as he walks behind the bar and washes his hands. Sierra moves to a customer at the other end of the bar.

"What a great surprise," Raj says, pouring some nuts into a little dish and sliding them toward me. "Do you know how much you helped me with my screenplay? I just wrote another scene during my break. And I have a zillion new ideas."

"Really? Because of me?"

"Hell, yeah," he says as he wipes down the bar. "Now don't keep me waiting any longer, how was the audition?"

I'm about to tell him about Thomas and his brown derby when Sierra cuts me off. "Raj, wonderful, wonderful Raj. Can you cover for me tomorrow? I have an audition."

"Sure, no problem," he says. I think I see him sweating a little.

"And is there any way you would go downstairs to the walk-in and get more pineapple juice? I'd do it, but that one chef is always asking me out and it's totally creepy."

"Of course," Raj says. "Be right back, Becca."

He heads to the elevators, and my heart sinks a little.

"What a mensch," Sierra says. "He's nervous about this screenplay contest, but I think he'll nail it, don't you? He's so brilliant." She lifts a glass of ice water with slices of lemon in it, and we clink glasses. She smiles at me and for a moment I am so jealous of her that it stings me like a jellyfish. I want her skin, her willowy confidence, her agent, and weirdly, her proximity to Raj.

THIRTEEN

"SO YOU'RE JEALOUS," Suzi Simpson writes in a chapter titled "I Will Survive." "Well, whoopty-flippin-doo. We're all jealous! No matter how far you get in life someone is always going to have it better. I know that probably doesn't help. I know it doesn't make you feel better. But what if I told you that jealousy can be a tool—just like rejection? That's right. The same way that rejection can be your fuel, jealousy can be your GPS. The next time you start to feel yourself 'go green' (and I'm not talking about recycling, though Lord knows we should all be doing that, too!), whip out that little notebook I told you to buy back in Chapter 2 (you didn't skip it, did you?), and write down what the other person has that you want. Circle it twice and call it a GOAL."

I did not skip Chapter 2, I tell Suzi in my head as I pour myself another cup of coffee at my kitchen table, which only wobbles the tiniest bit, and pull out my list. I already know my number-one goal.

1.	Get an (agent).	— Met with Athena at Talent Commune. Follow up on SAG.
✓ 2.	Get curtains.	
✓ 3.	Get a pillow.	
✓ 4.	~~Bu~~...	

I circle the word *agent* twice. Then I skip to Chapter 6, which begins with Suzi's advice about how to get representation and ends with a list of agencies in Los Angeles. I've read it a bunch of times, but I read it again.

"Okay, kiddos, bad news first," Suzi writes. "It takes an agent to get an agent. But here's the good news. You already have one. Look in the mirror and meet the person who's going to make your dreams come true. That's right—YOU!"

"Everyone wants digital submissions these days," Suzi writes. "But I believe that nothing stands out like a high quality photograph, the kind you can actually hold in your hand, delivered in person by you—the most neatly groomed and presentable version of yourself, that is."

I've been there and done that, and I only got one receptionist to take one measly Polaroid, but I don't know what else I can do, and I have to do something. Maybe it'll be different this time. Maybe I don't look like I just got here anymore—this will be especially true if I can figure out eye makeup. I take a quick trip to the Mayfair, buy whatever I can from their small makeup section, and then watch several YouTube videos. By the time I go to bed, I can confidently check number seven off my list.

✓	5.	Get a kitchen table, bed, and a dresser.
✓	6.	Go to the grocery store and get ingredients for healthy meals.
✓	7.	Learn how to apply subtle yet effective eye makeup.
✓	8.	Get a job to make $ $ $!
✓	9.	

So on my next day off, armed with a bus pass, an outfit I borrowed from Marisol, and my *subtle yet effective eye makeup*, I set about hand delivering my headshots—again—to talent agencies. I make a list of fourteen agencies that I haven't been to yet. I address each cover letter and envelope to a specific agent. Then I plan out a route that starts in West Hollywood, continues to Beverly Hills, crosses to Century City, and ends in Santa Monica, where Marisol is going to meet me for what she calls the best happy hour on the planet.

"You like oysters?" she asked.

"Oh yeah," I said.

"Then, girl, get ready to feast. I'll see you at the Lanai Hotel at four."

Rejection is my fuel, I tell myself every time Alex creeps into my mind. And I swear, this little mantra is working. Instead of feeling sad, I feel pissed off. But that anger doesn't get me down. Instead, it gets me going. If I feel tempted to get off track and browse in a store, I remember that I am my own agent, working for myself, and I'm not about to slack on the job.

Many of the agencies have a mail slot with a HEADSHOTS HERE sign. It seems to defeat the purpose of hand delivering as I don't get to make any personal contact, but I think the universe is taking note. At some agencies you can just walk through the door like you belong there. I always smile as I drop my carefully addressed, handwritten envelopes off with the receptionist. Suzi tells me to say that I was "in the area for a dance class." I haven't actually taken a dance class since I was six, but I love the line and what it implies about my life.

"I was in the area for a dance class," I tell a gorgeous twenty-something in a modern office with a view of the Hollywood Hills. She's wearing full makeup and an expensive suit.

"There's a dance class around here?" she asks, wrinkling her nose. I nod. "Really? You mean the pole dancing class?"

"Yes! It's great for the abs," I say, smiling and making a quick exit.

"Hello? I was in the area for a dance class," I call down the hallway of an office in Beverly Hills that appears to be empty. I figure everyone is in a meeting, place my headshot on the empty reception desk, and slip out the door.

"I hope it's not a problem that I'm dropping by, it's just that

I was in the area for a dance class," I say to a girl in jeans and a T-shirt at a small office in Santa Monica.

"I read that book," she says, and she winks as she takes the envelope from my hand.

Later I meet Marisol at the Lanai Hotel. She's found a table in the bar area with a breathtaking view of the beach, and ordered us two glasses of crisp white wine. It must be Marisol's confidence, but no one asks us for ID. She looks timeless in a yellow maxi dress and a white shawl, her dark hair piled on top of her head.

"Come, my darling," she calls to me as I walk toward her. The air is sweet with salt and rosy with afternoon sun. Ropey-legged joggers run past the hotel in neon sneakers. Seagulls strut in the sand. The ocean roars in the distance. A chilly breeze sends goose bumps up my arms, as a waiter in a blue oxford shirt delivers an icy platter of oysters and a basket of warm French bread.

"We'll need two more of these," Marisol says, gesturing to our wineglasses, even though I've only had one bracing sip. "I took the bus, too," she says. "So we can really enjoy ourselves."

"You took the bus? But you hate the bus."

"But then I realized that we could party, and somehow my fear just"—she snaps her fingers—"went away." I laugh as she tips an oyster back into her mouth. "Now, tell me about your journey."

I go over all the places I visited today, and we eat like we own the town, taking advantage of every last minute of the happy hour. At six o'clock, after two hours of drinking white wine and stuffing ourselves with bread and oysters, our bill is seventy-five dollars, which is somehow so much more than I was expecting it to be. I'm a little worried about making rent this month, but I try not to think about it as I place my credit card on the table.

"Oh no!" Marisol says when she looks in her purse. "I forgot my wallet!"

"Don't worry, I got it," I say, even though the money I spend makes me feel a little sick. I could have just spent twenty bucks at the Mayfair on beans and rice and a bottle of cheap Chardonnay.

"Thank you," Marisol says, resting her head on my shoulder. "I'll get you back, I swear."

Marisol and I stumble out into the sand, take off our shoes, and watch the sun drop into the sea. My head is swimming with wine, and my limbs are loose and warm. We sit back-to-back, and she sings a song in Spanish. I try to join in with her, approximating the words as best I can because I don't know Spanish. Our voices grow louder and more dramatic, until we are nearly peeing ourselves with laughter. The sky dissolves into lavender, then indigo behind the Santa Monica Pier. Blue-and-red lights illuminate the outline and spokes of a Ferris wheel, like it's a giant unicycle about to spin across the Pacific.

For the moment I can forget about the college applications I haven't been working on. The one exception is the California Film School. I keep pulling up their website when I'm on the bus. It's so different from the other schools. I think I can ask

Mr. Devon, my theater teacher, for a reference again, but who can I ask to write my artistic reference? Who knows my voice when I'm not even sure what it is yet?

But as far as the other applications, I'm so behind. I feel nauseated with guilt. I take a picture of Ferris wheel lights with the moon behind them and text it to Mom.

Me: To here and back.

Mom: Always. Again and again.

Marisol ties her dress in a knot and turns a cartwheel in the sand. I take the Polaroid camera out of my bag and snap a picture for my collage.

FOURTEEN

I TRY TO KEEP a piece of that sunset with me when I waitress, and I've been waitressing every day or night. Expenses are adding up faster than I anticipated. The headshots set me back almost twelve hundred dollars, including the prints. For some reason the trash bill in LA is a hundred and fifty dollars a month. I was sure it was an error, but I called the sanitation department and there hasn't been a mistake. Apparently that's just what it costs to get rid of garbage here. And then there's my phone bill, the utilities, groceries, all of my little indulgences like coffee and pastries. I bring people hamburger after hamburger after hamburger and Coke after Coke after Coke. Lately, I've been catching the waitressing rhythm, and I think that I'm actually getting the hang of it. I can manage a medium-size section until the dinner rush, when I tend to get flustered. I even managed the night shift on Halloween, serving drunk people dressed up as sexy nurses and truly frightening zombies—though no matter the shift, Gloria makes sure she has at least one negative comment.

But tonight I've had a bunch of shitty tables. The latest is a pair of mothers with fake boobs and plumped-up lips with their two young daughters dressed up like princesses. They don't look like they belong in this neighborhood. I feel like they got lost on their way to Beverly Hills. It's almost 8:30 p.m. and the little girls are overtired. They're alternately giggling and whining, bouncing and collapsing, teetering on emotional extremes. The mothers are trying to have an adult discussion anyway. The mother dominating the conversation makes pointed eye contact with me and taps her watch. I cover my mouth, realizing that I've forgotten to put in their order. I flip through my notepad, find their order, punch it in the computer, and bring the little girls extra paper placemats to draw on.

"I don't know what they taught you in that fancy private school, but it wasn't common sense," Gloria says as she watches me scramble. I ignore her.

"Here we are," I say, when I deliver the food ten minutes later. "Careful. It's a little hot." No one looks at me. One of the little girls lifts up the bun of her hamburger. She sees sautéed onions and screams. Shoot. I forgot to tell the cooks to leave them off. "Just scrape them off," I offer cheerfully.

"They touched it!" the little girl shrieks.

I smile at her. "Tell you what? I'll have the chef make you

a new burger, with our most secret special ingredient that will make this burger the most delicious burger in the whole, wide world." She's on the verge of buying it.

"We don't have time for this. This is completely unacceptable," the mother says. The little girl's face goes blank as though the mother has siphoned the child's anger.

"I'm *really* sorry. Can I refill your drinks? I'm sure the kitchen can make you another burger very quickly."

"Is this really so difficult? We're dealing with fucking hamburgers here." She addresses her friend, but the comment is meant for me.

"It was a mistake. I said I was sorry. There's no need to be impolite," I say.

"I wasn't talking to you." Anger flashes across her face as she pushes the plate at me. I catch it but knock over a Diet Coke. The little girl scrambles toward her mother as if it's human blood that's dripping from the table. This sets the other little girl off. The children keen in eerie harmony. The whole restaurant is staring.

"Get me a new waitress."

"Michelle," her friend says. "Let it go."

With an inch-thick stack of napkins I mop up the Diet Coke that's now streaming onto the seat of the booth. My pinky finger accidentally grazes the child's arm.

"Don't you dare touch my daughter," the woman snaps. The child, sensing that this is her cue, issues a fresh wail from her very core.

"Go away! Are you fucking deaf, too? Are you fucking retarded?"

I've never been spoken to like this in my life.

"Michelle," the other mother says, more firmly. "You're making her cry."

"I want to see the manager!" Michelle points a shaking finger at me.

I turn away from the table, plate in hand, to see Gloria moving toward me like a 747. She pushes me out of her way. The hamburger slides off the plate and lands on the woman's shoes.

I drop to pick up the burger, but Manuel, the guy who trained me, gets to it first with a dustpan and broom. "It's okay. I do it," he says.

"I got it."

"Becca," he says in his lilting accent, his eyes round and soft with sympathy. "I do it. Take break."

"Thank you." I stand up, wiping my sweaty hands on my apron. I run through the swinging kitchen doors and burst into tears.

"Was it a customer? Or is Gloria being a bitch?" Peanut asks. I cover my face, embarrassed to be crying in front of the three cooks. "Ignore Gloria," Pablo says. "She's crazy. Don't listen to anything she says."

"I can't get fired," I say through my hands, thinking about the money I've been spending, especially my credit card bill. It started when I put the headshots on there, but these little things—like dinner with Marisol on the beach—are adding up.

"Don't let her see you cry, pretty baby. Don't let her see you cry," Pablo says. I nod, brush away the tears on my cheeks, and wipe my nose on my shirt. He hands me an institutional brown paper towel from the cook's hand-washing station. "And don't wipe your nose on your shirt. You're better than that."

Gloria puts their meal on the house, then takes the cost of the entire check from my tips, making sure to tell the woman that this is what happened. She sends me home early and I'm suspended until Saturday. I leave with six dollars, two of which are in change. I'm going to get a new job as soon as I possibly can.

As I step out of the restaurant I check my voice mail. An agent call would make this whole evening disappear. It would lift me up as if on wings. Maybe, just maybe, all of my pavement pounding has paid off. But no. I have no new messages.

If anger is fuel, then I've got plenty of gas in the tank. I walk home so fast that I feel like I'm on the verge of flying. The nights have started to get legitimately chilly, and I wrap my thin sweater around my body, wishing that I'd brought a winter coat. Marisol says it's not safe for me to walk from Los Feliz to the Chateau this late by myself, but I feel pissed off and invincible. I can't imagine that anyone in my high school class has had to deal with what I did tonight—that woman's tone of voice, the utter disrespect in her eyes when she looked at me like I was dirt. If I were in college, inside the gates of some great institution, I would be held in some esteem. People would know that I had a place in the world. Actresses and waitresses don't exactly get a lot of respect—even if we are doing something braver.

As I cross Western Avenue, I see a stray dog on the other side of the street, heading toward me. He's lean and so light on his feet that he's practically dancing. For some reason, I'm not afraid of him. It's not until we actually pass one another that I realize that's no dog—it's a coyote who has probably come down from the dry hills in search of food and water. Once I'm at a safe distance, I turn and watch his silhouette, my heart pounding hot and fast. He's ragged, proud, and oddly elegant.

When I get back to the Chateau Bronson, I don't want to be alone. Marisol is dogsitting for her boss tonight, so after I shower off the smell of hamburgers and rage, I visit Raj. He's been working on his screenplay for the last few hours and is ready for a break when I show up.

"I saw a coyote," I tell him.

"Really? Where?"

"On Western. Just walking past the gas station like it's no big thing."

"Cool," Raj says, though I can tell he's distracted.

"So did you write the essay or make a collage for California Film School?" I ask, sitting on his bed.

"Essay," Raj says. "And I submitted a short film I made in high school. Why? Are you thinking of applying?"

I nod.

"That's awesome," he says, his voice rising. "You would love it, and all actors these days have to create their own work."

"Really?" I say, considering this.

"Hell, yeah. And you have to come with me to the awards banquet in January now. I'll introduce you to everyone."

"Thanks," I say. "That would be great networking."

Wait a second. Is he asking me out?

"I could use your creative talents, actually. I'm stuck again," he says, rubbing his eyes. "Want some tea?"

"I'd love some," I say, and kick off my shoes. "So, give me the update. What's going on with the script now?"

"Okay, well, there's a lot more tension in the scenes now, but there's something I keep bumping up against."

"Hit me with it!" I say, taking a seat on his neatly made bed.

"I don't know why they can't leave the hotel. Like, what is it that's actually holding them back and keeping them there?"

"That seems important," I say.

"Um, yeah. It's the key that's going to unlock this whole thing, and I have no idea what it is."

"Huh."

"Oh no. Where's your enthusiasm? You think it's a terrible idea now, don't you? It's never going to work, is it?"

"Relax. Of course it's going to work! I'm just thinking."

"Sorry, I'm just freaked-out. I'll get your tea. Mint okay?"

I nod as he disappears into his kitchen nook. Then I lie back, close my eyes, and think.

"So, my drama teacher used to tell us that if we got blocked, we should get personal."

"What do you mean?" Raj asks, returning with my tea. He

smiles ever so slightly at the sight of me lying on his bed. He places the tea on his nightstand. I sit up to take a sip. He sits next to me, and I'm aware there's only an inch separating us.

"I think what he meant was that if you invest something truly, deeply personal into your work—the uglier and more embarrassing the better—that you'll get unstuck. So I guess the same applies to writing, right?"

He massages his temples.

"Am I hurting more than I'm helping?"

"No, it's just a lot to think about. A screenplay has to be so carefully planned and perfectly constructed, and I can't believe I'm halfway through this thing without knowing the ending."

"Maybe you have to let go a little and just see where the writing process leads you."

"Do you have any idea how uncomfortable that makes me?" he asks.

"Sounds like you're onto something then," I say.

"I see what you did there." His eyes light up. "Get out of here, I have to write. Go, before you uncover any more of my issues."

"Okay," I say, feeling so much better, so much more human, than when I left the restaurant. "Can I take my tea?"

FIFTEEN

"BUT I DON'T want to hibernate! I can't BEAR it! I want to stay up and celebrate Hanukkah with Goldie Lox." I sit on a chair, taking a dramatic pause, and continue. "Tell us, Goldie, what is Hanukkah?"

I'm at a small theater on Santa Monica Boulevard in Hollywood. It's situated across from a gas station and between a Delish Donuts and a medical marijuana shop. I'm auditioning for my first paid acting gig, which I found listed in *Backstage* just this morning. Since my suspension, I've been more determined than ever to audition for anything and everything: "Seeking all types for series of children's holiday play *Baby Bear's First Hanukkah*. Auditions from 12 p.m.–5 p.m. Come dressed to move. Pay is $350/wk."

Three fifty a week sounded really good to me. Three fifty a week would mean I could cut way back on waitressing. I knocked on Marisol's door and brought her along with me. We had to wait in line for almost two hours to audition, and Marisol didn't make it past the first round, but the director, Dawn, has asked me twice now to stick around. Marisol, who apparently just isn't bear material, is waiting for me in the back of the theater. I'm surprised to have made it this far, hopeful that they want me to stay, and excited by the prospect of being chosen.

"Cut!" Dawn says now, using one hand to pull back her long, wavy hair, which hangs past her waist. Before I went on, the stage manager warned me that Dawn was in a bad mood after a long day of auditioning. "Don't take it personal," she said.

Papa Bear bulldozes past the command to cut. "Don't be silly, Baby," he booms as a fine spritz of his spit settles on my forehead and nose. His odor is 80 percent cigarettes, 10 percent booze, and 10 percent everything bagel.

"Time out! Time out!" Dawn makes the T-sign with her hands. Papa Bear, immersed in the scene, pushes me back in the chair and continues.

"We BEARLY know anything about Hanukkah," he bellows with both hands on my shoulders.

Dawn waves her hands in the air. "Hello, Jeff. Earth to Jeff. Stop. Jeffrey Peter Plotkin. Stop." Papa Bear is silenced. She shoots him a frustrated look, exhales through her nostrils, and turns to me. "Please stand up," she says. I do. "Don't ever, ever, ever"—she bobs her head for emphasis, holding her hands in a prayer position—"ever use a prop that isn't yours. It's like some-one is touching your body without permission."

"Oh."

"How would you like it if someone just walked up to you and touched your body, just touched you all over your body without your permission?"

"I wouldn't like that. But, um, what prop was I touching?"

Her eyes widen with amazement. She holds her arms out in a questioning position, stomps a foot, and leans forward, the choreography of someone asking a question. "Where were you sitting?"

"On a chair?"

"AHA!" She says, pointing a dramatic finger. "A chair is a prop."

"Oh."

"That chair doesn't belong to us. That chair belongs to *Eat Me*, the incredibly hot show who's very generously letting us use this space for auditions. For all we know, that chair could be designed to break the moment someone sits on it."

"Okay." That seems unlikely. I can see Marisol in the back, struggling to keep a straight face.

"Okay. Enough for Stagecraft 101," says Dawn. "Let's take it again from page fifteen, 'Papa Bear! Papa Bear!'"

We go through the scene again. At the end of it Dawn whis-pers with the stage manager and an assistant, consulting on my performance.

"Jeffrey, get down here," she says to Papa Bear. She announces to the room that she can talk to him like that because he's her husband. Papa Bear hustles off the stage and joins the huddle. I'm left alone to contemplate the set of *Eat Me*. Forgetting my lesson in Stagecraft 101, I sit down on a sofa but stand up before anyone sees me except Marisol, who laughs at how quickly I've hopped to my feet.

"How tall are you?" Dawn asks me.

"Five feet."

"Are you willing to wear a bear suit?"

Never did I think I would be asked this question, or that my answer would be an unequivocal yes.

"And you can rehearse and perform during the day?"

"Yes," I say without hesitation. I'll have to just work weekends at Rocky's, the dreaded Sunday brunch, but at least I'll be making most of my money as an actual actress.

"And you have reliable transportation? Preschoolers will be counting on you. All of my bears must be on time."

"I'm extremely punctual," I say, avoiding the transportation question altogether. The bus is reliable, right?

"It's twenty hours a week of rehearsal, and starting November fifteenth, it'll be four shows a week. Can you commit to all of these performances?"

"Yes."

"Looks like you got yourself a part." She consults my head-shot. "Becca Harrington."

At the back of the theater, Marisol gives me a standing ovation. I'm smiling so wide that it hurts. I know it's just a children's play, but I'm so happy that I'll finally get a chance to do what I've come here to do. I have a part. An actual part!

"We have to celebrate," Marisol says when we head back out onto Melrose. "Where should we go?"

"First stop, Delish Donuts," I say.

"Good call. Those sprinkles are calling my name," she says. The doughnut shop is weirdly connected to a liquor store. "You know this is going to help you get an agent."

"You think so?" I ask, browsing the doughnuts, which are glistening with sugar.

"They have kids, too," Marisol says, and digs into her purse for quarters.

"I'm buying you yours."

"I can buy myself a doughnut," Marisol says, though the fact that she's counting pennies makes me think she's really struggling.

"Come on, let me be your sugar daddy," I say. Marisol bursts into laughter. I turn to the kid behind the counter. "The young lady may have whatever she likes."

"You slay me," she says, and puts her change away.

Once we have our wax bags of sprinkled snacks, I throw an arm around her shoulder.

"Now to Hotel Uno!" Like most of the moments I share with Marisol, this one is so much sweeter, bigger, and brighter because she's here. "But we need to get our bathing suits. The pool there is sick."

SIXTEEN

"CHECK THIS PLACE OUT," says Marisol as we step onto the rooftop.

"Isn't it amazing?" I ask.

We take in the scene together: the white mid-century modern lounge chairs, the perfectly blue pool, and the view of downtown LA. Somewhere in the distance is the sound of traffic, but it's so far away it doesn't pierce the bubble of this cool, freestanding universe. Unlike the last time I was here, it's overcast and pretty empty. Except for a couple sitting at a table by the pool and a few people at the bar, we're the only ones here.

I wave to Raj, who is wiping clean glasses.

"Becca," Raj says. "I love that you're making this a habit."

He maintains eye contact with me as we weave our way over, smiling the whole time. "What's up, Marisol?"

"We're here to celebrate," Marisol says. "Becca got her first part today. She's playing Baby Bear in *Baby Bear's First Hanukkah*."

"The title role!" Raj says. "You got it? On the spot? Holy shit!"

His enthusiasm is contagious, and I find myself feeling even more excited about this than I was when it happened.

"How does it feel?" he asks, gripping my shoulders. "What's it like to be a working actress?"

"It's great!" I say. He surprises me by kissing my cheek.

"What can I make you? How about a mojito? We had a special on those last week."

"I'm not a rum girl," Marisol says. "But I love champagne."

"Of course. To celebrate." Raj pours us two glasses of champagne.

"The downside is that I'll have to wear a bear suit," I say, the reality sinking in.

"Doesn't sound like a downside to me," Raj says. "But then again, bears are my spirit animal."

"Really?" I ask.

"If I could be any other animal, I'd be a bear. Hands down. No contest. Wouldn't you?"

"No."

"Then what would you be?" he asks. I'm about to respond when Raj cuts me off. "You're going to say dolphin because you're a girl and all girls love dolphins."

"I resent that gender stereotyping," Marisol says. "Even though I do love dolphins. I mean, who doesn't? Only an asshole doesn't like dolphins."

"I was going to say beaver," I say. "They're both industrious and romantic."

"Really?" asks Marisol, sipping her champagne.

"They mate for life. They mate face-to-face as they swim slowly forward in the spring." I smile blissfully and pantomime a sidestroke.

"I'll drink to that," says Raj, and sneaks a shot of vodka. "How can you not love a woman whose spirit animal is a beaver?" He cocks one eyebrow, which I choose to ignore.

"A woman? I'm not a woman! I'm a girl," I say.

"You're a woman," Marisol says. "I hate to break it to you."

"I don't want to be a woman yet. I'm not ready."

"You're a girl-woman," Raj says as a couple standing by the bar signals to him. He goes to take their order. Sierra steps behind the bar and clocks in on the computer.

Marisol nudges me. "When are you just going to give in and let that man love you?"

"Raj is the best," I say, watching him mix a drink for a customer. The way he maintained eye contact with me did send an unexpected flutter though my system.

"Hi, Sierra," I say.

"Oh, hey, Becca." She flashes her million-dollar smile and then pours some chips in a bowl and hands it to us.

"You have beautiful skin," Marisol says to Sierra. Then she locks arms with me. We're a team, the two of us. I could face the prettiest girls in LA like this and not feel inferior.

"Oh, thanks," Sierra says.

"Do you know that you are talking to a working actress?" Raj says, coming back over.

Sierra cocks an eyebrow. "Oh, yeah?"

"Becca just got a part on the spot in a very prestigious children's theater," Raj tells her.

"I don't know how—" I start, but Marisol places a hand on my arm to quiet me.

"She came out here with no agent, no friends, no school, no nothing—bravest person I've ever met," Raj says, looking right at me.

"To LA," Marisol says, holding her glass up for a toast. We down our champagne. She leans in close. "Let's never leave this town. Let's stay here together forever and be true bohemians."

She holds up her pinky, and we swear on it. "When I finally make it, I'm going to live in a loft down here. With a pool on the roof. And an herb garden."

"I'm going to live at the beach," I say, thinking of our sunset a few weeks ago.

"Yes, Venice." Her breath is sweet with pink champagne. "I'll grow arugula and tomatoes!"

"I've never been to Venice," I say.

"It's perfect for you. And that way we'll have a town house

and a beach house, and all of our artist friends will gather at one or the other every weekend. We'll have literary salons."

"And outdoor movie screenings."

"And go for moonlight swims."

"It's going to be a great life," I say. Suzi Simpson says that actresses have signature drinks. I don't know much about drinks, but I decide now is a good time to pick one. I take in my surroundings and try to let an idea arise from my subconscious.

"Raj, I'd like a Sea Breeze! It's my signature drink."

"Whatever the lady wants, the lady shall have," he says, and rolls up his sleeves.

"Be right back. I'm going to the loo," I say, hopping off of my stool.

"Then it's pool time," Marisol says. The music has changed to hip-hop. I dance my way to the bathroom. I look in the mirror. This is the best day of my away-from-home life so far, I think to myself.

Me: Mom, I got a part!

Mom: What? Honey, tell me more!

Me: It's in a children's play. Baby Bear's First Hanukkah.

Mom: I'm so proud!

Me: Everyone has to start somewhere, right? And it pays!

Mom: Yay! And now you can write that on your college applications—a paying role!

Me: Yes.

The college applications are due in six weeks. I hold my breath.

Mom: Have you started?

Me: Yes.

Technically this isn't a lie. I did fill out the basic information for the California Film School, in addition to adding to my collage, which is growing in unexpected ways. I've started to add sticky notes with dreams, ideas, and quotes.

Mom: Good going, Becca. I can't wait to see you in December!

Me: Me either. I'm planning a fun Christmas for us.

Mom: Gotta run into a meeting. Doctor is ready for me. Keep me posted. LYTTS.

Me: AB.

I don't want my guilt over my college applications to ruin this day. I splash some cold water on my face and then pat it dry with one of the real towels that are artfully rolled up on the counter. I squirt some of the fancy lime-scented lotion on my hands.

When I come out of the bathroom, a classic hip-hop song is playing. I wave to Marisol and Raj. As I lip-synch I do one of my favorite moves. It involves rapid slicing of the air with stiff, bladelike hands. Marisol tilts her head back with laughter. Raj makes a lasso gesture. I mime being pulled toward the bar, throwing a kick in the air, and hoist a leg up on the barstool Marisol's been guarding.

"That was insane," Raj says, smiling.

"It was avant-garde," Marisol says. "Does that move have a name?"

"Yes," I say, and think of something on the spot. "The urban warrior."

"Perfect." A smile spreads across Raj's lips. "For the urban wilderness."

"Exactly," I say.

"You didn't tell me you could move like that," Marisol says.

"There's a lot you don't know about me," I say, trying to sound mysterious.

"Do you have an alter ego?" Marisol's eyes invite me to play.

I shrug. "Of course."

"I gotta hear this," Marisol says, looking at me like I'm the most interesting person she's ever met, like she's never been so delighted by another human being in all of her days. She hops off of her barstool and links her arm with mine. "Let's head to the pool."

"Have fun, girls," Raj says, looking as if he wishes he could join us.

"Women," Marisol says over her shoulder.

"Oh, yeah," Raj says. "Women. Or woman and girl-woman."

"Who's your alter ego?" Marisol asks.

"Miss Nancy. I'm British and I teach PE at a very proper private school in Boston." I'm thinking of my own PE teacher, Ms. Bishop, who I adore. Marisol giggles.

"I believe in freedom of movement!" I say, quoting Ms.

Bishop. "It keeps the body alive!" *Body* is especially fun to say in a British accent.

Marisol laughs as she strips down to her bathing suit and delicately steps into the pool.

"You're leaving your hat on?" I ask.

"I just got a blowout," she says. "Tell me more, Miss Nancy."

"I wake up every morning at four to greet the day, as one must," I say, taking off my sundress to reveal the vintage two-piece bathing suit I borrowed from Marisol. "I eat an egg with sliced to-mah-toes, and I do my Chinese exercises."

"I'd love to see those," Marisol says.

"They're quite invigorating." And with that I jump into the deep end, letting the soft pool water envelop me. Without coming up for a breath, I swim toward Marisol with open eyes. I rise to the surface in front of her.

"You're a true original," Marisol says. "You know that? A classic."

"I am?" I ask, dropping character. "Wait. Me or Miss Nancy?"

"You. I've never met anyone like you. You're going to make it. I feel it so strongly right now."

"Thank you." It feels so good to hear this. It also feels foreign, new. "You know . . . I think Alex basically broke up with me because he didn't think I was good enough."

"Wait—what?" Marisol says, tilting her head, her eyes swimming with compassion.

And suddenly, without warning, here on the rooftop of

Hotel Uno, I remember our breakup conversation. The parts of it that I pushed away. That I don't want to remember. "He didn't think we belonged together because I didn't get into college. He didn't say that exactly, but that's what he meant."

"Wait a second, here," Marisol says, holding my arm. "He didn't believe in you?"

"I thought he loved me." I hold my breath to try not to cry.

"Honey," Marisol says, placing her hands on my shoulders. I stare into the water. My tears drip into the pool. "Look at me."

I look up. Behind her, a dull layer of sunlight pushes through the clouds and pollution. The water catches the muted rays, reflecting triangles of light on our faces. We both sink down so the water is chin level.

"Just the fact that you decided to take a year off to find out what you really want to do makes you stand out. Every other person in your school is going to college, right? You're unique because you decided to do something different, something so daring. You could've taken the safe path . . ." she begins.

"No, I couldn't." I shake my head, then drop my voice to a whisper. "I didn't get in anywhere."

"Okay," she says, as if this is no big deal.

"No one accepted me. No place wanted me. I applied to eleven schools, and they all said no." The tears come faster now. "I'm sorry I lied."

"Don't worry about that," Marisol says. "Besides, you weren't lying, you were just spinning the truth."

"Same thing."

She shrugs. "You didn't know me. You thought I was going to judge you, because everyone around you did, even the person you trusted the most, the person you loved."

"In the end, he thought I was a loser like everyone else did. Rejection is, like, contagious."

"What a dingbat," she says, shaking her head with disgust. "Dingbat and idiot. Look, I don't know why you didn't get into college, but it's total bullshit. I know people whose parents paid thousands of dollars for some published author to write their kids' essays for them and still didn't get in to their top choices. It's all so unfair and none of it makes any sense. It doesn't say anything about you. It just goes to show how screwed up and random the admissions system is. I want you to know that I would never, ever judge you," Marisol says. "You're so positive. You're unpretentious. You see the best in everyone you meet. You're so funny and honest. You're not afraid to just be yourself. Personally I think you're a genius. Hey, you already have a part in a play."

"Marisol, would eleven colleges reject a genius?"

"If they didn't have the skills to recognize one, yes."

"Sometimes I feel like a Polaroid picture that can't develop," I say. "I keep trying to show up but no one can see me."

"Whoa. First of all, you just proved my point that you're a genius with that metaphor," she says. "And you know who sees you? I do. I see you."

"Thank you," I say, nodding, unable to contain my smile. The tears I'm crying now are tears of relief.

"And if there's one thing I know for certain in this crazy world, there's nothing ordinary about you."

I tip my head back, look up at the sky, and believe her.

When we get home, hours later, I smile as I check number eleven:

✓	1.	Get a friend. (friends?)
	10.	Get a new style, new wardrobe, etc.
✓	11.	Become a working actress!
	12.	♡ Get Alex back. ♡

SEVENTEEN

THE REHEARSAL SCHEDULE for *Baby Bear's First Hanukkah* is a jam-packed three weeks. We're expected to be off book, which means have our lines memorized, after one week. During my waitressing shifts I go over my lines in my head. I keep pages of my script tucked into my apron, and when I have a down moment, I duck into the coffee station and study them. I finally seem to have the knack for waitressing as long as it doesn't get too busy and no one yells. Ever since my suspension, I stay as far away from Gloria as possible. When she criticizes me for not looking neat enough or being too slow or saying, "I'll have to check," when a customer inquires about every single ingredient in the Cahuenga salad (there are eighteen), I don't make eye contact with her, but focus on a spot on the wall, nod, and just say, "Okay."

One day after Gloria reads me the riot act over a mixed-up order, a bodybuilder leaves me a crisp hundred-dollar bill as a tip on a twenty-dollar check. I can't believe my luck. It would ruin it completely if I spent it on something practical, so I pop into a cute new boutique in Los Feliz and buy a shirt that costs seventy-five dollars. I know it's stupid to spend so much on a single shirt, but it's a deep red that brings out my coloring, and the fabric is fine and soft, draping over my body in just the right way.

And then, even better, there's a new waiter, a musician named Jimmy. Gloria focuses on him for several shifts, allowing me to fade into the background. I had to cut back two of my shifts in order to make all the rehearsals. When I tried to figure out how I was going to cover my bills this month, I realized there was no way that I would. I put the most basic things, like food, on my credit card and try not to think about it even though the balance is creeping north of three thousand dollars. My limit is five thousand dollars, so I need to be careful. But the truth is that if I were to keep my head above water in LA, I'd never have time to pursue acting. Denial is part of this adventure.

Almost every day I meet Marisol at the café near the Chateau. We don't like our jobs and have made a pact to not discuss them so that we can spend as much time as possible focusing on our real lives, our acting careers. I take the last bite of avocado salad. This salad, which has a whole avocado and two hard-boiled eggs, has become our staple. It costs eight dollars. We figured out that if we split the salad and ask for extra bread and butter, it's enough food for two. We always eat at the same outdoor table.

I look at my watch. "Oh shit, I've got to go to rehearsal."

"Wait. There's this agent workshop thing on Saturday, and I know they have some spots left. I signed up for it this morning. It's at a place called Entertainment Connection Studios. You pay seventy-five bucks and you get to audition for four commercial agents." She scribbles ECS and a number on a napkin. "Call this number to make an appointment."

"Why are you going to one of these things when you have a commercial agent?" I ask.

"Because I want a better one," she says. "That guy hardly ever sends me out."

"It's seventy-five dollars?" I ask, even though I've just spent that very amount on a shirt.

"If we get commercials, we can quit our jobs. You can make fifty thousand dollars for a national commercial."

"Really?"

"Think about it. I know a girl who booked three commercials in LA in one year. She bought a bungalow in Echo Park."

"Wait, are you going home for Thanksgiving?" I ask. It's next week, and the closer it gets, the more bummed I am to be spending it alone.

"Nope," Marisol says. "I thought I was spending it with you."

"Really?" I ask.

"Of course," Marisol says. "We'll think of something fun."

"We always do."

She blows me a kiss.

Raj and I have developed a routine. I bring us coffee in my Ikea mugs, which just so happen to be the exact right size for the Corolla's cup holders, we walk to wherever his car happens to be parked that day, and he drives me to the theater before heading to work.

On the way, we discuss his screenplay, which he's making great progress on. I don't think I've ever seen someone so into something. Raj is eating, breathing, and dreaming this script, which is now called *Hotel California*.

"So I still don't know why our protagonist Olivia can't leave the hotel. What's the psychological reason the spirits are holding her there?" he asks as we make a right onto Santa Monica Boulevard. The traffic is thick.

"I'm going to be late," I say, checking my phone.

"All the more time for you to help me get to the root of this problem. I mean, not that I want you to be late of course." He places a hand on his chest and smiles at me. "I only have your best interests at heart, despite the fact that you're awesome at constructing a story."

"Flattery will get you everywhere," I say as a Nissan Altima cuts us off and then slows down so that he makes it through the light, but we're stuck at the red. "Damn!"

"Why'd you have to do us dirty, Mr. Nissan?" Raj asks, shaking his head.

"Talk to me," I say, surrendering to my tardiness. I'll have to hope I can sneak by the moody Dawn.

"Olivia is a control freak. That's her character flaw. So she needs to get over that in order to escape. She's going to have to think about her world in a completely new way, but I need to put a finer point on it, and make the psychological fear take a visual, tangible form."

"So let's think about this," I say. "What is being a control freak all about?"

"Being a perfectionist," Raj says. "Not wanting to hear anyone else's point of view."

"Yeah, yeah," I say. "I think it's about . . . avoiding chaos. Why do people avoid chaos?"

"They're scared," Raj says.

"Right. They don't want to get hurt," I say. Of course I'm thinking of Alex, who chose to cut me off emotionally so that he didn't have to deal with the messiness of being separated from me. "They want to avoid pain."

"Yes!" Raj says, barely making it through a yellow light.

"So in order for Olivia to escape the grip of the hotel . . ." I begin.

"She's going to have to deal with some ancient pain."

"Something that's been haunting her," I say as he pulls into a loading zone in front of the theater. "Only now, it's literally haunting her!"

"I'm going to have to park and write this down," Raj says.

"Are you sure you don't mind all these rides?" I ask, stepping out of the car. "I should at least reimburse you for gas."

"It's on the way to work."

"No, it's not," I say, with a smile. Of course, he blushes. Now I've lived here long enough to know that Raj is definitely going out of his way to bring me to rehearsal.

"It's fine. It's actually really selfish of me because you help me talk through all my script issues," he says. "I owe you."

"You can thank me by giving me a part when you're a famous director," I say.

"You got it," he says, and I run around the theater to the back door, hoping to avoid Dawn.

"Guys, something's up with Dawn. I'm ten minutes late and she just winked at me," I say as I walk into the small, co-ed dressing room at the theater. It's our final rehearsal for *Baby Bear's First Hanukkah*.

"She's in a good mood," Jeffrey, or Papa Bear, says. "This is what they call an upswing," he adds gravely.

"I guess that's better than a downswing?" I say, and find an empty metal folding chair in the tiny room. It's about eighty-six degrees in the dressing room with all the bodies crammed into such a small space. Naked lightbulbs border the mirrors.

Costumes hang on racks. The wire hangers are labeled for each character with tags fashioned out of masking tape. Little pots of makeup—tiny bowls of blush, eyeliner, lip liners, and jars of cold cream—crowd the counter. I take off my cardigan to reveal my lucky red shirt. I catch my reflection in one of the many mirrors; it was worth it.

Sally, aka Mama Bear, is in her slip, laughing at something Max, aka Hunter Green, has said. Sally, as true to her part as ever, is our actual den mother, always making sure that everyone's okay. She's in her fifties with pockmarked skin and the easy laugh of someone who's had a lot of therapy and gets life's ironies.

"Hey, sweetie," she says. "You look cute today."

"Thanks, Sally. This shirt was way too expensive, but I bought it anyway."

"The price us dames pay for beauty," she says, and bats her eyelashes.

Jeffrey's dressed and ready to go a full hour before showtime. He's sitting in front of the dressing room mirror with his feet on the counter pontificating to Anya, aka Goldie Lox, who is complaining about her Republican boyfriend.

"You've got to be a Democrat when you're young, and a Republican as you grow older," Jeffrey tells her, then adjusts his bear costume.

"He *is* fifteen years older than me, but I still don't think that's any excuse to be a *Republican*," she says.

"How old are you?" I ask.

"Never ask an actress how old she is," Jeffrey says. "Trust me."

"I don't believe in that garbage," Sally says. "I'll be fifty-six in May."

"A Gemini! I knew it!" Anya says as she takes off her shirt to reveal a surprisingly antiquated pointed bra and grandmother-style underwear. Jeez. Is Anya, like, fifty, too?

"Do you think these costumes have ever been washed?" I ask Sally, as I slip a leg into my bear suit.

"Not in the seven years I've been doing the show," she says, and ties an apron around her furry waist. As much as I like Sally, I say a silent prayer that I won't be wearing this bear suit seven years from now.

After rehearsal, I head to Entertainment Connection Studios. I tried to simply sign up for an "agent workshop" over the phone, but the young woman on the end of the line insisted that I "schedule a consultation."

It's in a modern building in West Hollywood, and only a short bus ride from the theater. ECS has glossy wooden floors and sleek, modern furniture. I walk down a hallway lined with advertisements for headshot photographers until I reach a reception counter. The pert receptionist adjusts her headset and smiles up at me.

"I have an appointment with Danielle."

"You're going to love Danielle," the receptionist says, and presses a button on her phone.

Danielle appears from around the corner. Her nose looks

like it's being pinched by a clothespin. She extends a hand for a limp handshake, and it feels like it's made of bird bones. She leads me back to her cubicle, pulls out a chair for me like we're on a date, then sits and studies my headshot and résumé.

"You're like me. You look so young. And you're very commercial, though I can tell that you're capable of dramatic roles as well." She cocks her head to the side. "You might benefit from some headshot advice."

Ugh. The headshots again.

Then, after extracting enough smiles from me to feel we have bonded, she begins a line of questioning: "Have you ever had representation? Do you even know what you're looking for in an agent? Do you have any idea what the different agencies offer?" She tilts her head like a puppy. "No? This is all so new, isn't it? What you need is our full membership program."

"What is that? How much is that?"

"Let me tell you what it includes. For starters, you get individual career counseling, priority admission at high-demand workshops, pre-printed mailing labels—"

"Is it free?"

"Hold on. You also get fifteen percent off of a professional headshot consultation—"

"Yes, but how much does it cost?"

She smiles stiffly. "It's nine hundred and ninety-eight dollars for the first year."

"I just wanted to sign up for the workshop with the commercial agents."

"You can do that, but that's going to cost you seventy-five dollars, which I could just put toward your membership. Twelve more workshops like that and you'll have your membership, and the classes will basically be free! You'll get unlimited use of our Macs and printers, a copy of our 'Taking Charge Actor's Handbook.'"

"No, thanks. I can only afford one workshop."

"I don't think it's a valuable use of your time or your money. You've got to see yourself as having your own corporation. It's called Becca Inc. You have to spend money to make money. These headshots, for instance, really aren't going to be much use to you."

"I like my headshots," I say.

"If you don't put your absolute best foot forward for the industry, I have to wonder how you feel about yourself." She pulls a calculator from her desk drawer. "We could work out a payment plan."

"I just want to sign up for the Saturday audition thing next week."

"All I can tell you is that you're lucky there's even room. And that's because of the holidays. The workshops with the good people, anyway—I mean, everyone we bring in here is good, but with the really well-known agents, those workshops fill up right away. In an hour sometimes. Last week one filled up in twenty minutes."

"Danielle." (*Danielle, who are you? Where are you from, you little snake?*) I take a deep breath and sit taller. I'm even shaking a little. But I know when someone is trying to take advantage of me, and after so much waitressing, I've learned how to stand up for myself. When I say her name I feel that I'm taking the power back. "Danielle. It's a risk I'm just going to have to take."

"Okay." Her shoulders slump, and she reluctantly prints out a sheet of paper and hands it to me without making eye contact. "Tara will take care of you at the front desk."

When I get to the lobby, I hand the sheet of paper to Tara. "Do you take credit cards?"

"Sure," she says. I feel a little sick as I hand over the card.

As I'm leaving the building, I pass Juice Man, who's on his way in. He's on his cell phone and does a double take when he sees me. Who is this omnipresent man?

"Are you following me?" he asks, grinning.

"I was going to ask you the same thing," I say. He laughs and continues his conversation.

"See you later," I say under my breath.

EIGHTEEN

ON SATURDAY, I'm back at ECS. This time I'm in Studio Three, a mock TV studio, facing the panel of four agents and twenty other actors, ranging from ages twenty to late sixty. I'm wearing my seventy-five-dollar shirt, jeans, and a pair of flat boots that Marisol insisted I buy, telling me they looked so good that it would be "irresponsible NOT to get them." I glance at the advertising copy, even though I've memorized it.

"When I graduated from college, my mom gave me a bottle of Di-Arrest. Some graduation present, huh? I was about to go backpacking in Europe. 'Trust me,' she said. Whatever, Mom! But, boy, was she right. Thanks to Di-Arrest, I had a super time, and diarrhea never stopped my fun, especially when I met Paolo! *Grazie*, Di-Arrest."

I look up at the four agents I'm auditioning for and await their reactions.

"I guess I'll start," says the guy who looks like a former actor. "There's something very dark about you. I can't put my finger on it. It's like you've got this cute face, but inside you're a dark person." He shrugs and rests his chin in his hands.

"Okay." I'm really not sure what to do with that. I look at the next agent, a woman built like a football player with Miss Piggy–style hair.

"Hi, I'm Marie," she says in a cloying voice. "You're nervous, but you've got a good smile. I won't call you in, probably. Good luck."

Good luck to you, too, Mama Marie, I think. This is the advice I paid seventy-five bucks for?

"You need to decide what makes you different," says the next agent, a weasel-like man. "Anyway, I really only work with the ethnic market, so I don't know how I can be helpful to you except to tell you that you hit the notes, you got the tone, but I get the sense that you don't really know who you are."

"Um, okay." Ethnic market? Can he really say that? I shoot Marisol a glance as she bites back a smile.

"I'm going to be honest with you," says the next man, a guy from Ace, the best agency here. "I only work with models. So I don't mean this to be an invitation—please don't call me. Seriously. But I disagree with these guys. I think you're excellent. You're totally relatable—a breath of fresh air. Get in front of as many people as possible. You might want to take a class in commercials just to get comfortable with the camera. But I think if you have the guts and the gumption to hang in there, you can do this. You might have to wait a while, though." He winks at me, and, without thinking, I wink back. He chuckles.

"Next!" says Danielle.

I see the man who works only with "the ethnic market" light up as Marisol steps onto the stage. I high-five her, and as I turn around, she pinches my ass. I yelp a little.

"She loves it when I do that," she tells the panel confidently. They all laugh.

Marisol begins, "When I graduated from college . . ." I can tell that she's nervous, but as I watch her on the monitor, her eyes are sparkling. When she says, "Some graduation present, huh?" she looks like she's talking to me. This dumb line of copy feels real. Marisol's a natural. A Girl Next Door with Leading Lady potential.

"That's what I'm talking about! You're going to be a hot commodity," says the weasel. Marisol beams.

On Thanksgiving, Marisol and I go to In-N-Out and order hamburgers double-double animal style, and sneak them into the movie theater. I wish Raj could join us, but he's gone home to Michigan. I miss him in a way I didn't expect.

A week later I wake with a start. The garbage trucks are making a racket outside, and they yank me from a dream in which Alex and I are on a ski trip and he's introducing me to the instructor as "his lady." For the briefest second, I forget how much I hate him. I check my phone to see if I have any calls, texts, or e-mails from agents. Not only are there no messages from agents, there's a reminder that today is the Jones concert—the day I was supposed to see Alex. No wonder I was dreaming about him. Is he still going? I wonder. Did he sell the tickets the same way he sold Ruby?

I roll over and pull the blanket around me, hoping that I'll tip back into the world of sleep, but my foot is itching like crazy. It had been bothering me all week, and I kept hoping that it would just stop, but when I confessed my situation to Mama Bear, she told me to google athlete's foot. I had a clear case.

It's not only my itchy skin that keeps me from sleeping. It's also the fact that rent was due three days ago and I haven't paid it because I don't have enough money. I stick my foot in the air, hoping the elevation will somehow help, and reach into my nightstand drawer where I keep my tips. I take out the cash and count it again slowly, praying that somehow this time it will add up to the eight hundred dollars I need to pay rent. The grace period for rent is four days, and I've been counting on it, trying to squeeze in as many shifts as I can. But they let me go early yesterday, even though I was supposed to have a double. I actually begged to stay, but Gloria told me that Chantal and Jimmy deserved the work more than I did.

Pablo gave me three awesome scones on my way out the door, but I have a feeling that the landlord won't accept payment in scones, even if they do have apricots in them, and he won't take a partial payment either. Last month, when I accidently put seven hundred and eighty dollars under his door, he returned the entire amount to me with a note that explained the rent needed to be paid in full or else it was considered delinquent.

I text Marisol my issue. I promise her scones, and fifteen minutes later she's at my door, wearing her kimono and bunny slippers and carrying two mugs of coffee. Her face is soft with sleep.

"Here you go."

"Thanks. I made some, too."

"But this is the real stuff. The best. Now let's brainstorm."

I take a sip of the coffee and scratch my foot through my sock. "I'm sorry, I know this is disgusting. I have athlete's foot."

"Yuck. Do you know where you got it?"

"The bear suit. Apparently last year's Baby Bear had athlete's foot."

"That's gross."

"It gets worse. He also had jock itch."

"From now on, double underwear and no thongs," Marisol says, taking a seat at my little kitchen table.

"Too late."

"You have jock itch?"

"Well, the pharmacist thinks it's a yeast infection due to stress and possibly exacerbated by the bear suit."

"You're a little . . . fungus fairy, aren't you?" Marisol picks up the medicine and reads the back. "This is going to help you. And if it doesn't, there's a free clinic on Sunset."

"Where am I going to get the forty bucks by the end of the day?"

"Forty dollars isn't that much. I wish I had extra money to give you," she says as a little line has creased her brow. "But I'm so broke, too."

"It's okay," I say.

"We'll think of something," she says.

"I don't know how you do it," I say. "I don't know how you don't worry."

"It's all going to work out in the end. I know it is. You need to believe it, too. And of course I worry, but it's just fear."

"Where do you get your confidence?"

She shrugs. "I've got this commercial shoot next week, so I know money's on the way." After our auditions at ECS, Marisol had two agents fighting over her. She had a bunch of auditions and booked a cereal commercial. She'll get five hundred dollars for the day and possibly tens of thousands of dollars in residuals. She's got the perfect amount of quirk.

"You're really talented, Marisol."

"Oh, please. It's all luck."

"That's not true. I saw you on the monitor. You're such a natural. I can't believe you're going to make five hundred dollars in one day." She smiles and I have to tamp down a flicker of jealousy. I slip on an oven glove and take out the hot scones from the oven. Pablo made me promise that I wouldn't put them in the microwave.

"Okay, let's think," Marisol says. "Is there anything you could sell?"

"My bed?" I put the scones on a plate.

"You need a bed," Marisol says, breaking off a steaming piece of scone.

"I wish I could play an instrument. I'd stand on the corner somewhere in a velvet skirt with an open guitar case or whatever."

"Damn, this is good," she says with a full mouth. "I can't do anything like that either. Hey, let's do a Shakespeare scene by the Echo Park Lake. It's like Shakespeare in the Park, LA-style."

"Logistically complicated. Besides, we'd have to memorize the scene. We don't have that kind of time." I refill my coffee and top off Marisol's. Without thinking, I look up to see if anyone else needs coffee. I'm waitressing even when I'm not.

"I wish I knew someone who could give us advice."

"Marisol, that's it."

"What is?"

"We'll set up an advice booth," I say.

Marisol beams at me. "On the Venice Boardwalk. With all the other street performers."

"Two dollars for a solution to your problems," I say. "That's such a deal!"

"I'm going to find us the perfect outfits," she says. "We're going to be so good at this. We'll probably make hundreds."

"Then we could get more oysters," I say.

"And the jeans that you truly deserve," she says.

NINETEEN

"MARISOL, DO YOU think we need a license? Like for street performing or something?" I ask.

"If anyone asks us for a license, we'll just play dumb," she says, and sets up the two folding chairs and the TV table we brought in the back of her car. "Remember the fine art of making shit up?" I nod. Marisol motions to a dreadlocked white dude playing a bongo drum and laughing to himself. "I mean, do you think that guy has a license?"

"I don't know, maybe?"

It's an unusually hot day for December in LA. We're wearing what Marisol deemed 1970s therapist outfits, including non-prescription eyeglasses. Mine are black and cat-eyed, and Marisol's are tortoiseshell and take up half her face. We decided to go with an old Woody Allen therapist look. We fast-forwarded through *Annie Hall* and *Manhattan* for fashion inspiration. I'm in high-waist pants and a blouse that ties at the neck, and Marisol's in a long-sleeved, calf-length dress with a high, ruffled collar. Marisol tapes a poster board sign to the table. It reads ADVICE: TWO DOLLARS A QUESTION. I tape a "tips" sign around a coffee can, in case someone feels like paying us above and beyond our fee. All we need is twenty customers and I'll be able to pay my rent.

Raj texts me: Turned in Hotel California. Ninety-eight pages of thrills and chills!

Me: CONGRATULATIONS! We need to celebrate!

Raj: Not yet—I just need to finish all the rest of my work. I have to write a web series pilot BY TUESDAY.

Me: Do you have an idea?

Raj: Kind of.

Me: Maybe I can help? Can you hang out for a little while? I haven't seen you since you've been back!

Raj: Yeah. Where are you guys?

Me: In Venice. On the boardwalk. We've set up an advice booth!

Raj: I feel like I need to see this. And I DEFINITELY need some writing advice. You're my secret weapon, ha-ha!

Me: Yes! Please come!

Raj: Send your coordinates. I'm on my way.

"Raj is coming," I say after I text our location.

"Nice," Marisol says, studying me.

"What?" I ask.

"You're blushing!" Marisol says.

"I am?" I put a hand on my cheek. I feel warm.

"You're blushing so hard. You like him!"

"Maybe I do," I say, feeling that same flutter I felt when we were hanging out at Hotel Uno. Oh my God, do I like him?

"This is great news," Marisol says. "I'm going to touch you up." She whips out a lip gloss palette. "Let's define this lovely pucker of yours." She paints my lips with the tiny brush. "So remember, with the people who come to our booth today. They're not customers. They're clients. Go like this?" She rubs her lips together, and I copy her. She holds up the compact to show me.

"I think we have our first client," I whisper, as a young guy in a Princeton crew T-shirt and running shorts approaches us. He has red hair and a soccer player's body. He smiles at us.

"Oh, I just love a redhead," Marisol says.

"So, hi. I actually really need some advice," he says, catching his breath. Marisol and I spend about fifteen minutes discussing his roommate situation with him until we arrive at the conclusion that he shouldn't break his lease. He gives us our two-dollar fee as well as a five-dollar tip. He also gives Marisol his number.

"That was easy," I say.

"That was wonderful," Marisol says.

"Only seventeen more clients to go."

Twenty minutes later, a man in his mid-fifties wearing a tracksuit approaches us. "So, what's this? How does this operation work?" he asks us in a weird accent. He's standing a little too close. His rests his hairy sausage fingers on Marisol's kitchen table.

"For the price of two dollars, you ask us a question and we'll give you advice," Marisol says.

He smiles as he stuffs two dollars in the jar. "Here's a question: How come my girlfriend won't let me eat her pussy?"

"EW!" I shriek and cover my face. "It's not that kind of advice."

"I paid my two bucks, I want an answer."

"Go away," Marisol say. "You need to get out of here! Go away."

He walks off, laughing. "That was worth two bucks."

I take out a Sharpie and add "No Dirty Talk!" to our sign. When I take my seat again, Raj is walking toward us with three iced coffees in a tray. He waves and I wave back, feeling brighter at the sight of him. It's like one of those California breezes that sweep through my apartment.

"Raj," I say as he hands me the cold drink, "thank you." Our hands touch, and his fingertips are pleasantly cold.

"So let's talk about this web series assignment. What's it about?" I ask. "Come on. Hit me with it."

"All right, here goes. It's called *Can You Watch My Computer?*"

"Okay," I say.

"You know how when you go to a café, people are always asking if you can watch their stuff if they go to the bathroom or have to move their car or whatever—"

"Sure," Marisol interrupts.

"So, I'm thinking this guy asks this girl, 'Can you watch my computer?' But instead of just sitting there for ten minutes, all this stuff happens, and she has to, like, do ninja moves and stuff to keep his computer safe. And it gets really weird and then he comes back and he's like, 'Thanks' and she's like, 'No problem.'" Raj throws his hands up in the air as if to say, *That's all I got.*

"That's funny!" Marisol says.

"Yeah, what's wrong with that?" I ask. "You might need to work on the ending a little."

"Yeah, yeah. It totally needs a tag or something. But the bigger problem is that this is supposed to be a pilot, so it needs to be an idea that can carry a whole series."

"This would make a good web series," I say, glancing around at our cozy setup. "Kind of like Lucy with her advice booth— but modern and with some grit."

"That's genius," Marisol says. She turns to Raj. "I keep telling her she's a genius, but she doesn't believe me."

"You think I don't know this? She saved my screenplay," Raj says.

"You guys, stop," I say, though I have to admit it feels really good to hear I'm smart. After all, not one of the eleven colleges I applied to thought I was up to snuff. "But seriously, though.

I think I'm onto something. Each episode could be a different client with a weird problem."

"That's a great idea," Raj says. He's wearing one of my favorite shirts. It's a long-sleeve T-shirt with three buttons at the top. The shade of ivory looks so good against his coffee-colored skin.

"It is?" I ask.

"Sure. It's an amazing concept. It's so self-contained—and cheap."

"That's important?"

"Money is always important," Raj says. "I'm going to need a kung fu expert to play *my* lead. Sometimes that costs money."

"And this idea has a simple framework," I say, getting it.

"Right. Damn, I wish I'd thought of it," Raj says.

"You can have the idea," I say. "Take it."

"No way," Raj says. "This is yours."

"But your project is due on Tuesday. And it's not like I'm going to do anything with it."

He considers it for a moment and then seems to think better of it. "I'm not in the business of stealing concepts. Talking out *my* ideas at great length with a supersmart girl-woman, yes. But stealing, no. Besides, you *should* do something with it."

"He's right," Marisol says.

"Improv something right now," Raj says.

Marisol and I lock eyes. Hers are sparkling and I bet mine are, too. Why not? I think, feeling giddy. "Will you shoot us?" I ask, handing him my iPhone.

"Sure," Raj says.

"Okay, I'm the therapist, and you have a problem," I tell Marisol.

"What is it?" Marisol asks, totally game.

"It's got to be kind of absurd but real at the same time," Raj says.

"How about if you're your boss and you're wondering how to get your assistant to like you?" I suggest. "Because you're actually afraid of what she thinks?"

"I can totally be Agnes," Marisol says.

Raj gets a shot of our sign as Marisol and I take our seats on opposite sides of the advice table. I pull my hair back in a tight bun. Marisol smiles at me—a conspirator. She takes off her glasses, shakes out her hair, and applies a thick layer of lipstick.

Raj crouches down so that the iPhone is level with our faces. "Action," he says.

"Tell me more about this assistant of yours. What's her name again?" I ask, holding a pencil to the notebook.

"Her name is Miranda," Marisol says in a perfect British accent. She sighs. "Miranda, Miranda, Miranda. She's not a very good worker, and she doesn't realize how lucky she is to have a job with me."

"And you continue to employ her. Can you tell me what that's about?"

"I don't want to let her go until she admits that she admires me. Just thinking about her gives me a headache."

"She's both the headache and the cure," I say, as a breeze lifts my hat from my head. "Oh!" I chase my hat down the beach, catch it, and return, breathless, to the table.

"You almost lost your hat, there, Doctor," Marisol says, laughing.

"But not my head," I say gravely. "And I think there's a message in that. Let the wind blow off our hats, for perhaps they aren't what's holding our heads together after all."

"Cut," Raj says. "That was totally weird and completely perfect."

In what feels like a bold move, he takes my hand. I don't let go.

"Want to try another?" I ask.

By 2:00 p.m., not only do we have the first three webisodes recorded, we've also had several "clients": a cute couple talking about who should move in with whom, a housewife wondering if she should have lunch with her high school boyfriend, and a pair of girls in sixth grade who wanted to put a spell on their teacher. There's also been some dirty talk despite our sign. We've made twenty-three dollars in two hours.

We're debating how to get more people to visit us, when I see someone walking down the boardwalk.

"No way," I say. It's Alex. He's too far away for me to see his face clearly, but I know that walk. Even though he's wearing a simple white button-down that every person who lives within a ten-mile radius of a Gap owns, I feel like I know that particular shirt. It's definitely him.

But what is he doing here?

Without thinking, I stand. I can almost feel the workings of my eyes as they focus on him. This is so weird. I just had that dream about him last night, so it's as if he stepped out of my subconscious. The air feels suddenly rich with the smell of the ocean. I can taste the salt in my throat. As he walks in our direction, a prickly heat radiates from my gut and I fall back into my chair.

"What?" says Marisol.

"It's Alex." I'm so shocked, I barely have enough breath to speak.

"We can't understand you, honey," Marisol says, bending toward me.

"I feel like she needs some smelling salts," Raj says.

"Alex," I say.

"Her ex. Oh, God," Marisol says, looking up. "Where?"

"Wait, who?" Raj asks.

"The blond guy in the white button-down," I say.

"Are you sure?" Marisol asks.

I look up. "It's definitely him." I cover my face with my hands and sink lower.

"What's the big deal?" asks Raj.

Marisol whispers in my ear. "He's coming toward us. He knows it's you. Come on. Smile and wave."

"I can't!" I say.

"Yes, you can!" Marisol hisses. "You *have* to! You're an actress—act!" I look up and wave as Marisol continues to whisper in my ear. "You're Grace Kelly, the picture of elegance."

"I'm the picture of elegance," I repeat as Alex approaches. My stomach sinks as I remember that I'm sitting behind a sign that reads ADVICE: TWO DOLLARS A QUESTION. NO DIRTY TALK!

"Becca?" Alex asks, picking up the pace as he strides toward us. "I thought that was you. Nice glasses." He laughs. "This is crazy!"

I push the glasses up on my head and stand. "Alex, I can't believe this. What are you doing here?" I lean over the table and hug him. His hands on my back are stiff and nervous as he pats me. I am dizzy with the incongruity of the moment.

"I'm here for the Jones concert."

"Oh," I say, and feel a pinch in my chest that he's still going—without me. "You didn't sell the tickets?"

He shakes his head no.

"Who'd you come with? Your new girlfriend?" I can't disguise the edge in my voice. If I have to meet his new girlfriend, I'm going to barf.

"No, I'm here with my roommate. I never said I had a girlfriend, by the way."

"Whatever."

"I'm Marisol," Marisol says, stepping toward me protectively and placing a hand on my shoulder.

"Raj." Raj nods hello. He's off. His face has fallen so far, he's almost unrecognizable to me.

And it's so weird to have them standing so close together. I don't like it. It's like my old world—with all of its pain and history and longing—is bleeding into my new world, which for a moment felt so full of promise. I'm not ready for my old world to see my new world. I also don't like the way that Raj is standing—his shoulders hunched, his usually relaxed posture tense.

"Marisol, here, is booking commercials left and right, and he's a filmmaker," I say. I almost tell him about *Baby Bear's First Hanukkah*, but think better of it.

"That's cool. . . . So what are you up to?" Alex says. "What's this all about?"

"Well," I say, glancing at Marisol. Her brown eyes widen, urging me to make shit up. "I'm making a webisode."

"Starring and directing," Marisol says.

"I just hold the iPhone," Raj says.

"Really?" Alex asks, his voice full of concern. I nod with too much enthusiasm and a shadow crosses his face. "Becca, do you . . . need some money?" He pulls a couple of twenties out of his worn leather wallet.

"NO!" I say. Oh, God. Doesn't he understand how humiliating this is? He sticks a twenty in the can.

"We are not looking for handouts," Marisol says. "We're offering a service."

"While making art," I add, fumbling.

"Dude, you paid the fee—just ask a question," Raj says. His voice sounds lower than normal, and he looks like he wants to punch Alex.

"Raj and I are going to take five," Marisol says, glancing at her watch-less wrist.

"Huh?" Raj asks, looking pale.

"This is a union gig," Marisol says, leading a reluctant Raj away. "We're entitled to breaks."

"This is nuts," I say, shoving my sweating hands in my pockets. I've fantasized about running into Alex so many times. In none of those fantasies was I dressed like a Woody Allen character and sitting with a coffee can.

"It is what it is," he says, looking at the ground. "Okay. Advice time. What should I get Granny Hopkins for her birthday? She's turning ninety."

Oh, Granny Hopkins. Alex's most captivating relative. How I love her.

"Take her on a date. Somewhere really elegant. Pick her up at eight in a coat and tie."

"Nicely solved." His eyes flicker with recognition. "But you've always been good with presents."

"It's true," I say, thinking of the last present I got him. A T-shirt from an amusement park that we both went to as kids, but was shut down a decade ago due to safety concerns. We both loved the roller coaster. I found the shirt at a Goodwill in Rhode Island. It took all my strength to hide it from him until Christmas.

"I brought that T-shirt to Stanford," he says as if reading my mind.

"It's a great shirt," I say, and he smiles at me.

"It's on the house." I take his twenty from the can and hand it back to him.

"Take it. I insist. I'm supporting the arts." His cell phone beeps with a text. He checks the message and replies.

"So, you're okay?" he asks, eyes squinting with genuine concern.

"YES! I'm great! I'm acting. I'm directing. I'm following my passion. I'm doing what I love. But what about you? Are you okay? Do you like Stanford?"

"Yeah," he says, his face registering surprise at the question, because of course he's okay. He's at Stanford, after all, fulfilling not only his parents' dream for himself, but also my mother's dream for me. "It's fucking awesome."

"Is it?" I ask, because although I can't really explain it, something about him inserting the word *fucking* indicates that it's actually not that awesome. Alex is not one to swear casually.

"I mean, it's hard. But it's Stanford, so . . . of course it's hard."

"Yeah, of course it is," I say, holding his gaze.

"I've got to go. My roommate is waiting for me. I'm sorry about the phone call, Becca. I'm sorry that I wasn't more . . . forthcoming."

Alex and his vocabulary. As charming as it is, it's also distancing.

"It was rough," I say. He nods, and we hug again awkwardly.

"Take it easy," he says, and walks away. A second later he

turns around and says, "Don't worry, I haven't forgotten about your camera." And then he's off.

"So, that's him," Marisol says. She and Raj take their seats on either side of me.

"That's him," I say, kind of numb.

"I mean, he's okay," Marisol says. "If the whole Captain America thing gets your motor running."

I stare into the middle distance.

"Resist the dark side," Marisol tells me. "There's nothing for you there."

"He apologized," I say.

Marisol snorts. "I should hope so. I mean, after that phone call."

"You've been talking on the phone with him?" Raj asks.

"Just once," I say. "It was awful."

Raj nods. A little while ago we were holding hands, but I feel so confused and muddled right now.

"Good news, fungus fairy," Marisol says. "Our scheme worked. Forty-three dollars. You can pay your rent."

I check my phone. Please make an agent have called. Please let one of my headshots have landed me something. But there's only a missed call from an 888 number, which I know is a robocall from the phone company telling me I'm late paying my bill, and must do so immediately to "avoid a disruption in service." I have an ache in my belly, and I hate that seeing Alex has created it. Being reminded of the pain of rejection upon rejection is like a punch in the gut. I sit in the chair and place my head in my hands. The Rastafarian's drumming isn't helping. For the second time today, I think I might pass out.

"Doll?" Marisol asks, rubbing my back.

"Yeah."

"How about we make both our lives a little easier and you move in with me next month?"

"I'd like that," I say.

She puts an arm around me. "We'll sell my coffee table, and you can sleep in my trundle. How does that sound?"

"Like just what I need," I say, and put my head on her shoulder, which smells like perfume, salt air, and just a touch of pig placenta.

TWENTY

"YOU WERE BEGGING? On Venice Beach?" Mom asks. I'm lying on my bed with my limbs bent and splayed in a pose of defeat, like an actor on a Civil War reenactment battlefield.

"I wasn't begging, Mom. I was giving advice. I was providing a service," I say into the phone. I sit up and stare at my Polaroids, which I've been sticking to my mirror in no particular order.

"On the beach?"

"Kind of. I was more on the boardwalk. But, yeah."

"Whatever. It was outdoors. It was begging."

"You wouldn't say that if I'd been playing the flute in a velvet skirt," I say, placing the picture that Raj took of Marisol and me next to the one of her doing a cartwheel on the beach. So far the collage looks kind of messy, but I'm messy inside right now, too, so at least it's authentic.

"What was Alex doing there?" Mom asks.

"He was going to see that Jones concert that we'd bought tickets to back in June. He went with his roommate."

I tape up the other two pictures I have from today, one of our bare feet in the sand, and one of Raj listening to me, his hand curled under his chin like *The Thinker*.

"He wanted to see you," Mom says. "And I think maybe you wanted to see him, too."

"It was a total coincidence," I say. "I promise."

"That you went to Venice, where the concert was being held?"

"The concert was in Santa Monica," I say.

"Close enough—on the day you knew Alex had the tickets. I don't know, honey. I really think you should come home." I hear her spoon hit the side of her tea mug. She sips the drink, and I listen as she takes a bite of what I know is toast with apple butter on it, because it's December and we always have toast with apple butter in the winter. I feel a pang, wishing I were with her.

"I can't come home." I'm surprised by my own certainty.

"What do you mean you can't? Pack up your stuff, get on a plane, and come home. You can use my credit card."

"I'm not ready to surrender." I close my eyes and fall back on my bed. "Besides, I'm in a play."

"The bears one?"

"Yes," I say, annoyed by her tone. "It's a real play, Mom. And they pay me. And I have an idea for a web series."

"LA is a big city. A big, expensive city. You obviously can't afford it, honey."

"Yes, I can. I made my rent. And Marisol and I are going to move in together. We decided today."

"What about the college applications? You have less than five weeks. They should be just about done now. Are they?"

"Almost," I say, though this is not the case at all. And it's not just because I feel a little sick every time I open the Common App. It's also because I don't want to give them the chance to reject me all over again. And I'm not sure if I belong in college. What if Marisol is right, and I'm a genuine artist who doesn't really need college? "I'm not ready to give up on acting, Mom."

"Have I told you about my old classmate Caroline Windsor?"

"No," I say. My feet are starting to itch again. I peel off my socks.

"We were tied for valedictorian in high school."

"You can tie for that?" I ask, threading my fingers through my toes to get to the really itchy places.

"Sure. She went to Harvard. And then she became an actress. She's a pretty lady, too. At least she was. Time has not been kind to her. All that hard living, I suppose. She crashed on couches and ate ramen long after the rest of us moved on. She had bit parts here and there, but she never had a break. The whole thing is very sad if you ask me."

"Maybe her big break is right around the corner," I say, putting her on speaker and carrying the phone to the bathroom so that I can wash my hands.

"Oh, honey, that's the kind of thinking that got her in trouble in the first place. Grandma told me that she still asks her parents for money on a regular basis. At thirty-eight. A Harvard graduate. Can you imagine? At one point, she was a clown. From Harvard to the circus. She's the antithesis of the American dream. You don't want to end up like Caroline."

"Jeez! Aren't you being a little judgmental? Maybe she enjoys being a clown." I remember that California Film School offers clowning classes, and smile to myself. It sounded fun to me. The hot water feels good and I decide to soak my feet. "Maybe she brings people happiness. Did you ever think of that? Besides, don't you believe in me?"

"Oh, I believe in you. I believe you are a beautiful, intelligent, incredible young woman. And I want to see you succeed. I don't want you to miss out on college. If you let these next few weeks get away from you, I promise that you will regret it. What are you doing? Are you taking a bath?"

"I'm just soaking my feet," I say, then realize if I tell her I've contracted athlete's foot from a gnarly bear costume, she'll use it as ammunition. "To, um, relax. Anyway, I'm not going to let anything get away from me, Mom. But I do love California."

"You can apply to schools in California, honey. But I'm not going to sit back and watch you let the years go by, sitting on the sidewalk with a coffee can, all because you can't get a part in a chicken soup commercial. It's beneath you, and you know it. Don't you want to succeed?"

"Of course." Monistat and antifungal foot cream are on the sink. My black waitressing sneakers, the toes curled up with wear, are in the spot I kicked them off last night. Next to the toilet is *Making It in Hollywood!* From her author photo, Suzi Simpson looks at me with her kind, no-nonsense expression. I grab the Polaroid and capture the scene. Then I tuck the undeveloped picture into the mirror.

"Promise me that you won't miss those deadlines. I'm on your side, you know. No matter what, I'm always on your side."

"I know," I say, wincing with pleasure as I slip my feet into the hot water.

"Tell you what. I'll pay the application fees."

"Really? Are you sure?"

"Absolutely. I'll send you a check tomorrow. In return you have to promise me to apply."

"Thanks, Mom. I promise." I debate telling her about my application in progress—my collage for California Film School—but for some reason I don't.

"And you know, maybe you should call Caroline. She might have some advice. I'll e-mail you her contact info. I'm sure I have it somewhere."

"Maybe I will," I say, though deep down, I have to admit that her life seems pretty depressing, even if she does occasionally bring happiness to others. "She sounds like a very brave person." Mom sort of grunts. "It was an adventure today, Mom. There was this guy next to us playing drums, and Raj brought us iced coffee, and I think Marisol met a guy. And the beach, Mom. It's just beautiful. I think you'd love it out here, actually. Maybe you could do, like, a Murphy's Soap commercial."

"Murphy's Soap? I'm not that old."

"You're getting there," I joke.

"I'm hanging up. I love you to the sky."

"And back," I say.

We hang up. I glance at the Polaroid picture. It's not ready yet, but I have a feeling when it develops it's going to be heartbreaking.

❊

Later that night, Raj knocks on my door. I'm a little embarrassed about the state of my studio since his is so neat and tidy. But he doesn't even seem to notice.

"I want to show you this footage," he says. He sits on my bed and I sit next to him. He shows me the scenes we recorded on his iPhone, and we both laugh. It's not just the improv between Marisol and me that works, it's the places that Raj zooms in and pulls away. It's who he chooses to focus on and when.

"Do I think this is funny just because of the Ikea effect?" I ask.

"Do you mean because we made it?" he asks.

"Yeah," I say.

"No way," Raj says. "There's poetry here. I like how you recovered when your hat blew off. It was this totally real moment, and I love that you just went with it. A lot of people might have frozen up."

"Wait, is my wall down?" I ask, grabbing his hand.

"I think so," Raj says, and turns to me. For a moment we're both very still, and then I realize what's about to happen. He leans in for a kiss, and I pull away.

"I'm sorry," I say, my heart racing. "I can't."

"Becca, I really like you."

"Yeah, but . . ." I freeze. I feel like I'm watching the scene from a distance. Something deep inside of me has gone numb. If my wall was down today, it's back up now.

"It's because of Alex?" Raj asks, and I wince at the sound of his name. *Is it because of Alex?* I was feeling something this morning. I was so easy, so free with Raj. I feel smarter around him, better than my normal self. So why do I feel so locked up inside? Raj's jaw tightens. His eyes flicker with pain, and I feel desperate to get out of this moment. "You want to get back together with him?"

"No," I protest. "I mean—I don't know. I should be over him by now. I *know* that, but it's like I'm stuck." He sighs and stands up. "I'm confused. I feel—"

"You don't have to say anything," he says, backing away. As he's about to leave, he pauses in the doorway. "Remember when we were talking about *Hotel California*? You were the one who said that avoiding pain is what keeps people running in circles, staying in the same place."

"How can I be avoiding pain when I'm in so much pain?" I say, holding back tears.

"I'm sorry," he says. "I didn't mean to do that."

I stand up and open my mouth to speak, but no words come out. Instead, I feel something sharp and foreign in my chest, like a rock. No matter which way I move today, something hurts.

TWENTY-ONE

THE NEXT MORNING, I knock on Raj's door.

"Hey," he says quietly. I don't want things to be awkward between us, but there's no doubt about it, they are. Normally he invites me right in. But today he's standing in his doorway.

"I thought of how your idea might work," I say. I gesture inside. "Do you think I could . . . ?"

"Um, sure," he says. And now I see why he was guarding the door. His usually meticulous apartment is messy. Not by most people's standards, but definitely by Raj's. There's a pizza box on the floor with a half-eaten pie in it, his bed is unmade, and there are papers all over his desk. "Sorry."

"Doesn't bother me," I say. Ugh. My voice sounds too bright and cheerful.

"It bothers me," he says. And now that I look at him a little more closely, I see circles under his eyes and even a stain on his rumpled T-shirt, which is the same one he was wearing last night.

"Do you want to hear my idea for *Can You Watch My Computer?*" I ask.

"Sure," he says.

"So, in every episode, someone asks something else of a person—doesn't have to be the same girl, but it could be. You just take questions strangers ask each other and expand them to their fullest capacity. Like holding someone's spot in line? Asking for the time? I'm not really sure. I just had the thought and wanted to tell you."

"Huh. That's pretty good," Raj says. Though his interest has perked, I don't sense his usual enthusiasm or warmth. "Thank you very much."

"Oh," I say. And that's it. That's all he says. And before I know it, I'm back in my apartment. Alone. I guess this is how it's going to be now.

Mom's check to cover my application fees arrives in a few days, and I waste no time cashing it. Every day for the next two weeks, I sit down at my computer and start the Common App. Every single day. But every time I get to the essay, I stop. The perfect question awaits me.

"The lessons we take from failure can be fundamental
to later success. Recount an incident or time when you

experienced failure. How did it affect you, and what did you learn from the experience?"

My failure is so obvious. I failed to get into college. I am a freak among my peers. So why can't I answer this question? What did I learn from the experience?

I learned that rejection sucks, I write. I learned that it's contagious. I learned that it spreads and infects every aspect of your life.

Then I delete it.

There are other questions on the Common App, and I take a stab at each of them, but none of them resonate like this one. This is the one I need to answer. I know it. As Ms. Bishop would say, I can feel it in my stomach-brain. But I can't bring myself to type a response. Something that feels like a cross between goose bumps and internal poison ivy starts to creep up my throat every time I try to begin this essay. Is it possible that failure can become its own circle? That once you enter into it, there's no way out?

Every day I sit here at my vanity-table-turned-desk and sweat for a good thirty minutes in front of my laptop. I sweat salt and coffee, and munch on my cold, hard toast, and clutch my stomach until I can't take it anymore. I shut the computer and tell myself, Tomorrow. Tomorrow I will apply to college. And then, if it's warm enough, I go for a swim in the Ramada Inn pool. The water is always soft and warm. The sound of distant traffic from the 101 has started to sound like the ocean to me. I swim laps, counting each one as I turn somersaults at the ends of the pool, and emerge thirty minutes later transformed. Calm. Ready for the rest of my day.

One day I manage to write to Mr. Devon for another letter of recommendation. I tell him it's for the California Film School. He agrees with a cheery "good for you." I still don't know who else I can ask.

The two-week run of *Baby Bear's First Hanukkah* is a success. Every performance is a full house. The Pull-Ups crowd loves us. In fact, *Baby Bear's First Hanukkah* is the hottest preschool show in town, and inevitably toddlers who didn't plan ahead are turned away at the door. There are only forty seats in the theater, but I never fail to find the line around the block impressive. Raj and Marisol surprise me on my opening afternoon. I didn't expect to see Raj, even though I put a note under his door to invite him. He's been so distant—and I don't blame him. But he's there. He cheers me on, then leaves immediately afterward to get to work.

Marisol attends all four performances on my opening weekend. I take her out for tea afterward and she tells me all about her blossoming romance with Dave, the cute redhead we met on the boardwalk. It turns out he's not only hot and smart, but he has a great job in an advertising agency.

"Are you in love?" I ask her, my breath snagging on the question. Even though I adore Marisol and want her to be happy, I don't want to lose my best LA friend to a boy. Not yet.

"I don't know," she says, and I have the distinct feeling that she's never been in love before. Because it's not something you have to think about.

Vivian drives in from Pasadena to see my show the next weekend. She's brought me flowers and a gift certificate to Trader Joe's for her little "starving artist."

"It was cute," she says, when we get back to my apartment. "It was much cuter than I thought it was going to be."

"Jeez. What did you think I'd gotten myself into, Vivian?"

"I wasn't sure, but those kids sure did love it, and the theater was nice. I'm not going to lie, Becca, you can rock a bear suit. When you shook your butt spinning the dreidel? I mean, I was genuinely laughing. And my heart was racing when that hunter was chasing you. I'm not kidding."

"See? I can do this. I can be an actress."

"I don't know about this apartment, though," she says with a grimace. "That bathroom—"

"That bathroom is *clean*," I say.

"Becca, the paint is peeling everywhere. There's water damage on the ceiling. I'm proud of you, but I'm also worried about you. What would your mom say if she was here?"

"She's coming out here soon. And you don't have to be," I say. "I'm fine. And anyway, I'm moving in with my friend at the end of the month." There's a knock at the door. "I bet that's her now." I open the door and see Marisol all dolled up for her latest audition. I think it was for Wendy's. "Marisol, this is my cousin Vivian. Vivian, meet Marisol. Best friend and future roommate."

"Nice to meet you," Marisol says.

"You too," Vivian says with a smile. "Please tell me your apartment is bigger than this, otherwise I don't know how two of you will fit."

"I'm going to sleep in her trundle bed," I say.

"What are you, twelve?" Vivian asks.

"Sort of," Marisol says, and giggles as if this is a good thing.

I see Raj pass by the open door and call out, "Raj, any word on the screenplay?"

"Not yet," he says, peeking his head in.

"Let me know when you hear something, okay?" I say. I miss him. I really do. I miss discussing plots and psychology with him. I miss all of our conversations.

"You got it," he says.

"This is my cousin Vivian," I say.

"Nice to meet you," she says.

"She finds our building a little less than satisfactory," Marisol says.

"It's kind of grim," Raj admits. "But that's why artists like us can afford it." He shoots me a conspiratorial smile, and I feel like he's back—just a little. And then he heads down the hall.

"Would you like some tea or coffee, Vivian? Are you hungry? I think I have some cheese sticks," I offer.

"How about I take you two out for dinner? At least then I can tell your mother you've had a hot meal. Do you want to bring your cute friend along?"

"Raj?" I ask. "You think he's cute?"

"Very much so," Vivian says. "I mean, he's not my type, but he looks like he could be yours."

"Yeah," I say. "I guess he does. I'll go ask him."

I try to catch him on his way out the door, but it's too late. He's gone. He must have nabbed a really good parking spot.

Marisol brings her boyfriend, Dave, to the final show, which goes off without a hitch. I show the appropriate amount of fear at the sight of the hunter, collide as planned with Mama Bear in the chase, and learn from Goldie Lox how to play dreidel. The kids love it. They shriek and giggle and clap. I have to pause for laughter no less than six times. The people laughing don't have fully developed brains, but it doesn't lessen the satisfaction. A little girl waves to me during the performance. Despite warnings from Dawn to never break the fourth wall, I wave back. Her face shows pure exaltation. Her mother, who looks like she could use a nap, mouths, "Thank you."

When I'm taking my bow I think I see Juice Man standing in the back with a toddler on his shoulders! I can't be sure it's him, and before I can take a second glance, I have to step back so that Goldie can take her bow, and she stands right in front of me.

After the show, I ask Dawn if she has any idea who that guy was. "The one standing in the back with the kid? He had brown hair and glasses?"

"Brown hair and glasses? Honey, we had a full house, I can't get a biography on every member of the audience."

"Just asking," I say. "Anyway, thank you so much for the opportunity."

She nods and tells me that she hopes I'll audition again next year. "You did a good job, and it ain't easy to find someone who can fit into that bear suit."

"Thanks," I say. While I'm flattered, I hope I've moved on by next year.

"You were so cute!" Marisol squeals after the show. Dave says that as a Jew he can officially say that it was a great explanation of Hanukkah.

"I'm going to bust out of this costume, then let's get out of here," I whisper to them, and head back to the dressing room. I affix a note to the bear suit, warning next year's Baby Bear about athlete's foot and jock itch. I slather on cold cream, wipe off my whiskers, and apply some lip gloss. I throw on a loan from Marisol, a vintage Diane von Furstenberg dress, and heels. There's something about wearing a bear suit that makes a girl want to look good. I bid farewell to my castmates, wrap my peacoat around me, and head into the cool, bottle-blue evening with Marisol and Dave.

I text Raj to see if he wants to join us, but he writes back that he can't. He's working extra shifts. I wonder if this is actually true or if he just doesn't want to be around me.

"All right, everyone. I'm going up!" I announce to the room full of strangers. It's several hours later, and Dave, Marisol, and I have migrated to a party hosted by Dave's advertising firm at a karaoke place in Koreatown. Earlier in the week they landed the Volkswagen account and they've reserved this place to celebrate. We've been at the party for almost two hours now, hanging out with Dave's boss, a guy in his thirties named Woody. Waitresses have brought us endless free drinks and Korean appetizers, and now I've hit a Sea Breeze sweet spot. My joints are loose and my spirits are high.

And the karaoke aspect of this party has been neglected. A heavily lip-lined woman from the accounting department has been dominating the microphone with Frank Sinatra songs. The only variation has been from a freckled executive in a day-to-evening dress who did a pitch-perfect but boring "Bette Davis Eyes," and two giggling receptionists who abandoned "Islands in the Stream" halfway through. I've been resisting getting behind the mic because I technically don't have any business being at this party. But I can't restrain myself any longer.

"Get ready to be entertained. Get ready to do 'The Humpty Dance'!" I say, and pump the air with my fist. I've learned from all the bar mitzvahs I attended in seventh grade that "The Humpty Dance" is an oldie but goodie—a classic that never fails to ramp up a crowd. The DJs played it for the parents, but it never failed to fill the dance floor.

Marisol claps and cheers. "I told you," she says to Dave triumphantly. "I told you she was a wild woman just waiting to unleash herself. Let's see what you got, Becca!"

"Are you sure you want to do this?" Dave asks, swallowing

nervously. His expression reminds me of Alex's embarrassment at my dance moves. I hesitate.

"What do you mean is she 'sure she wants to do this'?" Marisol asks.

"This is my job," Dave says. "And everyone knows I brought you guys."

"Yeah, and she's about to make you look like a damn genius," Marisol says sharply. She shoots me a look like, *Don't listen to him.*

"I sense trouble," Woody says. "What's going on over here?"

"I'm about to do the best version of 'The Humpty Dance' that you've ever seen is all," I say.

"Right on," Woody says, his curls falling across his forehead.

"Now, if you'll excuse me, I have a song to sing, even though I can't really sing." Dave is not amused. "Don't worry, Dave. I may not be musical," I say, patting his shoulder, "but I'm very, very dancical."

"Who is this funny little person?" Woody asks, gesturing to me with his drink.

"I'm a girl with a dream—an actress. I arrived three months ago—"

"Oh, shit," Dave says, wiping his face with his hand.

"Lighten up," Marisol chides.

"Yeah, I want to see this," Woody says.

I stand up, straighten my dress, put in my request with the karaoke master, and approach the stage. I tap the microphone.

"Testing, testing. One, two." I look out at the crowd of well-dressed professionals just waiting to be entertained. I know what

Suzi Simpson would say: "*You* gotta own it to sell it, kiddo." The music starts and I move to the beat, owning every footfall, every turn of the head and every snap of the finger. When I sing the words I know by heart, I own every syllable. I invent a catchy sequence: it's a closed-fist arm extension, followed by a sharp head turn, then side step/arm retraction, and a pelvic shimmy. I disappear into the performance until I feel like I'm flying, until I feel like it would be impossible to make a false move. In the space I'm in, there are no false moves.

"You're welcome," I say into the microphone when the song is over. I'm met with rapturous applause. Shaking with exhilarated delight, I take three dramatic bows, one for each section of the room, gingerly place the microphone on the stand, and skip back to my seat, high-fiving my new fans along the way.

"Dude, that was awesome," Woody says, standing. "You really are dancical."

The freckled executive in the day-to-evening wear puts her hands on my shoulders. "Weird Dancing Girl."

"YES!" Woody says, pointing at me. "She's totally it!"

"What do you mean?" I ask, sensing good news.

"Do you have an agent?" Woody asks me.

"No," I say, wilting with disappointment.

"Perfect. I have to clear it with a few of our peeps, but if I have any say, we're casting you."

What? These have to be the three best words in the English language! I can't stop myself from jumping up and down. "Yay!" I cheer, then ask, "In what?"

"Our Volkswagen campaign. One of our spots is Weird Dancing Girl, the spirit of the new Volkswagen yet-to-be-named subcompact car."

I'm delirious, both from my performance and the Sea Breezes. "I told you she's a genius, Dave!" Marisol says, and then spins me in her direction. "You're going to be in a commercial. And this campaign is huge. Dave's been talking about it non-stop. It's going to be everywhere! And this is totally going to help you get an agent!"

The next morning, still bleary, I update my list.

1. Get an (agent). — Met with Athena at Talent Commune.
   Follow up on SAG.
√ 2. Get curtains.
√ 3. Get a pillow.
√ 4. Buy pots and pans.
√ 5. Get a kitchen table, bed, and a dresser.
√ 6. Go to the grocery store and get ingredients for healthy meals.
√ 7. Learn how to apply subtle yet effective eye makeup.
√ 8. Get a job to make $ $ $!
√ 9. Get a friend. (Friends?)
10. Get a new style, new wardrobe, etc.
√ 11. Become a working actress! — Just call me Baby Bear!
    YAY VOLKSWAGEN!
12. ♡Get Alex back. ♡

TWENTY-TWO

THE NEXT DAY Marisol and I go to the Ramada Inn pool, aka our pool, which really is—as I know all too well—way too easy to sneak into. We don't even have to walk through the lobby, where the hotel staff might start to get wise to us. We just amble through the parking lot and open a back gate, and voilà, we're in our own little paradise. We're usually the only ones here, but today a pasty, middle-aged couple who look like tourists from the Midwest have crashed our party, sitting in lounge chairs and looking at those maps that show where movie stars live.

"I can't believe you broke up with him," I say.

"I can't believe that I didn't see his uptightness sooner," Marisol replies. "Usually I can sniff out an uptight person like that," she says, snapping her fingers. "My radar must be way off."

The couple turns around, startled by her volume. They continue to watch her, captivated, no doubt, by her vintage bathing suit and sunglasses, and all-around self-possession. She looks like a 1940s movie star as she takes off her sunglasses and says, "Besides, how could I be with a man who tried to silence you?"

The couple gathers their things and heads inside.

I laugh and she does, too. I'm glad to see her looking so happy and free. Marisol booked that cereal commercial and then quit her job. However, she hasn't booked another one since.

"We need to celebrate my new single status and your career advancement. Let's go out again tonight!" She claps her hands and rubs them together.

"I can't jinx it. My official audition is tomorrow at eight. But tell me everything you know about commercials."

She pulls out two iced teas from her purse and tells me that a national commercial on this scale would earn an actor between twenty and sixty thousand dollars. The actor gets paid a flat fee for the day of work. That fee varies depending on the actor, the part, the product, and if the commercial will run on cable or on the networks. It's usually about five hundred bucks. If an actor's in the Screen Actors Guild, he or she earns a small amount of money every time the commercial plays. This money is called residuals, and it's where the twenty to sixty grand comes in. Because I'm not in SAG, I won't get residuals. The payment for the day will be my only payment.

"Without an agent, you're really going to have to fight for yourself." Marisol dives into the pool, swimming to the end underwater before coming up for air. "But you need to negotiate hard."

I put my head in my hands. "The last thing I negotiated for was twelve dollars an hour for a babysitting job. Working up the guts to do that gave me a stomachache for a week." I slide into the pool. "How will I know how much to ask for? How will I know I'm not being ridiculous?"

"Well, they want your dance moves. They made that very clear." She floats on her back. "You have *special skills*. I know one girl who got six grand for a day of work because of her *special skills*."

"Jesus. What could she do?"

"Speak Japanese and juggle fire. But you're a really good dancer. Play hardball and see what happens."

⁂

This conversation is running through my mind as I sit on a red leather sofa in the slick Santa Monica offices of the advertising agency. I had a brief audition for Woody and some Volkswagen executive earlier in the morning. I danced and lip-synched to Michael Jackson's "The Way You Make Me Feel" in a large conference room. I wasn't trying to be funny, but they laughed when I said the one line of copy, "I love the way you make me feel, Volkswagen," and offered me the part on the spot.

Marisol insisted that I wear a short skirt and heels, so now the backs of my knees are sticking to the red sofa. I take a deep breath as I get to the page in the contract that specifies the amount paid for services rendered. "I'd love to do this for a thousand dollars. However—"

"That's more than they usually pay for a day of work," Woody says.

"But because I'm not in the union and this isn't a SAG shoot, I won't be getting residuals. . . ."

"I don't mean to be a jerk, but that's part of the reason we went non-union. Dealing with agents is just . . . ugh. It's a nightmare."

I think of Suzi Simpson. I need to be my own agent. Suzi Simpson says you can always walk away.

"I'm not sure this is going to work out," I say. "I realize I don't have an agent, but that means I have to really look after my own interests here."

"What would you consider fair?" Woody asks, jingling change in his pocket.

"I was thinking . . . five," I say, feeling the color rise in my cheeks.

"Five *thousand* dollars?" The change stops jingling.

"Most actors would make at least thirty thousand with residuals. So, like I said, I won't see a dime of that because this isn't a SAG gig. I understand if there's another actress you'd like to go with, but personally, I need to pay my rent and put some food on the table. I mean, what would you do?"

He smiles. "Let me see if I can get you two."

"Five," I say, holding five fingers in the air.

"I'll be right back." He opens the glass door of his office, then sticks his head back inside and smiles. "Balls of steel, by the way. Love it."

The second he's gone I peel my legs off the sofa and start panting with anxiety. I fan my shirt away from my perspiring body and gulp the Diet Coke Woody gave me from his personal mini-fridge.

Woody bursts back into the office so suddenly I almost spit the soda all over him. He grins and opens his arms. "Tell you what, Becca. You have us over a barrel. Five thousand it is."

All I can think is that Suzi Simpson would be so proud. I should have asked for ten.

❧

Me: Mom, I'm going to be in a commercial!

Mom: What? That's amazing! What for?

Me: Volkswagen. Can you believe it?

Mom: How did this happen?

Me: Karaoke! I was picked out of the crowd at a bar.

Mom: Amazing! Wait, how did you get into a bar?

Me: Mom, that's not the point!

Mom: Okay, okay. I know, but I can't help it. I'm your mom. When can I see it?

Me: I don't know. I'll tell you when I do.

Mom: My baby is famous!

Me: Ha! Not exactly. I gotta go. I have to get my beauty sleep.

Please don't ask about college applications, I think. *Please, please.* The only one I've made any progress on is the California Film School one.

My favorite thing about the day of the actual shoot is the terminology. I have a *call time* (time you need to be at the set), a *wardrobe fitting* (they pick out your costume), and a *hair and makeup call* (self-explanatory). It's a rainy December morning, and I treat myself to an Uber to make sure I get to the set on time. It's in a studio in a weird area near downtown. As instructed, I check in with the *AD* (assistant director). I stop by *craft services* (free food!) for breakfast. Later, I'm outfitted in a bright blue dress, and my hair is trimmed and blow-dried while a pretty girl with a super-stylish Afro does my makeup.

"You have great cheekbones," the makeup girl says.

"I do?" I ask. Even though I've heard this before, it feels new and special coming from a real makeup artist.

"And good lips, too," she says, smiling. "Let's listen to some music. Do you like Joan Armatrading?"

"I love her," I say, even though I have no idea who she is. When they're done, I check myself out in the mirror. I know it's a total cliché, but I can't believe I'm getting paid for this.

The director, Doug, wears a sweatshirt and jeans with holes in them. I have to dance to "The Way Make You Make Me Feel," a bunch of times before I'm in the groove. But then, it seems, I get it right. Five thousand dollars for only five hours of work!

"That was it," he says on the fifth take. He shakes my hand. "That's a wrap."

When I get home I really want to see Raj. I get as far as standing in front of his door, but for some reason, it doesn't feel . . . appropriate. I hate the word as I think it. Why isn't it appropriate for me to share the best news ever with the person who will be the happiest for me?

Because I've hurt him, I think. Because even though I like him, I can't return his feelings. And yet, I miss him so much in this moment, this joyful, over-the-top, victorious moment, I'm on the verge of crying.

TWENTY-THREE

I DEBATE QUITTING my waitressing job. It would feel so good to march out of this restaurant. But instead, when the check clears I decide to pay down my credit card. Now that I'm in a commercial, waitressing doesn't make me feel so crappy. In fact, Gloria has ceased to be scary. I used to fantasize about telling her off and quitting on the spot, but when I watch her counting bills now, she looks tired and small behind that ridiculous old-fashioned cash register, which looks even more ornate in contrast to her plainness.

"Is your commercial on TV yet?" Chantal asks after she drops off food to a table of hipster chicks who are all dressed like nineties schoolteachers for some reason.

"I just shot it," I say. It's a slow morning, so I'm drying and sorting silverware until more customers come in. "I don't know when it's going to air."

"I hope you told my cousin about it. I still can't believe she didn't take you on like this." She snaps her fingers. "You're my people. Therefore, she's supposed to give you preferential treatment. I think she did it to get back at me for telling her mom about that weekend in Vegas."

"It was so unbelievably nice of you to get me a meeting, and for her to meet with me. I sent her an e-mail about the commercial, but she didn't write me back, so I don't think there's anything else to do. Besides, she's not a commercial agent, she's a legit agent, so it probably doesn't mean that much to her."

"She's going to regret it when you start making serious bank," Chantal says.

"Becca," Gloria calls from the front. "You have a visitor."

It's Raj! Standing at the counter in his fedora and a wool coat. He looks like a proper gentleman. Chantal actually whistles. A couple with a set of twins walks into the restaurant behind him, and Gloria seats them in my section.

"I'll get them," Chantal says. "You go see your *visitor man*."

"Hey, Raj," I say. I motion for him to join me by the twirling stools in the back. "Now it's my turn to get you something to drink. What will it be? A Coke? A Sprite? A root beer float?"

"Water's fine," he says, and takes a seat. I pour some for him and sit on the stool next to his.

"I just wanted to come by and say that I heard about the commercial, and I'm so proud of you. I hope that doesn't sound condescending or anything."

"No, it doesn't. Thank you."

"So tell me about it?"

"It was awesome. It was fun and I felt good at it. And they had these delicious tacos for lunch. They let me keep the dress I wore. It was the best!"

"That's awesome. I'm really, really happy for you."

"Me too. Have you heard about your screenplay yet?"

"Not yet. But I should any day now," he says. "I don't want to jinx anything, but I have a good feeling." Chantal is lurking by the soda hoses. She's pretending to wipe down glasses, but I know she's eavesdropping. I catch her eye and wave her away. "And I also wanted to tell you that I want to be friends."

"So do I! I miss you so much—and not just for the rides."

"I have a plan for New Year's Eve, if you're up for it," he says.

"I'm up for it. Whatever it is. I'm up for it!"

❀

After my shift, I buy an eight-dollar juice and I don't even finish it. I stop by the fancy boutique with the seventy-five-dollar T-shirts, feeling like I have a right to look, even if I don't buy anything. My mom is coming in two weeks, and I want to get her the perfect gift. I'm sure a part of it is guilt that I haven't filled out my college applications.

But there's another reason. She's worked so hard for so many years to take care of me, and no one's really ever taken care of her. Not since she was a kid. I pick up a gauzy cashmere scarf that's two hundred and fifty dollars. It's an emerald-green color that would look amazing against her pale, Irish complexion.

But it's not quite what I have in mind for her. I want to, somehow, get her something life changing. I'm folding the scarf and placing it back on the shelf when my phone rings—it's an LA number that I don't recognize.

"Hello?"

"I have Carson Smith at the Ace Agency on the line for you," a young female voice says. "May I put him through?"

"Yes," I say.

Oh my God! It's an agent. An actual agent! My legs go numb.

"Becca, hi, it's Carson."

The second I hear his voice, it hits me. Carson Smith is the agent who liked me from ECS.

"Hi," I say, stepping out onto the street. I immediately turn down a quiet alley to make sure I don't miss a word.

"A client of mine is in a show at Company One. Do you know it?"

Do I know it? Yes. I sent my headshot to them. It's the hot theater company run by Kingman Brewster. He's a theater director, an indie filmmaker, and husband to the blockbuster movie star Amelia Kirk. Kingman is a huge supporter of young artists. He gives the best experimental playwrights a shot at having a real production, and he always casts from *Backstage* cattle calls, never through agents. I went to audition for them once, but over two hundred actors beat me to it, so I couldn't get a slot.

"Yes," I say. "And it's so nice to hear from you by the way. Do you know I was in a Volkswagen commercial?"

"Listen, Company One opened a new show last week and

they need a replacement actress who's small and can pass as a ten-year-old onstage. I thought of you. Are you available?"

"Oh my God, yes!" I say. Carson gives me the information and tells me that I need to meet the assistant director tonight. "This is going to be a very fast process if you get it. You'll maybe have one or two rehearsals, then you're on. Can you do it?"

"Yes. Thank you so much. Um, does this mean you're my agent?"

"I only work with models, hon," Carson says, "and you're—"

"A character, I know. But then why are you doing this for me?"

"Someone did it for me once. Break a leg." He hangs up before I can thank him again. I float home, warm and buoyant despite the first LA rain I've ever seen, felt, or smelled, soaking my jeans and seeping through my sneakers.

1. Get an (agent). — Met with Athena at Talent Commune.
   — Follow up on SAG.
   — Carson Smith, ACE Agency, remembered me and got me an audition!.
√ 2. Get curtains.
√ 3. Get a pillow.
√ 4. Buy pots and pans.
√ 5. Get a kitchen table, bed, and a dresser.
√ 6. Go to the grocery store and get ingredients for healthy meals.
√ 7. Learn how to apply subtle yet effective eye makeup.
√ 8. Get a job to make $ $ $!
√ 9. Get a friend. (Friends?)
10. Get a new style, new wardrobe, etc.
√ 11. Become a working actress! — Just call me Baby Bear!
12. ♡ Get Alex back. ♡

YAY VOLKSWAGEN!

TWENTY-FOUR

A BRIGHT YELLOW flag with a giant "1" hangs outside the door of Company One Theater in a recently revamped part of Hollywood. The lobby is spare and narrow with dark hardwood floors. Artful posters from past productions line the walls. An upright piano stands in the corner. The place is packed with a young, fashionable crowd sipping imported beer from bottles and red wine from plastic cups. They have good haircuts and thoughtful shoes.

"Stand in the back. We're oversold," says Jesse, the assistant director, to whom I've just introduced myself. She tells me to look at the part of Young Anna and hurries down a flight of stairs, speaking into her headset.

I make my way through the crowd and find a spot by the

...th. The set is simple: Astroturf, three large wooden ...xes, and a screen where a dynamic night sky is projected. A three-piece jazz band plays stage right as the audience files in. A guy bends into his bass, one plays his clarinet with his eyes closed, and another hits his drums in a loose, solitary joy.

I stand between two couples, but I'm not lonely. I could be a part of this. The house goes black. The audience quiets. The band bursts into a new tune as twelve actors run onstage, and it's clear the audience is in the hands of experts. To prevent heartbreak in case I don't get the part, I search the cast for a weak link or proof that this isn't any better than Baby Bear, but I find no such evidence. Everyone is good. One guy is so gorgeous I can't take my eyes off of him. He's lithe, agile, and confident, electricity shaking off his body like salt. I check the program. His name is Reed. He's from Seattle. He went to Yale.

The performance hums along, surprising and electrifying me. The jazz band plays throughout the show, and I realize that I like jazz. I mean, I *really* like jazz. As of this moment, it's not just pretend. I want to be out there with the actors so badly that I'm afraid I'll jump onstage or raise my hand. Young Anna is a small but memorable role. In her one big scene, the character delivers a stream of consciousness diary entry as she fends off "cosmic ninjas," played by the chorus: three guys and two girls who appear throughout the play as townspeople, demons, and a PTA committee. The language in the monologue is by turns grounded and fanciful. The actress playing the part has an edge of sarcasm. I think it would be funnier played straight. After the show, I linger in the lobby as the rest of the audience files out. Jesse approaches me.

"Well, what did you think?" she asks. Her stance is wide and confident.

"I loved it," I say quietly. We schedule an audition for the next day. The actors emerge from the dressing rooms. Reed is even better looking offstage. He's taken a shower (they have showers here?) and he's wearing jeans and a broken-in leather jacket. He looks like he smells good.

I tap his shoulder. "You were incredible up there." My breath gathers in my throat as I take in the alarming blueness of his eyes and the health of his skin. If I had a little more restraint I wouldn't speak at all. I can't trust myself in the face of this kind of attraction. "You were, like, glowing," I say, feeling my face redden. To him, compliments are probably as common and meaningless as pennies.

"What a beautiful thing to say." He takes my hand. Instead of shaking it, he just holds it. We softly swing our connected arms. My smile grows until it breaks into a soundless laugh. "Hi," he says, tilting his head, smiling.

"Hi."

"Who are you?"

"Becca," I say. My pulse gallops. My heart knocks.

Still high from hand-holding/arm-swinging the night before, I practically skip to the audition the next day. I wonder if I'll see

Reed again. He's so good-looking that he almost doesn't seem real. Like he stepped from the pages of a J.Crew catalog. He's crush material: distant, sparkling, and as easy to crave as ice cream.

It's cold today. Not Boston cold, but LA cold, and I wish I'd worn a jacket. I hustle from the Hollywood and Vine Metro stop to the theater, passing people dressed up as Marilyn Monroe and superheroes—people do this for tips—and laugh as I remember that the last time I was here I was auditioning for that *Hamlet*-in-the-nude play. In fact, I start laughing so hard I get a few looks. I really wish I'd brought my ballet sweater. I'm wearing the rest of what has become my audition uniform: my red T-shirt, jeans, and zebra flats. Once the theater is in sight, I mentally salute the yellow Company One flag. I pass a girl who looks at me suspiciously and imagine that she's just come from her audition. I meet her gaze and smile. We each size the other up, but for reasons I can't explain, I don't feel intimidated.

I check in with Jesse, then pop into the bathroom to take some deep breaths and to add a touch of lip gloss. I wait on the piano bench in the lobby that had been so crowded the night before. Now I can hear the activity in the pipes.

"So just go ahead and do the monologue when you're ready," Jesse says. Her voice is slow and liquid, giving the impression that she's listening at the same time she's speaking. Her head is cocked to the side as she settles into her seat. "I'll be right back," she says when I finish. A minute later she returns with Kingman. He's the kind of slender, fine-featured man who'd make a beautiful woman.

"Take it from the top," Kingman says. I do, and afterward, Kingman is beaming. "Well, you're definitely an actress," he says, wiping his chin with his hand as if stroking an imaginary beard. "You understand we don't pay? You can get great exposure, but we don't pay."

"Yes."

"You have someone who can vouch for you? A director from another play?"

"Yes." Dawn from the Hanukkah play will be cool, I hope.

"We're seeing a few more people. We'll know by tomorrow morning. Thanks for stopping by."

TWENTY-FIVE

ALL MORNING I listen for the phone. I curl in my warm sheets, thinking about Reed, how his hand felt and how he looked at me. I think about sitting at a diner with him late at night, talking about movies and plays. I think about sinking into the seats of a movie theater, resting my head on his shoulder. I think about having him in my bed, rolling around with him until dawn. He'll wake me up with his warm hands and kisses. I'll make him chocolate-chip pancakes, and he'll make bacon. Even if we only hook up and none of these other moments come to pass, I bet I'd still enjoy it. I've never had a random hookup before, but maybe that's what I need. Maybe that will help me get over Alex, finally. As Marisol says, maybe I need to "cleanse the palate."

Except for my mom and Marisol, who each call twice to see if I've heard anything, the phone is silent. My mood grows increasingly sour as the hours march by like staggering zombies. Maybe I've grown overconfident because the Volkswagen commercial came so easily, but I thought I was going to get this part. I went to bed last night feeling like I got it.

Kingman said they'd know by morning, so when my Ikea clock hits twelve, disappointment clamps my chest. I tell myself that for some, morning might extend until the afternoon, until 2 p.m. even. But 2 p.m. comes and goes as quietly as a cat. I decide to work a little more on my collage, which is taking on a narrative of sorts. I add the pictures from *Baby Bear's First Hanukkah*: one of the theater exterior, with a giant Jack in the Box soda cup rolling past the entrance, another of Goldie Lox's bra on a hanger labeled with her character's name, one of Sally—aka Mama Bear—applying her makeup, and one of me in the bear suit, looking conflicted. At three o'clock, I knock on Marisol's door.

"Are you in there?" I ask. "Do you want to go for a hike?"

"I'm napping," she calls back. "Come back in a half hour."

I knock on Raj's door. I feel sort of weird about it, but he did say that he wanted to be friends.

"Come in," he says.

I open the door and ask him if he'll go on a hike with me.

"I'm writing," he says, looking up from his laptop.

"What are you working on?" I ask, leaning in the door frame.

"Another screenplay. This one's a kind of forties-style mystery."

"Oh my God," I say, taking in the Post-its on the wall. There are twelve rows of them, all in perfect lines. "What are these?"

"Those are scenes. I'm not like you. I can't just improv my stuff. I have to go into it and write out every detail."

"This is awesome," I say, seeing how he's color-coded each scene according to whether they are the A, B, or C plotline.

"Can't you take a break?" I ask. "Maybe it would do you good."

"I promised myself I'd write out the first act. Can you wait a few hours?"

"I need to do something now," I say. "I've been waiting around all day and it's killing me."

"For what?"

"To know if I got this part at Company One."

He finally stops typing. "Oh my God, Becca! That would be amazing!"

"I know! Hence all the anxiety."

"Can't you go for a hike by yourself?"

"I'm too scared," I say.

"Of what?"

"Rattlesnakes and rapists."

"Rattlesnakes and rapists, huh?" He sighs and rubs his eyes. "I'll go with you later. In the meantime you need to channel your anxiety through creativity. Make another one of your webisodes. You don't believe me, but it's a great idea. I brought it up in class, actually, and my professor used it as an example of a perfect concept for a small-budget production."

"Really?" I asked, flattered that Raj would mention it to his professor.

"Yeah," Raj said.

"All right," I say. "That's what I'll do. I just need to rally Marisol."

"Good luck with that," he says.

I walk back down the dim, carpeted hallway to my apartment, wait Marisol's requested thirty minutes, and then float the idea by her.

"What do you say?" I ask.

"Sure. But can you think of another good character?" she says, and narrows her eyes.

"What if you were one of the extras that you met this morning?"

Marisol has landed a gig as an extra on a soap opera.

"That's easy," Marisol says. "There was this girl today who made sure everyone there knew that she was Eva Longoria's body double, but it was all so desperate. Kind of sad, actually."

"Perfect," I say.

Since Raj isn't available to record us, I set up my computer to do it. We get on a roll and record a bunch more. Once I start thinking of characters, I can't stop. Marisol and I trade places, so that she's the therapist and I'm the client. I become the security guard at the Mayfair, Oh Fucky, Miss Nancy, Gloria. In addition to her love of country music, Marisol has a huge collection of hard-core rap and we take dancing breaks in between takes. Before I know it, several hours have passed.

"Okay, I need another nap now," Marisol says after we have over an hour of recorded sessions. She yawns and heads back to her apartment, which will soon be our apartment.

I'm watching the footage on my laptop when Raj knocks on the door.

"It's too late for a hike, but we could go for a walk?" he says.

"Actually, want to sit on the roof with me? I want to show you what we did."

"Sure," he says. "But it's kind of dark out."

"Like a movie theater," I say, closing my laptop and tucking it under my arm.

"How do you feel about your screenplay so far?" I ask as we climb the stairs to the roof.

"This one's going well, I think. Hey, so remember that banquet at the end of January I told you about? Do you still want to come with me? As friends, of course. That way I can introduce you around and make you want to go there even more. They're going to announce the winner of the screenplay contest then."

"I'd love to," I say, stepping outside. It's cold again today and on the verge of rain. Dark clouds hang over the mountains. "Are you nervous?"

"Totally. Can you imagine—a hundred thousand dollars to tell the story I want to tell. If I can do this, if I can make it happen, then I can start looking for agents, too."

I show him the footage and he laughs throughout, pointing

out why some episodes are better than others. Pretty soon, a pattern emerges. "Marisol is hilarious, but you're the star of this thing. The British PE teacher is the best. Miss Nancy?"

"She's based on a real person from my high school, Ms. Bishop."

"I love the line: 'Only moments of pain and beauty change our lives.' Okay, let's pick the best four and put them up on YouTube and see what happens."

"Can you help me edit them and stuff?"

"Sure," he says.

I feel my phone ring in my pocket and almost have a heart attack. "Hello?"

"It's Jesse. We'd like to offer you the part of Young Anna."

"Really?" I squeal.

"Really," she says, laughing, and tells me she'll text the rehearsal schedule.

"I got the part!" I say to Raj.

"Becca, you did it." He high-fives me.

I want to jump into his arms, but I hesitate. Would this be leading him on? He rolls his eyes as if he can read my mind, then smiles and gestures *come here*. I leap and he catches me.

❀

Me: Mom, I'm on fire! I'm going to be in a play at
    Company One.
Mom: What? What's that?

Me: It's a theater that's owned by Kingman Brewster
    and AMELIA KIRK!
Mom: Honey, that's fabulous! You're having an
    amazing month. Is Amelia Kirk going to be in the
    play?
Me: No, but I think I'm going to meet her.
Mom: I can't wait to tell my friends at work. I'm so
    proud of you!
Me: I'm doing it, Mom. I'm really, really doing it.
Mom: Yes, you are, honey! And once you get those
    college applications behind you, you're going to
    feel even better.

I sigh and press the phone into my pillow to keep from
throwing it. Why is she so obsessed with college applications?
Why can't she just let me have this moment without making it
about college? I take a breath and text her back.

Me: Right now, I'm just so happy about the play. This
    is a HUGE deal.
Mom: I know. And I'll get to see you in it, right? I'll be
    there in a week!
Me: Yes! I can't wait!

TWENTY-SIX

TWO DAYS LATER, it's my opening night at Company One. I'm sitting in the bathroom-size dressing room in my schoolgirl costume. I've had only two rehearsals prior to tonight, both led by Jesse. The only people I've rehearsed with are those in the scenes with me: a girl named Molly, who plays my sister, and a guy named Jack, who plays a bartender/poet. I haven't met the rest of the cast, nor have I seen Reed or Kingman again.

I've arrived early to meet Jane, the costume and makeup person, who gives me a ziplock bag of (free!) MAC makeup and shows me how to apply it to make myself look younger. When she's finished, I look in the mirror and see Young Anna. I see someone who has never worked for twelve hours straight or freaked out about her bank account. Jane dusts off her expert hands before she gathers her black leather bag and heads out, leaving me alone to await the arrival of my castmates.

"I thought I heard someone in here." Reed stands in the doorway. He's wearing a blue T-shirt, a beige Carhartt jacket, and jeans. From the arches of my feet to my eyelids, I'm burning up.

"Hi."

"You okay?" he asks. I nod, smiling. "I was hoping that when they said Becca had been cast that it was you."

"It's me," I say, and shift back in the chair, striking an understated pose.

"I can see that." He leans against the door frame. "You're here early."

"Makeup." I hold up the ziplock. He sits next to me.

"Are you nervous?"

"A little."

"Everyone's really nice. It's a great show." Heels click down the hallway, the doorknob turns, and I smell the perfume seconds before Pam enters. She's Carson Smith's client, who plays Anna. Pam is from Kansas and older (twenty-six; she volunteered her Northwestern graduation date in the program bio), but her stature, dark hair, and bold features give her a foreign, worldly appearance.

"Everyone's nice, except Pam," Reed jokes. "Pam" doesn't suit her. She should be named Consuela. She should be standing on a balcony in a red dress, drinking cognac.

"I heard that, Reed," she says, and punches his arm gently.

"Oh, hey, Pam," he says with exaggerated surprise. Does Reed like her? How could he not? I feel his hand on my back. "This is Becca, our new Young Anna."

"Carson told me about you," Pam says. "Said you were spunky. Isn't he a doll?"

"A total doll," I say, though the comment sounds strange coming out of my mouth.

"I'll let you ladies get dressed," Reed says, and gives my shoulder a squeeze. His thumb touches my neck. He shuts the door behind him. I wipe my brow.

"You all right, there?"

"Hmm?"

She laughs. "Be careful," she says. "That boy is a player."

The door opens. Shoshanna, who plays a clairvoyant waitress, arrives in business attire and sneakers. She carries her work shoes in a tattered Rite Aid bag. She drops the bag on the floor and kicks it under the counter.

"Well, my day sucked," she says, then peels off her coat and heads to the bathroom.

"Shoshanna works full-time at some evil real estate corporation," says Pam under her breath. Pam takes off her shirt and unhooks her bra, revealing a pair of perfectly matched, magnificent boobs. I stuff my head in my purse and paw around in there to avoid an eye-to-nipple exchange.

"So do you have a job, Becca?"

"I do commercials," I say. It's not technically a lie.

"That's it?" Pam asks. "You must work a lot."

"I mean, I'm a waitress, too," I say, a little embarrassed to have been called out. "But I just did a commercial for Volkswagen." When I resurface she's zipped up her dress.

"Cool. I heard your audition was amazing, by the way."

"Really?"

"Apparently there was no contest." She speaks evenly so as not to disturb her makeup application. "You blew them away."

"Thanks for telling me," I say, and feel myself glow.

Shoshanna reenters, strips to her thong, and applies her makeup. I'm already in my costume, but I contemplate undressing just to fit in. A few minutes later, Molly rushes in. Molly promptly puts in her earphones and turns up her iPhone to a dangerous volume, focusing so intently on herself in the mirror that she could burn a hole in it. She rocks out as though she were alone. Her elbow nearly takes out one of my eyes. I put my hand to my face.

"Could you move over?" She's loud, unable to gauge her own volume. Her skinny fingers pitch a tent on her pale, unblemished décolletage, a word Marisol has taught me. "I, like, don't have any room to get ready."

Pam locks eyes with me, then rolls them in solidarity. I escape into the cooler air of the hallway. Inside me, butterflies beat their wings.

"Fifteen minutes! Fifteen minute call!" Jesse shouts down the hallway.

Then: "Ten minutes."

Then: "Five minutes."

Then: "Places."

The entire cast is in the first scene. I've never rehearsed this scene because my only job is to stand there for a few minutes, listening to the live music like I'm in an old-timey jazz club. I guess Kingman figured I could do that without practice, but I'm nervous as I crowd backstage with everyone else. I hear the audience rustling in their seats. Reed rolls his neck. Molly jumps up and down. Pam inhales huge whale breaths. It's so dark back here. The drum thunders. The clarinet sings. The door is thrown open. We charge the stage. It's ten degrees warmer under the lights. For a full three seconds I'm Becca, orienting myself, holding my breath, looking around. Reed, now in character as a rough poet/bartender, holds out a burning, hand-rolled cigarette. I take it and inhale. It stings. The tobacco sticks to my teeth, and Reed is taking off my knee socks with his eyes. This is going to be fun.

Forty minutes into the show, when I hear my cue, I fly onstage. For the next several minutes, I'm in the zone. When I exit I hear laughter, and my heart swings in my chest.

I have various backstage duties throughout the show. They include everything from helping Pam apply bruises to her arms, to hoisting a tree to center stage between scenes, to handing off a broom, to pulling a curtain aside for Shoshanna's complicated entrance with a tray of drinks. Jesse made it clear to me that if I'm not on top of all my duties, I could screw up the entire show. I follow my script with a miniature flashlight. I forget only one thing: to fill a glass with iced tea meant to be bourbon for Reed.

"Sorry," I mouth to Reed.

"You'll remember tomorrow," he whispers. "Besides, my character is supposed to be totally wasted at that point, so he might not even notice that his drink is empty."

Jesse fixes us with a hard stare to shush us. Reed squeezes my hand in the darkness, then takes off for his next entrance, once again leaving me with a rabbit's pulse.

At the end of the show the cast runs onstage, holds hands, bows, and runs off. I never practiced this bit and just follow along. I have a small part, but no one would guess it by the reaction to my bow.

"You've got chops," Kingman says as I file out of the dressing room in my jeans, wrap sweater, and of course, my zebra flats. "Good night for it, too. *Variety* was here."

"*Variety?*" I ask. Every agent, casting agent, and director in town reads *Variety*.

"It was one of the good guys, too. Some of them are just assholes."

"I didn't know they covered theater," I say.

"They cover *us*. Be cool, okay? See you at the party." He claps my back. A woman who looks rich—flawless hair, teeth, and clothes—taps him on the shoulder. "Patricia!" he says, and kisses her, European-style, on both cheeks. "Thank you so much for coming." He takes her arm and disappears into the crowd before I can ask, *What party?*

I rush back into the dressing room, where Pam is pulling on high-heeled boots over black tights. I'm glad to see her and not

Shoshanna or Molly. I ask about the party and she tells me that it's at Kingman and Amelia's house in the Hollywood Hills.

Amelia Kirk's house? In the Hollywood Hills? Holy shit, *this is real*.

"Whatever you do, don't get dressed up," Pam says as she writes the address for me. "This one girl showed up in a gown. It was really embarrassing. Also, FYI, Amelia just wrapped a movie, so there'll probably be some other celebs there."

Oh my God—I'm going to be at a party with celebrities!

I fold up the address and put it deep in my pocket. When I look up, Marisol and Raj are walking toward me. I fly into Marisol's arms and semi-collapse.

"You're a star," she says.

"A constellation," Raj says.

"Guys, come here." I pull them into a quiet corner near the bathrooms. "Do you know what I have in my pocket? Kingman and Amelia's home address in the Hollywood Hills. I'm invited to a party there, and I need you two to come with me."

"No way!" Marisol cries.

"This is going to be great networking," Raj says. "I wonder if her producers will be there. Kingman's house? This is where things happen. Where cards get handed out and deals get made."

"Really?" I asked.

"Who knows who's going to be there?" Marisol says. "The important thing is that we're invited."

I read in an interview once that Amelia likes white flowers. The three of us stop at a grocery store where I pick out a simple bouquet. We grab an Uber to the party and chat about the play, which Marisol and Raj both seem to have genuinely enjoyed.

As we're about to cross Sunset, a bus stops in front of us with an ad that takes up the entire side of it. I see hundreds of ads like this a day—on billboards and bus stops, on coffee sleeves and plastered repetitively, Andy Warhol–style, on the sides of buildings—but I'm taken in by the girl in this ad for American Express. She's a waitress, and the slogan is about dreams being priceless.

Just as the last traveler steps aboard, I realize that I know this girl's face, and know it well. It's Brooke. Brooke Ashworth, huge and groomed within an inch of her humanity, pretending to be a waitress. Which I actually am!

"Holy shit," I say.

"What?" asks Raj.

I point to the bus. "I know that girl. She's going to NYU. She's not supposed to have her face on a bus yet!" An inflight safety video is one thing, I think, but this is a whole other level. "She's supposed to be taking pantomime classes and listening to lectures on the history of theater."

"That's a nice gig," says Marisol. "I went out for that. It's a big deal. Print, TV, the web. I'm talking international."

"That little hack. How? How did she do it?" I look at Marisol pleadingly, like she might really have the answer. "How?"

Marisol holds up her hands as if she's under arrest. "I don't know. I don't know everything, you know. She made a lot of money, though. And that's a union job for sure."

"Ugh! Why'd I have to see this right now? It's going to ruin my night!"

"Don't let it," Raj says.

Like it's that easy. The Uber car ascends into the Hollywood Hills, where the roads are impossibly narrow, steep, and twisting.

"You're right," I say. "I know you're right." I open the door of the Uber in front of Kingman's address. No matter what Brooke is doing, she's not going to a party with celebrities tonight. And neither is Alex. This night is mine.

TWENTY-SEVEN

IT DOESN'T LOOK huge from the outside, but this place is amazing. There are probably fifty people here, enough to make it feel like a big party, but few enough that I feel selected. I spot Pam talking to a salt-and-pepper-haired gentleman. I think I see Reed outside with Jack and some of the rest of the cast. The other guests are adults, full-blown adults. Dancing, laughing, partying adults. I feel this wave of triumph over Alex, who even with Stanford and his family's connections would never get invited to a party like this. At least not as a fellow artist. He thought I'd never make it. He felt sorry for me when he broke up with me, again when I called him, and the worst was seeing him feel sorry for me in Venice. I take a Polaroid and stick it in my coat pocket. Then I take another picture with my phone and post it to Instagram: #HollywoodHillsParty #TheGoodLife. And then I just can't resist . . . #Blessed.

In your FACE, Brooke and Alex! Ha!

Brazilian music plays. At first I think it's live, but then I see a DJ spinning out by the infinity pool.

The style of the house is modern with bohemian touches. There are real works of art on the wall and careful-yet-casual arrangements of black-and-white photographs. There are also movie posters and theater posters, all framed. There's a grand piano. There's an open glass door that leads to the pool. There's a fireplace. I feel like I've landed in a magazine. I take in the views of the blinking city.

"Pick your jaw up off the floor," Marisol whispers.

"I'm totally screwed," I say, and shake my head.

"Help me follow your logic," says Raj, who's stuffed his hands in his pockets.

"Well, I can never be something normal now."

"Who said anything about being normal?" Marisol asks.

"And I can't settle down someplace like Portland, Oregon, and, like, work for an environmental nonprofit."

"Why?" asks Raj.

"And who knew you had these secret plans?" says Marisol.

"Because this is what I want. And now I have proof that it's possible. All you need to do is be a successful actor."

"Or director," Marisol says, nodding at a guy with black glasses and red hair.

"Malcolm Barclay," Raj says, and pales. "I need a drink."

I spot one of the cast members from *Saturday Night Live* laughing as he sips a glass of wine. "Shut the fuck up," he's saying. "Shut. The. Fuck. Up."

"Join us," a barefoot Kingman says to me as he gestures to the party.

"Thanks for having us." I hand him the flowers and introduce Raj and Marisol. "No one else brought flowers, did they?" I feel suddenly embarrassed.

"No one else has such good manners," Amelia Kirk says in her trademark Southern accent. She's wearing jeans and a T-shirt. She's so tiny. There's no way that she's taller than me. She must weigh only enough to survive, and yet she emanates health, her skin glowing as if she's been brushed with starlight.

"Follow me to the kitchen and we'll put these in water and get you a little something to wet your whistle. I'm so glad you could join us. I'm Amelia, by the way."

"I know," I say as Raj, Marisol, and I follow Amelia and Kingman to a modern kitchen.

"Well, I know who you are, too," she says. "And you were dynamite tonight. You have a luminous future."

"I do?"

"I think so," she says.

"Oh, thank you," I say, my hand to my chest. "Thank you."

"What can I get you to drink?" she asks as she unwraps the flowers and quickly arranges them in a vase. All three of us are silent. "How about some red wine?" She wipes her delicate hand on her jeans.

"That would be lovely," I say.

Someone calls her name from the other room and she sighs. "I'm being summoned." She hands me a bottle of wine and points to a cabinet on her way out. "The glasses are in there."

I look up at Kingman as if to confirm that a real movie star, one of the biggest of our time, told me that I was luminous.

"Make yourself at home," he says, and follows her out.

"Luminous!" Marisol says. "She thinks you're luminous." Marisol and I jump up and down in a victory dance. Raj points to a Post-it on the fridge on which is scribbled *Malcolm* and a phone number. "Um, this is Malcolm Barclay's number, right here on the fridge, in the same spot where I have my Hollywood Pizza magnet."

Oh my God! I silently exclaim. As Marisol and I do another victory dance, Raj uncorks a bottle and pours us each a generous glass of wine. We raise our glasses in a giddy toast.

"She's got to be over forty. How does she look so good?" I ask.

"If we had a nutritionist, a trainer, a makeup artist, and a personal shopper, we'd look that good at forty-five, too. Come on. Let's find a bathroom. I'm going to do our makeup," Marisol says.

Raj looks at us, panicked. "What do I do?"

"Mingle," I say.

"But I have social anxiety."

"Raj, you're a bartender," Marisol says, with one hand on her skinny hip.

"I hide behind the bar," he says. "Sometimes literally."

"You do not," I say, and without thinking, I give his hand a squeeze. I look around for Reed, but I don't see him anywhere.

Once in the bathroom, Marisol pulls out her makeup bag. "I've got to teach you how to do this yourself. I'm really not helping you. I need to teach you how to fish instead of just handing you the sea bass." I laugh as she opens her lip gloss palette.

Two hours later, the crowd has thinned and Raj is playing Bob Seger's "Old Time Rock and Roll" on the piano. The *Saturday Night Live* star, now totally wasted, is singing along. "Duh-duh-duh-duh-duh-duh-duh!" He bellows as Raj pounds the opening chords. I see Amelia sitting on the sofa, talking to a woman with almond-shaped eyes, narrowed in concentration. I pull up a cowhide-covered stool. I smile as they continue to talk about some island I've never heard of. I try to find a place to chime in, but it doesn't feel natural, so I wait, smiling, for them to change the subject. The woman with the almond-shaped eyes excuses herself. For a second, Amelia's face goes blank, so blank that I wonder if she's fallen asleep with her eyes open. Maybe the lighting isn't as good in this corner of the house, or maybe her makeup has faded, but for the first time she looks her age. Amelia leans forward on the sofa as if to stand. I sense that the party is winding down; this might be my last chance to talk to her.

"Hi," I say.

"Hi, there," she says, snapping to life.

"So you know how you said that you liked my work?" I ask. She nods slowly with wide eyes. "That means a lot to me, obviously, coming from you, and I wanted to say thanks."

"You're welcome."

"The thing is—and I have no idea what your experience was like as a younger actress—I mean, I know you know this. But if I want to, you know, um, be seen, well, it seems that what I really need is an agent."

"It's true," she says. "And you'll find one. My momma used to tell me that the cream rises to the top." She smiles a closed-lip smile. She stands; so do I. I think about one of Suzi Simpson's anecdotes. She approached a casting director in a supermarket and it led to her first gig. "Take a risk, kiddos," Suzi wrote at the conclusion of the chapter. "C'mon, what do you have to lose?"

"So. Is there any way that you could help me?" I ask.

"Hmm?"

"Well, since you said I have a bright, um, luminous future, I'm just wondering, do you think you could tell your agent about me?"

The last vestige of her smile vanishes. "My agent has been my agent for seventeen years. He only works with established artists."

"Of course." Air seems to be pooling at the bottom of my lungs. "I didn't know if maybe you knew someone. Or he knew someone, or he knew someone who knew someone, or maybe a casting director you knew wouldn't mind setting up a general. I have this web series on YouTube. It's called *Talk to Me*. And I think—"

"I'm going to stop you," she says, placing a moisturized hand on my elbow.

"Oh."

"You should know that this is not really something one asks at a private party. It's very awkward. This is my home. Okay?"

"I didn't know," I say, shaking my head. "I'm sorry." I open my mouth, wondering how I can possibly turn this horrible moment around. There has to be a way. But nothing comes to mind. My cheeks are so hot I feel like I must have a fever of at least 103 degrees. I look at the floor and she slips away.

I walk though the party on gelatin legs, toward the backyard, wondering how quickly I can get out of here. Kingman's earlier request that I be cool now seems like an ominous warning. As I catch my breath in the hallway, I'm met with a portrait of Amelia taken by Annie Leibovitz. She's in a white gown, seated on a horse, her eyes fixed on something distant and miraculous.

I slide the glass doors open and sit by the pool on a lounge chair. There are a few other people out here, smoking pot by the hot tub, but I don't recognize them.

"Hey, you okay?" a voice asks. I turn around to see Reed, practically glowing in the moonlight.

"Yeah," I say, too embarrassed to tell him what just happened. "Just getting some fresh air. You were incredible tonight, by the way."

"You don't think I was too restrained?" he asks.

"No, not at all," I say.

"Even in the second scene, the one with Dylan?" He sits next to me. "I feel like I was a little off."

"Not at all," I say again. I can tell that it's all about him, and that's fine with me. It's a relief actually. "I think it was your best scene."

"Really?" he asks, and his pinky finger grazes mine.

"Really," I say, meeting his gaze. Even his jaw is muscular. Even his mouth is hot.

My phone buzzes with a text.

Marisol: Where are you? Raj and I think we should leave on a high note.

I wish I'd gotten this text before my gaffe with Amelia.

"Who's that?" Reed asks.

"My friends want to leave on a high note," I tell him.

Reed inches closer to me so that our legs are touching. "I don't think you've hit your high note yet."

"No?" I ask. My heart pounds. Maybe someone like Reed is just what I need. Someone who is so hot that his touch can burn away my memories of Alex. Someone whose feelings are hard to find, even if his intentions are clear. Someone to help me forget this night.

"Not even close," he says.

Me: I'm staying. See you guys tomorrow.

Marisol: Have fun!

Me: I think I'm going to.

TWENTY-EIGHT

AN HOUR LATER, I get into an Uber with Reed under the pretense that we're sharing it to our respective abodes, but somehow, I find myself at his Echo Park apartment.

"Come in here," Reed says, taking my hand and pulling me into his bedroom. The apartment smells like a boy; it has the vague odor of dirty hair. He, however, smells like sandalwood soap. I kick off my heels, my bare feet sinking into the suspiciously crunchy wall-to-wall carpeting.

"You're short," he says.

"What are you going to do about it?" I ask in a husky voice, which sends him into a fit of laughter.

"I'm going to rest my chin on your head," he says, pulling me close and doing just that. With his palm on the small of my back he presses me close to him. I shut my eyes and lean into him.

"I feel dizzy," I say.

"Then you'd better sit down." He leads me to the bed.

"Or maybe I'd better lie down. Just as a safety precaution." I stretch out on his pilling navy-blue comforter. I roll onto my side and pat the space next to me. "You'd better lie down, too."

"You're funny," he says, lying next to me. I move closer and kiss him. His lips are warm. I close my eyes. "And hot." He unzips my dress and slips his hand down my back. I lift the dress over my head, shivering.

"Are you sure you want to do this?" He looks me in the eye.

"Yes," I say. "I'm sure."

"As long as you know that I'm not really looking for a commitment."

"Let's just go with it and see what happens."

"Okay." He pulls off his shirt, revealing the cut body I've only touched over his clothes. He pulls off his jeans, smiling at me. His body is so beautiful, I feel like I'm watching a movie. He hooks his fingers in my underwear and pulls them off. I'm really glad I wore nice ones today.

Then he produces a condom from a bedside drawer, and it happens. It happens fast and is over even more quickly than it began. He rolls over and within seconds is asleep. I just had sex, I think as I stare at the ceiling. S-E-X. I've only ever had sex with Alex. I can't even wrap my head around it, let alone my feelings.

At 4 a.m., after several hours of trying to sleep, I find clean socks and a T-shirt in his dresser drawer and venture to the bathroom. The shower curtain has a map of the New York subway, showing that at one point, Reed had an inspired moment—a thought that he was going to decorate his bathroom with something cool—but this spirit was obviously quickly abandoned. The yellowing, once-white towels droop over the top of the shower. I peek inside. The white rack that hangs from the showerhead has left a rusty print of itself on the tiled wall. An old bar of soap has molded itself to the bottom rung. The tub is faintly gray.

I shut the shower curtain and turn to the medicine cabinet. I open it, hoping to scrounge up some kind of sleeping pill. I scan the contents of the cabinet. There's a pack of condoms, a tampon (relic of another girl?), and a bottle of antifungal cream, whose package I recognize from my battle with athlete's foot. There's a box of Theraflu that expired six months ago and—yes!—generic sleeping aids. I pop two in my mouth, stick my mouth under the tap, and swallow them.

I take a seat on the closed toilet and check out the bathroom literature. Next to the toilet is a stack of *Maxim* magazines with a couple of *Men's Health* thrown in. Beneath them is porn. I've never seen porn before, but the expression that you know it when you see it holds up. It's so strange. The breasts look like inflated birthday balloons. The hairless vaginas and anuses are fanned out with fingers. It's almost scientific. I guess I hadn't thought too much about what porn was or what it looked like, but I thought it would be more romantic or sensual. I thought that maybe the ladies would be eating chocolate naked on animal-skin rugs or standing under a waterfall or wearing nothing but velvet capes and masks. This is so bare and unadorned. I can't even tell where the women are. Are they on the floor? In a bed? In jail? This is what guys want? They want to look at close-ups of waxed assholes? I hear heavy footsteps approaching and instinctively throw my hand on the doorknob, which twists, with some pressure, against my hand.

"Occupied," I say, the porn spread on my lap.

"Oh, sorry," a voice grumbles. It's not Reed. Must be his roommate.

"One sec," I say lightly, and carefully put the porn back under the stack of *Maxim*s. I needlessly flush the toilet and turn on the tap as if I'm washing my hands. On second thought, I should absolutely be washing my hands after leafing through those periodicals. After a thorough scrubbing, I open the door for his roommate, a Viking type clad in boxer shorts and a stained white T-shirt. The porn must be his. Reed is a hippie of sorts. Hippies don't like porn. Right?

"Hey," the roommate grumbles.

"Hey," I say with a bowed head, pulling the T-shirt over my thighs. I make my way back to Reed's room. I get in bed next to him, under the unfamiliar quilt. He shifts a little but doesn't put an arm around me. I'm glad. I'd like him to want to put an arm around me, but not to actually do it.

It takes time to really feel something for someone, I think, looking at his chiseled, peaceful face. I turn away from him, curled on my side. I close my eyes, hoping that the sleeping pills will kick in.

I bet at our next rehearsal we'll kiss backstage, or at least hold hands. Maybe we'll become a Hollywood power couple, I think. I imagine us drinking coffee and reading *Variety*, then later helping each other with our lines. We'll go to parties together—parties like last night. And through the ups and downs of our acting careers, which of course will be mostly ups, we'll encourage and celebrate each other. As two artists we'll really understand each other. I'm getting ahead of myself, I know, but still. I turn and face him. He's snoring quietly, but I'm awake like a traffic light on a dark, desolate street, changing color for no one.

"Becca, time to wake up." Reed is shaking me. I try to sit up, but the sleeping pills seem to have added several pounds to my head; it feels like a turkey. I glance at the digital clock. It's 8:30 a.m. "I'm working brunch today," he says. "We've got to be out of here in, like, five minutes." So much for chocolate-chip pancakes. He hands me my balled-up dress.

"You okay?" Reed asks, quietly laughing, as I walk into the door frame.

"I'm in a bit of a fog," I mutter, rubbing my head. I find the bathroom and brush my teeth with my finger. I pull my dress on and check my voice mail for messages. Nothing.

"Hey, do you have an agent?" I ask when I get back to his

room. As I watch him get dressed I almost can't believe how hot he is. He has an actual six-pack.

"Yeah," he says, but doesn't offer any more information. He looks up at me as he puts on his shoes, grinning. "Wait, were you just using me for my connections? Sleeping your way to the top?"

"Ha-ha," I say. "Yeah, right!"

When we step outside his apartment building in Echo Park, it's raining in sheets. We stand under the tiny awning. I wrap my arms around myself. This would be a good time for Reed to offer me his jacket, but he's staring into the distance. I take a breath, hoping he'll say something romantic.

"Where's your car?" he asks.

"We took an Uber last night, remember? Anyway, I don't drive."

"I'd give you a ride home, but if I'm late, my manager's going to rip me a new one," he says.

"Don't worry about it."

"Hey." He lifts his chin in acknowledgement. "Thanks for last night."

My instinct is to say you're welcome, but that makes me feel like a hooker. Before I have a chance to respond, he turns his back. I watch his agile body dart across the street to his Hyundai with runner's form.

I take the bus back to the Chateau. When I get there, I pass by Raj's door and pray that I don't see him.

TWENTY-NINE

THE NEXT DAY, I wait for some kind of contact from Reed. Nothing. I don't get a phone call or a text. I remember Marisol telling me that I wasn't a damsel in distress and that if I want to talk to a guy, there's no reason I shouldn't just text him. But reaching out didn't exactly go well for me last time. The idea of having a conversation that has any possible echoes of the one with Alex is enough to send the blood pooling to my feet, forcing me to put my head between my knees.

I'm nervous to show up at the theater, not only because of Reed, but also because, oh my God, what if Amelia is there? I can't eat all day. How did this experience go from awesome to terrifying in less than twenty-four hours?

Reed nods hello when he arrives that night. I nod back. What are we, business associates passing on the street? During the show, he's polite to me, but he's not acknowledging what happened. I'm in uncharted waters. The only person I've ever slept with is Alex, and we had been together for a year before we did it. The distance Reed is keeping from me makes it hard for me to focus. Young Anna is anxious, too, I remind myself. She's out of her depths and trying to play it cool. I surrender to the feeling and do my best. But while my scene flies by, I feel like I'm a little out of sync. Still, when I take my bow, I get plenty of applause. After the show, I ask Reed if we can talk.

"Sure, sport," he says. *Sport?* "What's up?"

"Um . . . We had *sex* last night," I whisper. We're standing in a pretty public hallway of the theater. He blushes, like I'm embarrassing him by bringing it up.

"But I thought you understood," he says. "I told you I'm not looking for a commitment." Panic flashes across his face. "You were very clear about consent."

"Of course I was. I wanted to do it."

"I'm sorry, kid. I don't understand the problem."

Kid? "It wasn't permission to deny what happened."

"Okay," he says, watching the door behind me. "I'm sorry. I thought I was clear. I was, wasn't I?"

"I guess so," I say, feeling my brow furrow. I really do feel like we're nothing more than acquaintances.

"Can we be cool now?" he asks.

"I guess so," I say. *You've seen my naked body!* I want to shout. *You kissed my ankles!* But he's just looking at me like I'm his mail carrier or something.

"But listen," he says, giving me a penetrating stare now that he's been let off the hook. "You have an amazing energy. You should let go more. It's good for your acting."

"Thanks." I have to restrain myself from slapping his gorgeous face.

Anger is my fuel, I think and promise myself that I'll kick ass in this show every night. *Pour your energy into your art!*

Reed winks at me. Ugh. I could punch him. I get dressed quickly but linger to see if anyone is going anywhere tonight. I don't want to go home. Kingman is outside having a smoke by the stage door.

"Can I bum one?" I ask, stepping into the cool night air. I don't know why I'm asking. It just seems like the kind of thing a pissed-off actress should do.

Kingman looks at me sideways. "You smoke?"

"No." I shake my head.

"Then no fucking way," he says with a smile. "It's a totally disgusting habit."

The front door opens and slams and I gasp at what I think is the silhouette of Juice Man. He's walking away from us—I swear I could recognize his spritely gait anywhere.

"Do you by any chance know who that guy is?" I ask. Kingman furrows his brow as I point. "The one about to turn the corner."

"I really can't tell from here," Kingman says.

"I see him everywhere," I say. "It's the strangest thing."

"We did have a bunch of industry comps tonight," Kingman says. Industry comps are free tickets for people like agents, managers, casting people, and press.

"That's so cool," I say. At first I'm excited, but then I remember that tonight didn't exactly feel like my best performance.

"You were fine," Kingman says, as if he can read my mind. "Don't sweat it."

But I do sweat it, because the very fact that he's telling me not to indicates that something was off.

"I felt like I was kind of forcing it," I say. I realize that this is the longest social conversation we've ever had. If he thinks I'm a jerk for asking his wife for an agent, he doesn't show it. He leans against the railing and inhales his cigarette.

"Next time just take the shit out of it."

"Take the shit out of it," I repeat, trying to figure out what this means.

"Just do it. No big show of emotions, no scenery chewing. Just get onstage and go after what you want."

"Yeah," I say, getting it. "Okay."

"Don't worry about yourself, just try to make your scene partners look good. Where are you from anyway?" he asks as he blows a smoke ring.

"Massachusetts," I say.

"Mom and Dad paying the rent?" he asks without judgment.

"Nope," I say.

He lifts his eyebrows and nods his head with what I think is respect. Then he stuffs his cigarette butt into an empty soda can.

"See ya," he says, and walks inside. "And can you sweep this landing up? It looks like crap."

"Sure," I say. As I head toward the broom closet, I realize that I've just had the most profound conversation about acting that I've had since I arrived.

Afterward, I catch the bus across from the giant car wash on Santa Monica Boulevard. My mind is back on Reed. I didn't even like that guy that much, I tell myself as I step into the street and crane my neck to look for the bus. Two people who I think are prostitutes are standing on the other side of the street in short skirts and furry boots. This stretch of Santa Monica Boulevard is a famous spot for prostitutes to hang out. They're laughing and sharing a cigarette, calling each other *sugar* and *honey*. I don't even know Reed, I remind myself. A night with him was just supposed to be fun—no strings attached. So why does it feel like someone else just broke up with me? Was I lying to myself? Did I think it would be more than that, that he could get inside my heart and heal the wound that Alex left? Why do I even care?

A couple walks by with their hands shoved in each other's back pockets. The whole point of sleeping with him was to somehow burn off Alex. Did it work? Not really. I sigh as I pull my coat around my body. Except now I can't stand guys more than ever!

The bus pulls up at an alarming speed, screeching to a stop in front of me. It's almost empty, and the driver has a crazed look in his eyes.

"Come on in," he says with a weird grin. He's wearing headphones held together with duct tape. I step inside, take a seat up front, and clutch my purse.

THIRTY

A FEW DAYS later the *Variety* review comes out. At 7 a.m. my phone explodes with group texts from the cast. I could look it up online, but I want to see it in print. I don't bother changing out of my pajamas. I just slip on my sneakers. The streets are quiet and dark. I can see my breath in front of me as I jog to the Mayfair.

I pick the top paper from the stack and search for the review. I find it and let the rest of the paper fall from my hands. It's a rave. Most of it is about the play itself ("provocative," "sharply directed," "a gem"), with a focus on Pam ("stunning") and Reed ("raw and brave," "with James Dean looks") and the cast as a whole ("a winning ensemble"), but I have one line, one beautiful string of black ink on newsprint, dedicated to me: "The winning gamine Becca Harrington shines as Young Anna."

Gamine. I search the definition online: a girl with mischievous charm. It makes me smile. It's better than the Girl Next Door. I'm physically unable to stop smiling. I buy four copies of *Variety*.

I call Mom, right there in the parking lot of the Mayfair.

She answers on the first ring. "I'm getting ready to head to the airport, sweetie. Tell me, how cold—"

"Mom, go online and find the review of the play in *Variety*. Now."

"Okay, okay," she says. "Let me just get to my laptop. In the meantime, what are the temperatures like there at night? Should I bring a jacket?"

"Yes, yes, bring a jacket—have you found it yet?"

"I'm looking, I'm looking. . . . Okay, here it is. Company One, right?"

"Yeah—are you reading it?" I ask.

"Oh, sweetheart, this is good," she says as she reads it to herself. "This reviewer liked it. That must make you feel really good."

"Keep reading, keep reading," I say.

And then I hear her gasp. " 'Winning gamine Becca Harrington shines as Young Anna.' Oh my God! This is incredible. *Variety!* Honey, you're a star!" I pull the phone away from my ear as she screams with delight. "Jesus H. Christ, wait until I tell Grandma. I'm going to get this framed. First I'm going to get it blown up. They do that at Staples, right?"

"I don't know, Mom," I say, tears streaming down my face. It feels so good to have her be proud of me. It feels so, so good.

"I'm going to see you so soon, and, sweetheart, we are going to celebrate."

"I haven't gotten you a Christmas present yet," I tell her. Maybe I'll do one application today. Just one. For her.

"Nothing could be better than wrapping my arms around you," Mom says. "My *winning gamine!*"

After my morning shift at Rocky's, I'm thinking I'll get that application done. But instead, Marisol and I spend the afternoon celebrating. We go for a hike in Griffith Park, and then I take her out for coffee and croissants at the French place in Los Feliz, which has been completely decked out for Christmas. Streetlamps are decorated with wreaths, and fake snow has been sprayed inside store windows. I can't wait for Mom to get here. I can't wait for her to see the show tonight. Marisol and I go to the little boutique. Instead of completing an application, I buy Mom the gauzy scarf I saw last week.

"There's my star!" Mom says as she climbs out of the cab in front of the Chateau. I run toward her and throw my arms around her neck. I squeeze her neck and don't let go for at least a minute. The familiar smell of her rose soap catches me off guard, and my throat tightens up. The cabdriver unloads her bags on the steps of the apartment building, and when we're done hugging, Mom hands him a big tip.

"This is adorable," Mom exclaims after I take her up to my apartment. I've borrowed an air mattress from Marisol and made it up for her with Marisol's fancy sheets and the soft blue blanket that Raj bought for me. "From the way you described it on that first day, I was prepared for the worst. But it's clean and cute and even has a certain charm."

"Thanks, Mom. Would you like coffee?"

"You're a coffee drinker now, are you?" I nod. "Well, then yes, I'd love some."

As I scoop the coffee into the filter, I feel her watching me.

"What?" I ask.

"You just seem so grown-up. And you look, well, gorgeous. This outfit is so chic."

"Marisol found it for me in Goodwill. These jeans are Calvin Klein from the nineties."

And somehow, with my mom's stamp of approval, I feel like I can finally check off number ten.

✓	8.	Get a job to make $ $ $!
✓	9.	Get a friend. (Friends?)
✓	10.	Get a new style, new wardrobe, etc.
✓	11.	Become a working actress! —Just call me Baby Bear!
	12.	Get Alex back. ♡ YAY VOLKSWAGEN!

"Sounds like she has an eye for fashion," Mom says, checking out the contents of my refrigerator.

"She does."

"And thrifty, too," Mom says. "You know I admire that. Organic yogurt? Salad ingredients? Sliced fresh turkey? I'm even impressed by your fridge, honey."

"My body is my instrument, you know."

Mom nods, though I think I see her biting back a smile.

"I wish you could meet Marisol, but she's with relatives in Orange County for Christmas."

"Me too. I told all of my friends about your review in *Variety*," Mom says. "At least everyone I could text before I got on my flight. I stopped sending individual texts by the time I got on the plane, and then I sent out a mass message to all my contacts seconds before the flight attendant told us to shut off our devices. I'm so proud of you."

I beam as I hand Mom her coffee.

◈ ❊

"Hey, is your mom here?" Reed asks when he comes into the dressing room after taking tickets up in the lobby. Pam and I are chatting and applying our makeup.

"Yes, how'd you know?" I ask, adding just a bit more blush to my cheeks.

"Because she's your twin," Reed says. "She's really young, huh?"

"Don't get any ideas, Reed," Pam says.

"Yeah, that's a bridge too far," I say, disgusted at the direction this conversation is going.

"You really think the worst of me," he says. "I hate that. All I was thinking was that you two must have a deep bond."

"We do," I say. He's giving me puppy dog eyes, begging me to say, *Of course I don't think the worst of you*, but I won't say it. Tamera enters the dressing room, late as usual, and Reed's focus immediately shifts to her.

"Would you please scram so that we can get dressed?" Pam asks.

"Sure," Reed says, and closes the door behind himself, but not until he gives Tamera's shoulder a little squeeze.

"Be careful," I whisper to Tamera. She looks at me as if to say, *What could you possibly mean?* I just smile, because she knows exactly what I mean.

My mom is here, I think before I go onstage. This is my chance to show her I can do this. I take a deep breath and remind myself of Kingman's advice about taking the shit out of it, just doing the scene without any extra emotion. My job is to make my scene partners look good. I hear my cue, and I'm off.

My scene feels great. Alive and awake but not forced or pushed. The whole show feels great. It goes by fast, and I've found peace in the routine of it: the lifting of the tree, the handing off of the tray, applying Pam's bruises, the reliable music cues and audience responses, the pulsing electricity of a live performance.

After the show, when I spot Mom in the lobby reading over the program, she's smiling to herself so broadly, I take out Marisol's Polaroid and snap her picture without her even realizing it. Just as I'm about to greet her, Kingman taps me on the shoulder.

"Becca, this is Hal Conway, he's an old friend of the family and a producer at MTV." Kingman raises his eyebrows at me in this way that lets me know this is a big deal.

"Hi," I say. "Becca Harrington. It's so nice to meet you."

We shake hands. It feels for a second like a spotlight is shining on this moment. I can sense something important is happening, and I'm absolutely present.

"I just wanted to let you know you were terrific," Hal says to me. "I'm always on the lookout for young talent."

"Wow," I say, wondering if I might be sparkling from the compliments. Out of the corner of my eye I see Reed and Tamera holding hands, but I don't think anything could get me down right now.

"Normally I'd contact your agent, but Kingman said you're looking for one. . . ."

My breath leaves me for a second. I look to Kingman, and he smiles the smallest of smiles. It's hardly a gesture of reassurance. More like an acknowledgment of what happened.

"I don't, it's true—" I begin, but Hal cuts me off.

"That's okay. Do you have a website?" Hal asks.

"I don't have a traditional website, but I do have a bunch of work on YouTube," I say. "Webisodes."

"Excellent," he says. "Every actor needs to be creating her own work these days." He hands me a card. "E-mail me the link, okay? Let's keep in touch."

"Yes," I said. "I'd love that." We shake hands again and he walks out the door.

"Kingman, thank you so much," I say. He waves me off. I glance at Mom, who is watching this conversation with wide eyes and a smile as big as her face. I don't think she can hear us from where she's sitting, but she knows something good is happening. I give her the one-second signal. There's something else I need to do while I'm still high on this moment.

"So, I'm going to apply to California Film School."

"Good for you," he says.

"Is there any way you would write me a recommendation? It would really mean a lot to me." I feel a little light-headed, and my mouth is dry, but that spotlight is still on me. I can feel it. I have to take the risk.

"Sure," he says.

"Really?" I ask. "It's due in a week."

"How about this: you write it for yourself and then I'll sign it, okay? Assuming I agree with everything you write."

"Thank you so much!" I say.

"You're welcome," Kingman says. "Now, I think you have another fan."

I turn around and see Mom, watching from afar, beaming at me.

"That's my mom," I say.

"I guessed that," Kingman says, and he politely excuses himself.

Mom opens her arms and I leap into her embrace. I don't care if it looks uncool. Mom whispers in my ear, "I'm so proud of you."

"You're never going to believe what just happened," I say.

"What?" Mom asks.

"I'll tell you all about it in the Uber."

THIRTY-ONE

THE NEXT DAY is Christmas Eve. I have another morning shift at Rocky's, where the holiday spirit is alive and well. People are tipping well above the usual 15 to 20 percent. I wait on my mom at the counter, bringing her French toast and eggs, and Gloria comps it as a Christmas present. Afterward, Mom and I go shopping at the Grove. A mariachi band plays Christmas songs, and Mom and I drink Mexican hot chocolates as we shop.

The upscale outdoor mall is swarming with people, but the dancing fountains, the carolers, the elaborate Santa's cottage, and the Christmas tree the size of an office building are all putting me in the Christmas mood. Mom buys me a pair of shoes at Nordstrom, and I buy her a new lipstick from the Bobbi Brown counter after we both get our faces made up by the pretty girls in lab coats. We stop in J.Crew and try on some sweaters, but decide we should wait until they go on sale in January. We debate getting our picture taken with Santa for old times' sake, but the line is so long and both of us are hungry again. I take Mom's hand as we walk toward the new burger place that everyone in the cast has been talking about.

"So, Becca," she says when the hostess seats us. "I have to ask. What about those applications?"

"Well, they're coming along," I say, feeling both guilty and a little blindsided after all the positive feedback last night—she practically peed her pants when I told her about my conversation with the executive from MTV. "But given how everything is going, do you really think that's the best choice for me right now?"

"I am so proud of you," Mom says, squeezing my hand.

The waitress stops by, and we order some Cokes. "Anything else?"

"We need another minute," Mom says, and then she turns back to me. "But we had a deal. Even if in this moment you don't think college is right for you, you promised me that you'd apply, and I'm counting on you to stick to your word."

"I will. But I feel like I'm just getting some traction, and I've worked so hard for this—"

"I know. And this show you're in is great. I'm really impressed. But what happens after it ends?"

"This guy from MTV said he was going to be in touch, and I know that eventually I'm going to get an agent—"

The waitress returns with our Cokes and looks at us expectantly.

"We're still not ready," Mom says. We haven't even opened our menus. The waitress walks away. "You have to get a college education. Without one—oh, honey. I don't want to think about it. As your mother, I won't let you not apply. I love you too much."

"But—"

"I'll ask you again. How are the applications coming?"

"Some are coming along better than others," I say. This is not a lie. I did just ask Kingman for a reference last night, and I have Mr. Devon's reference ready to go. I've filled out the entire informational section of the CFS application, and my collage is almost complete. I haven't totally ignored the Common App. I've filled out the easy parts and uploaded my references from last year, even though they did me little good. It's that essay question that feels totally insurmountable to me, that stops me in my tracks each time.

"I know we talked about how the University of California schools would actually be much more affordable now that you're a resident, and of course I'd love to have you back in Massachusetts. Or at least New England, or even New York. Honey, you look extremely pale. Have a sip of Coke."

I do, in fact, feel like I'm about to faint. I sip the sugary drink. "Can we talk about this later. Please?"

"We can talk about it later," Mom says. "And we will. Right now I want to get some food in you. I think you need some iron. Do you think you're anemic?"

I open the menu and am perusing the burgers, when Mom grips my hand and shrieks. I glance up at her and her eyes are glued to something behind me. I turn around to see what has transfixed her. My Volkswagen commercial is playing on the TV mounted above the bar!

"It that you?" Mom asks, pointing to the TV.

"YES! Oh my God, YES! That's my commercial!" I'd been wondering when it was going to come out. There I am with the greatest haircut of my life, dancing in the bright blue dress. But I'm not just there, on this TV, in this bar. I'm on thousands, no millions, of TVs across the country. The volume on the TV is turned down. I watch my lips on the screen as they say, "I love the way you make me feel, Volkswagen."

"That's my girl!" Mom announces to the burger place. "That's my baby girl!"

I don't need college, I think to myself with a smile. I'm going to be a star.

❦

That evening Mom and I pick up a tabletop Christmas tree at Trader Joe's and some white lights at Rite Aid. We make popcorn and hot chocolate and watch my commercial online about a thousand more times. After we think we've seen it enough, we watch movies on my laptop. It's cold, and my apartment doesn't have heat, except for a small space heater that I picked up at Home Depot. Mom and I fall asleep together in my tiny bed. In the morning, she makes pancakes and coffee, and we open presents next to the tiny tree. She loves the scarf I bought her and puts it on over her pj's. Later, we go for a hike in Griffith Park, which is surprisingly crowded with families having picnics and playing soccer. I take her up the same route Raj took me. The sky is an almost alarming shade of blue. We stop every so often to check out a particular tree or flower, which feel incongruous with Christmas. On our walk home, we stop by the Mayfair and buy a chicken to roast, and some apples to fill with cinnamon and sugar and bake whole, just like we do back home.

"You're going to turn in those applications, Becca," she says to me before we fall asleep that night.

"Yes," I say.

When the cab arrives to take her to the airport in the morning, we both cry. And yet, when I watch the car turn down Hollywood Boulevard, I'd be lying if I said I wasn't just a little bit relieved.

That night Raj stops by with a few gifts. He's carrying a big white piece of cardboard, and what at first I think is a bottle of wine. It's a wine-shaped gift bag, after all. But when I open it up, I find a can of what looks like hair spray. I read the label. "Adhesive spray?" I ask.

"For your collage," he says. "I think it will hold your pictures better than that double-sided tape you've been using. And this," he says, holding up the cardboard, "is foam core, which is a lot stronger than that poster board."

"Cool! That's awesome," I say. I love that my collage, which has been buckling under the weight of everything I've added to it, will now be sturdy and substantial. "Thank you. Now, your turn."

I hand him my gift, which is in a more normal-shape gift bag. He smiles and pulls out two thermoses, the perfect size for the cup holders in his Corolla.

"I figure if we start teaming up again in the morning, these will work better than my coffee cups. Especially if you have to park up the hill somewhere."

THIRTY-TWO

I'M ACTUALLY GOING to miss this little apartment, I think as I lock the door and place the key into the padded envelope with the landlord's address on it. I was able to sell my entire Ikea collection for a whopping one hundred and fifty dollars to a guy just moving into the apartment downstairs. He's an aspiring model. Even though Marisol's apartment is nearly identical, and a whole lot nicer given her furnishings, it was kind of sweet having my own little corner of Los Angeles. Still, the relief of splitting the rent—and the damn trash bill!—is nothing to ignore. Even though I technically have this place for another night, Marisol and I decided I should just move in today before my afternoon waitressing shift. That way we could relax and enjoy New Year's Eve without thinking about hauling my stuff.

She cleared three drawers for my clothes and half a rack in her closet, which I've already filled. My Ikea sheets are on her trundle bed, waiting for me.

I pick up my collage, which I've transferred onto the foam core using the adhesive spray, and head over to Marisol's.

I knock on the door and she opens it wearing black jeans, a black sweater cape, and sunglasses. I don't think much of this look given her eclectic style choices.

"What's that?" she asks, dabbing her nose with a tissue.

"It's my collage," I say. I haven't shown it to her yet. I haven't shown it to anyone except Raj. But I just can't hide it from her now that we'll be living together. "I'm making it as part of my application to California Film School."

"You're applying?" she asks.

"I think so," I say. "And anyway, it's been fun to work on."

"It's so cool," she says. "Look, there we are with our advice booth! And ooh, is this that list you told me you made when you first moved here?"

"Yep," I say, blushing just a bit.

Marisol takes off her sunglasses to get a better look, and that's when I see that her eyes are bloodshot and wet.

"Oh my God, have you been crying? What's wrong?" Her face is streaked with tears. I take a seat on the sofa and motion for her to sit next to me.

"It's terrible," she says, shaking her head and holding an embroidered handkerchief to her nose.

"Oh, no." I wrap my arms around her. She sits down, gives

me her full weight, like a little kid, and sobs into my jacket. "What is it?"

"I can't tell you. It's awful."

"It's okay. You can tell me anything. Anything." I take her by the shoulders and look in her eyes. "Is it herpes? If it is, I've heard it's not as terrible as they make it out to be. And warts can be removed, regardless of their location."

"No, it's nothing like that," she says, shaking her head. She takes a deep, shuddering breath and lowers her voice. "I found a gray hair."

"Where?"

She looks at me with complete and utter disbelief, and then I realize.

"Oooh. I thought maybe you found one in your soup."

She laughs for a moment before the laughter morphs back into tears.

"I'm aging prematurely," she moans. "Today it's gray hair. Tomorrow I'll be hobbling toward a bus stop in my nursing-home shoes. And I've made nothing of myself. Nothing."

"This is crazy talk." I pull a napkin from the dispenser and hand it to her. "You're twenty. It's just a freak thing. Unless . . . are there a lot of them?"

"No, just one." Marisol delicately pats her reddened nostrils.

"You want my advice?" She nods soberly. "Say fuck it and pluck it." I smile, pleased with my cleverness. She laughs. And once again, before I can blink, she slides back into tears. I cover her hand with mine. "I get it. It's upsetting. But I think it's probably just one of those random things, you know? Is there something else going on? I've never even seen you cry before. Not once."

She sighs, resting her forehead in her hand briefly before she begins. "Well, something else happened this morning. . . ." She waves her hand in front of her face to fan away the rising emotion.

"Deep breaths."

"Yes." She inhales three times, exhaling dramatically. "This morning. I went to turn on the lights. And they wouldn't turn on." Her hand worries the handkerchief.

"Okay. Did you try replacing the bulbs?"

"You're a little slow today," she says, annoyed.

"I'm sorry," I say. "I don't get it."

"I couldn't pay the bill. I'm totally out of money. Totally and completely wiped out. I have nothing left and only a few weeks to go."

"A few weeks until what?"

"My birthday. I'm going home to Miami. Everyone will know I'm a failure. I said I could do this on my own, but I can't." She hangs her head, tears dripping directly from her eyelids to the lap of her skirt.

"Failure? What? No. Look, I know how you feel. Trust me. But we're supposed to be broke. We're actresses. We're teenagers."

"You're a teenager. I'm almost twenty-one."

"That's so young! Twenty-four is young. Twenty-eight is

young! Thirty-five is . . . Well, thirty-five is old, but we have a long way until then. Let me make us some tea." I walk to the kitchen and fill the kettle.

"But actresses don't age like other people. We age like dogs. One year is worth about seven."

"You've lost perspective. You're not even making sense." I place the kettle on the range, turn it on, lighting it with a match, and pop back out to the living room. "You know what Miss Nancy would say?"

"What?" she asks.

"Deep breath, duck," I say in my best Miss Nancy voice. "Imagine a shock of golden energy coming straight through the pelvic floor, up the diaphragm, and out the nostrils."

"You're ridiculous," she says. She slides out of the harsh sunlight that's streaming in the window and lies down on the sofa.

"You'll get another commercial soon," I tell her. "You obviously have the look."

"Things haven't picked up like I thought they would. I've only had three auditions since, and I didn't get a single callback. I thought after that ECS thing that I was going to be fine, but it turns out it was just beginner's luck."

"You'll get something soon. Or maybe you could find another job? Or maybe Agnes would hire you back. Remember how much you loved it when she gave you all those clothes? Not to mention this awesome furniture." Against her will, her mouth turns up in a smile.

"Stop cheering me up," she says. "I was prepared for a day of self-pity. I even dressed for it." She points to her black ensemble. "What am I going to do about the electric bill?" She lowers her voice. "It's so overdue that it's three hundred dollars. And my cell phone's been cut off, too. And honestly, I don't know how I'm going to eat. I'm lucky my car hasn't been repo'ed."

"Can't you put it on your credit card?" I ask.

"They're all maxed out," she says.

"I'll pay for it," I say. "I'll pay for your cell phone and even help with a car payment. And then we'll go grocery shopping."

"No," she says firmly. "No."

"Yes, yes, yes. We can't live in the dark." I sip my tea. "Literally."

"No," she says, shaking her head. "You've worked so hard to get out of debt."

I shrug. "And now I'm going to help you out. It's what friends do."

"Becca, I can't take money from you."

"You're not taking anything. I'm giving it freely. We need electricity. It's one of those things that define our first-world existence. What are we going to do, use headlamps?" I laugh, picturing Marisol in her vintage nightgown and an industrial-strength headlamp, going about her ten-step evening beauty routine. She starts to laugh, too. "Besides, what if that producer Hal loves *Talk to Me*? I might start making *real* money, baby. TV money."

"That would be so awesome," she says, and we both knock furiously on the wooden café table. "I'm going to pay you back as soon as I can."

The teakettle whistles. I return to the kitchen nook to make our tea.

"I always see this place on Western by that pho restaurant Raj likes. I think it's called the Cash Depot. It's one of those check-cashing places, and according to their neon sign you can pay bills there, too. We'll take care of this after we finish our tea."

She tilts her head and looks me in the eye. "Becca, I've never had a friend like you." Though she shifts her position on the sofa to avoid the glare of the sun, it keeps catching up with her. The light slides over her face again. I notice that there are a few tiny lines around her eyes. I would never tell her that I've noticed them. She would hate that, though they only make me love her more. They're the lines of someone who feels things and shows it. They make me feel like I know someone in this world.

"I'm going to make this up to you," she says, her dark eyes catching flecks of gold as I hand her a mug of chamomile tea.

Her Jeep has not been repo'ed. It's in perfectly fine condition, parked not even a half block away. We hop inside and drive to the check-cashing store, where we pay her electric bill and cell phone bill. The place smells like urine. The carpet is stained and fraying where it was roughly cut to fit this dark, cramped space.

The employees are behind bulletproof plastic. We pay the bill and fly out the door.

"Is that going to be us someday?" I ask her. Then I cover my mouth. "Oh my God, it is us. Today."

"Come on," she says, linking her arm with mine and steering us toward her car. "I need to cleanse your palate. Let's go to Silver Lake—there's a gorgeous new boutique on Sunset."

"My shift starts in two hours," I say.

"We'll just take a peek," she says. "Maybe try on a few things?"

I shouldn't. I don't have a prayer of finishing the Common App, but I can at least write that letter of recommendation for myself for Kingman to sign. And yet, I freeze at the thought. It's almost harder than the essay about failure. Marisol is looking at me.

"On to Silver Lake?" she asks.

"Yeah," I say. And just like that, I've decided not to apply to college. I feel like my insides are floating inside my body. It's freeing—horribly so. "Let's go."

THIRTY-THREE

"DOLPHINS," MARISOL SAYS, pointing to the sleek, arching bodies in the distance.

"Amazing," Raj says. "Are there four of them?"

"I see five," I say. "And I love each one of them. How do they move together like that?"

The air coming off the ocean wraps around me and coats my skin and hair. It's a bright January afternoon, warm and then chilly when a cloud slides across the sun. Raj, Marisol, and I are standing on the damp sand in Malibu on our own private stretch of beach, gazing out at the sparkling blue Pacific. Raj is housesitting for his "douche bag cousin," Brandon, and we are in what is essentially his backyard—the beach. We're all going to spend the night here.

Douche bag or not, he's got an amazing house: modern and minimalist, with the breath of the ocean soothing the place into a dream state. The freezing water nips my toes, and I suck in air, enjoying the sharpness of the sensation. The deadlines have passed. I never submitted the Common App. Honestly, it's a relief that it's over. Now with the cold sand under my feet, the salt stinging my skin, I feel suspended in the moment with the five dark dolphins dipping and rising through waves. The sun catches their fins, and college applications hardly seem to matter.

"I feel like dancing," Marisol says. "I feel like leaping. The spirit of the dolphin is upon me."

"Leap, Marisol, leap!"

"You can't ignore the spirit of the dolphin," Raj says.

Marisol takes off down the beach in surprisingly elegant ballet leaps as the wind whips her hair. Raj and I cheer her on. With his pants rolled up and his hair mussed by the sea air, Raj looks handsome. I can see him as an older person. I can tell he is the kind of guy who gets even better-looking with age.

"What?" he asks, his eyes wrinkling at the corners.

"Nothing," I say. He smiles and shakes his head. I swear sometimes that he can read my mind.

Later that night, we sit on the back deck, wrapped in mohair blankets and drinking hot cocoa. The stars above us are brilliant and infinite. Every surface is coated with sand. The ocean is so loud we have to speak in raised voices to hear each other.

"I didn't apply to college," I say, practically shouting.

I expect to see judgment or surprise on their faces, but instead they just seem to be listening.

"I think it's great," Marisol says with notes of wildness and glee in her voice. "It's fine. We're going to be fine." She's so certain. She's so free. "We're going to be perfect."

"Are you okay?" Raj says. "You were so close with CFS. That collage . . . ?"

"I know," I say, feeling my guts shrink inside me. "The only thing I had left to do was to write my own recommendation letter. Kingman said he'd sign it. And I just . . . I don't know. I couldn't do it. I panicked."

"There's so much you can learn outside of college," Raj says. "And you can always take a class or two."

"Besides, it's not like starting college at twenty would be the craziest thing in the world," Marisol adds. Twenty sounds old to me, worlds away, but I don't dare say this to Marisol, who is so freaked-out about turning twenty-one.

"I should've at least applied to CFS," I say.

"You don't need to worry so much, Becca. And you're not alone. We're in this together," Marisol says.

"But what if I don't make it? What if the phone never rings?"

What if an agent never calls me? What if my mom is right?" I ask.

"I know you love your mom more than anyone in this world. And I'm sure that if you had two lives to live, you'd live one of them for her," Marisol says. "But this is your life. Your only one. You have to live it for you."

"She's right," Raj says.

"The worst part is that I lied to her. I lied to my mom," I say, tears stinging my eyes. But they can't hear me. The wind has picked up and carried my words out to sea.

I wake up the next morning to my phone ringing. I'm under the mohair blanket on the window seat. Marisol is sleeping on the sofa, her mouth wide open and a notebook in her hand. I see the phone on the table with my half-finished mug of hot cocoa and leap to answer it.

"Hello?" My voice is thick with sleep.

"Is this Becca? I have Hal Fogel on the line for you from MTV."

"Yes, yes. It's me," I say. "Please put him through."

"I've got good news, Becca," Hal says.

"Oh my God."

"The execs love *Talk to Me*. We want to hire you to write your own pilot."

"Will I get paid?"

"Of course." He laughs. "That's what 'hire' means. It won't

be crazy. It'll be guild minimum. What is that? Fifty grand? You'll have to look it up."

Fifty thousand dollars? Fifty THOUSAND dollars?

"Wait, do I need an agent?" I ask, panicked.

"No! You already got the job. Why do you want to give away ten percent? Come on by the offices to meet everyone on Tuesday at eleven. Our people will get started on a contract. Sound good?"

"It sounds amazing," I say.

"Enjoy the rest of your weekend. Amelia was right about you—you were totally worth checking out. Congratulations."

"Wait. Amelia was behind this?"

"She told me to go see you in the show."

"Thank you," I say.

I guess my moment with Amelia Kirk, as dreadful as it was, did pay off. I'll have to send her flowers or wine or whatever it is that people send. "Thank you, Amelia," I whisper. "Thank you, thank you, thank you."

I'm about to wake up Marisol and Raj but decide to keep this moment for myself. I let it fill me until I'm light and buoyant. I stand on the window seat and watch the ocean push the shore. I touch the cold glass. I'm a part of things. I'm not on the outside anymore, wanting in. I'm on the inside—the sweet, bright inside of life.

When I get back to the apartment, I make an addition to my list and check it off right away:

1. Get an (agent) —Met with Athena at Talent Commune.
   —Follow up on SAG.
   —Carson Smith, ACE Agency remembered me and got...
√ 2. Get curtains.
√ 3. Get a pillow.
√ 4. Buy pots and pans.
√ 5. Get a kitchen table, bed, and a dresser.
√ 6. Go to the grocery store and get ingredients for healthy meals.
√ 7. Learn how to apply subtle yet effective eye makeup.
√ 8. Get a job to make $$$!
√ 9. Get a friend. (Friends?)
√ 10. Get a new style, new wardrobe, etc.
√ 11. Become a working actress! —Just call me Baby Bear!
                                    YAY VOLKSWAGEN!
   12. ♡Get Alex back.♡
√ 13. BECOME A STAR!!!

THIRTY-FOUR

MARISOL SENDS ME a text the next day.

> Marisol: Off to Miami! See you in a week. Can you water my succulents?
>
> Me: Succulents need watering?
>
> Marisol: And love. Just one drink will do it.

On Tuesday, the day of my meeting at the MTV offices in Santa Monica, I wake up before the sun. I'm just so ready for my new life to begin. It's time to tell my mom the truth. I'm not going to college. I'm going to be a TV mogul! It's so early that I catch her before she's at work.

"Mom, I have some news. I'm going to have my own show on MTV."

"What?" she asks. "Wait, wait. Are you joking?"

"I'm not joking, Mom. They are going to pay me to write and star in my own show."

"Becca! Oh, Becca, I'm so proud of you! Holy . . . I'm about to go into work, but I want to hear the whole story later!"

"That's not it, Mom. There's something else I need to tell you."

"Can it wait? I'm just about to step through the door. There's my boss. I can't wait to tell him. Oh, and I have to put in a special call to Connie Ashworth. Honey, I am bursting with excitement."

"I just had this feeling that I was going to make it," I say, unable to tell her about college. Maybe it doesn't matter now anyway.

"You were so right, baby! You were so right. I'm so proud of you."

As I open the door to the MTV Studios, I catch a glimpse of my reflection in the glass. I can't believe how *myself* I look. It's like my insides and my outsides are finally aligned. I wish I could take a snapshot of this and show it to my earlier self, the one who arrived in September feeling so lost.

Look, I'd say. *It's all going to be worth it. You're going to make it. There's nothing you can't handle.*

Instead, I take a picture with my phone and post it to Instagram: #MTV #DreamsComeTrue.

"Hi, I'm Becca Harrington," I tell the receptionist. "I have an appointment with Hal."

She wrinkles her nose. "He didn't call you?"

"Call me? About what?"

"He's no longer with MTV."

My stomach drops straight to the ground.

"There's got to be some mistake. We just talked on Thursday. He said we had a deal. He said they were drawing up contracts."

"Didn't you read *Variety* this morning?"

I shake my head. My heart is pounding in my chest, and it feels like there's a rock stuck in my throat.

"The whole digital department was fired. New management cleaned house a lot faster than anyone anticipated."

Cleaned house? Jesus, is the world this cruel? Can my dream be ripped away from me like this? My vision blurs as tears sting my eyes.

"So my project is just over?" I ask. I already know the answer by the way she's looking at me—looking through me. I once again feel like an actress coming "off the streets" without a headshot.

"I'm really sorry," she says.

Tears fall down my hot cheeks. I wipe them away with the back of my hand. This can't be possible. "Can I have his phone number? Can I call him?"

"No, no. I'm not allowed to give out private numbers. Soooorrry." She hands me a tissue box.

"Do you know where he is?" I'm openly sobbing now. "In a new office somewhere?"

"I think he said he was going to Palm Springs to clear his

head, but don't repeat that, because I really, really wasn't supposed to say it."

"As if it's of any help at all!" I blurt out, surprised by the rage in my voice. I'm so mad at this innocent receptionist. I'm so mad at Hal. At the new management. At the world.

"Um, you can leave now," she says, scoffing as she sits up a little straighter.

"Fine," I say.

I quickly push the elevator button ten times, but it can't come fast enough. I take the stairs, dash out of the lobby, and onto the Santa Monica sidewalk, which is bathed in the Southern California midday light. It's reflecting off the pale sidewalk and white building. It's so bright I can barely see.

I take the bus home, sitting in the back and weeping into the sleeves of my sweater. Once I reach the Chateau Bronson, I draw Marisol's curtains shut. I want to stay put in the apartment for as long as possible. I want to freeze the world outside while I figure out what the hell I'm going to do with my life. I visit college websites online. I pore over them, envious of the dorms and the classrooms, the structure and the safety. My old life, the one where I wasn't in LA trying to do something so difficult, living on a very sharp edge, fills me with a sense of relief so profound that I actually feel lighter within seconds of considering the possibility that I could have some form of it back.

I pull out my old notebook and pencil and start to put together a new list.

1.	Get a job.
2.	Enroll in whatever school will have me.
3.	Get a life.

I text Chantal and ask her to cover my shifts. Luckily, she's just bought a new Fiat, which is even cuter than Athena's MINI, and she needs more money to cover the payments. She says she's happy to cover my whole week.

Later that night, there's a knock on the door. "Becca. It's Raj."

I freeze, a woodland creature startled by a flashlight, holding the teakettle like a precious nut. I don't want to see anyone. I don't want to explain why I'm wearing pajamas, an inside-out T-shirt (which I've only just realized is inside out), and mismatched socks at 7 p.m. He knocks again.

"Becca, are you in there?" I hold my breath, and as I shift my weight, the floorboards creak beneath me. "I can hear you in there," he says. "I'm dying to know how it went with Hal . . . aaaand I have some really good news." I gingerly place the teakettle on the burner, and it makes a scraping sound. "Helllloooooo?"

I shuffle over to the door, fiddle with the locks, and open it up.

"What happened to you?" he asks. I run a hand through my hair as I watch him take in my disheveled appearance. "Jesus. Are you okay?"

"It's all over," I blurt out.

"What?" he asks.

"The MTV thing," I say, and collapse on my bed. I cover my face with my pillow. "It's not happening."

"Wait, what happened?" he asks, gently removing the pillow.

"The whole digital content team was fired," I say, sitting up. "And it's all over. Just like that." I try to snap, but can't seem to make that satisfying noise. Instead my clammy fingers slip past one another.

"Oh yeah," Raj says, his eyes full of empathy. "I actually heard about that. I just didn't put it together. Your thing seemed so . . . certain."

"Tell me about it," I say. "I guess the guy's in Palm Springs, 'clearing his head.'" I put air quotes around the phrase and roll my eyes. "Where am I supposed to go to clear *my* head to feel better? The *Mayfair*? The fucking . . . Scientologist castle?"

"No! This really sucks, but don't go there. They'll make you do hard labor."

"That's all I do anyway!"

"But they'll make you do it in ugly clothes."

"Who cares?"

"Becca? You're not really going to the Scientologists, are you?"

"No," I say, hanging my head. "I'm just so . . . disappointed.

And broke! I'm broke as a joke. A terrible, old, cliché of a joke."

"Aw," he says. "Come here." He opens his arms. I lean against him. I'm going to have to feel this now. My chest and throat contract as he hugs me. "Come on, give it to me," he says. "Give it all to me. Take a deep breath." We inhale and exhale. All the emotion that I've stifled comes out. Now that I have the comfort of his body, it feels as necessary as air. I grab him tighter. "It's okay," he says, rubbing my back. "You're not alone."

And that's when I start to cry. He holds me close and then even closer. So close that I can smell a mixture of his soap and shampoo at the base of his neck. And something else, too. His very Raj-ness. I hang my chin over his shoulder and let the tears spill down my cheeks and dampen his collar. After a minute he suggests that we go back to his place and get some takeout.

"I kind of want to take a shower first," I say. "I think I might stink from all this heavy emoting."

"Good idea," he says, with a teasing grin.

"I stink?" I ask, smiling for the first time since The News.

"Let's just say that I think a shower would feel good."

I tilt my head in the direction of my armpits and sniff. "Eek. Sorry."

"We're all just human-animals, right?"

"Right," I say. "Would it be okay if I showered at your place? I really don't want to be alone."

"Of course. Bring over your clothes, we'll order some food, you'll take a shower, and we'll chill."

"Sounds good," I say. I step into the closet to gather my stuff. "Hey, wait a second. What's your good news?"

"My screenplay is a finalist for that grant."

"What?" I say, flinging the door open. "What? That's awesome!"

"Yeah," he says. "I wanted you to be the first to know, because you helped me so much."

"Oh my God, Raj! I'm so proud of you!" I say as I gather my clothes and stuff them in a bag. "I knew you could do it!"

"Thanks," he says. "This could be huge for me. Now I just have to shoot a scene from it to be screened at the banquet."

"The banquet I'm going to with you?" I ask as I shut off the lights.

"That's the one. Now let's go browse my menus," he says. "I'm thinking Thai."

"Do you have any conditioner?" I ask from inside Raj's shower. Unlike Reed's bathroom, Raj's is spotless.

"It's in the shampoo," he says. "Don't they just make that part of all shampoo nowadays?"

"You're such a dude," I say.

"I'm going to take that as a compliment," he says. And I laugh.

After the shower, I put on my clean clothes.

"You look better," he says as he dishes the Thai food onto two plates and carries them to the futon.

"What do I do next?" I ask.

"You eat it," he says, handing me a pair of chopsticks. He pulls a plastic fork out of his pocket. "For backup."

"I mean with my life," I say.

"Tomorrow, we come up with a plan. Tonight, we laugh." He shows me his collection of cheesy eighties DVDs. "Are you in a *Beverly Hills Cop* sort of mood? *European Vacation*?"

"*Overboard*," I say, spying Goldie Hawn's goofy smile.

"I thought you might pick that one," he says. "Goldie Hawn is so funny in that."

I take a bite of the Thai food, and the spices clear my sinuses. "Jesus. This'll shock me out of my funk." I guzzle water.

"That was kind of the point."

Later, around midnight, I'm lying on the futon and Raj is in his bed. "Raj," I say into the darkness.

"Yeah?"

"Thank you."

"You're welcome," he says.

"I mean, really. Thank you. You're a great person."

"Well, thanks."

"That movie got me thinking. . . . Maybe I need to go on a cruise," I say.

He bursts out laughing.

"What? I'm serious."

"Have you watched *Titanic* recently?"

"No," I say. "But I'd like to wear those outfits and bring my things aboard in a trunk. I could peer out at the ocean and find answers."

"You'd probably be doing the Electric Slide and getting head lice." We both laugh.

"I want you to know how totally and completely happy I am for you," I say.

"I'm just a finalist," Raj says.

"Still, you're going to shoot a scene that the whole school is going to see. That's so cool. And just so you know, I'd be totally thrilled to play Olivia. Then that part on my fake résumé about being in a student film wouldn't be a lie. I could use it as part of my reel and it'll show my range."

There was a long pause.

"Raj?"

"Yeah?"

"What do you say?"

"I can't talk like that because I don't want to jinx anything."

I totally get it. Right about now I wish I hadn't told a soul about freaking MTV, and I regret typing #DreamsComeTrue with my entire being.

"Raj, can I come in bed with you? I mean, for warmth's sake?"

He pauses. "Sure."

He opens up the blankets, and I crawl inside. It feels nice to be next to another body, and his pillows smell clean. "Thanks." I put my feet on his legs.

"How are your feet cold, even through socks?"

"My feet are always cold. So are my hands." I lay the back of my hand on his cheek, and he pulls away, then takes my hands in his and breathes on them. We face each other now, our knees touching. I inch closer, sticking one of my shins in between his. His hands close around mine. His head bows in toward mine. Our noses are now touching. We're moving closer and closer, until our lips touch. There's a literal electric shock. We both laugh. I close my eyes and we kiss. A warm current runs through me.

"Becca." He pulls away. "You're so distraught. You just need to sleep."

"I don't want to sleep." I'm breathless; I pull him closer with my leg. I kiss his neck.

"Are you sure?" he says, but his legs are intertwined with mine. I lift his shirt and mine so that a band of our bellies touches.

"This is wrong," he says. "I'm taking advantage."

"Making love keeps the body alive," I say in my Miss Nancy voice. With my hands on his back, I feel him laugh and see him smile in the dark. He brushes hair from my face. I take his hand, kiss his palm, and place it on my chest.

"Becca," he says.

He looks at me with deep recognition and awe, and I can feel then that Raj loves me. He loves me the way that I am—rejections and all. We kiss again. This time it's a long, deep kiss that goes on and on. The rest is like swimming at night in a place that you've been to a hundred times during the day. Only now it's quiet. The stars are out. The rocks you've known during the day have changed. They have the same shape but seem to be made of something else. And when you jump in the water, you know it's not just the place that's different. You are, too. You're exhilarated, swimming with your eyes open, rising to the surface, skimming the moon. You're fearless and whole and anything is possible.

THIRTY-FIVE

I WAKE UP AT NOON. Raj has gone to school. I remember him kissing me good-bye. "Stay as long as you want," he said. I see the imprint of his body against the sheets, and place myself in it. Then I remember. It's Marisol's birthday. She's coming home tonight. I need to get back to her place and clean it. I draw a big heart on a piece of notebook paper and leave it on his pillow.

On my way down the hall I leave Marisol a voice mail.

"Happy birthday, Marisol! You're probably with your family, or maybe you're on the plane by now, but I wanted to be one of the first people to wish you a terrific birthday. Also, I have news. I have some bad news. But I also have some good news. I can't wait to see you and tell you everything. Okay, so this is me, giving you a big fat birthday kiss." I make a kissing noise and hang up the phone.

In front of Marisol's door is a padded envelope. It's too big to fit into our mailbox, so the mail carrier brought it inside. As soon as I pick it up, I recognize the handwriting: it's from Alex. He's written *Photos inside, please do not bend.* And I know instantly that this envelope contains the pictures of our trip. I open our apartment door and sit on the bed with the envelope in my hands. I debate throwing it out before even seeing what's inside, but I can't help myself. I rip open the envelope, and the pictures fall out. My heart races as I read the note, written on a scrap of notebook paper.

Becca, Here are the pictures you've been asking for. My roommate thought it would be cool to develop the film for his photography class and I didn't think you'd mind. For what it's worth, he says you're a good photographer. Anyway, I hope you're well and that you finally got that agent you've been wanting. As for these pictures, we had some good times, didn't we? I realize that I've found the perfect word to describe my feelings for you right now. Fond. I'm fond of you and what we shared. That's it! I've got to run to class.

—Alex

I taste what I think is bile in my throat. Fond? He's fond of me? I look through the pictures: Alex and me with our arms around each other in Maine, ankle deep in the ocean in North Carolina, eating ice cream in Texas, kissing in Utah, posing outside a casino in Nevada, tangled in sheets in Palm Springs, the moment right before he broke up with me in Pasadena.

My heart is beating so fast, like I've had too much coffee. I'm short of breath. I can't seem to get enough oxygen. I have to move my body. I have to do something to escape this feeling.

I pull up the shades, put my hair in a ponytail, and blast music. I sit on the fire escape and clean the windows. As I perch on the iron grate and go to town with the Windex, I wonder, What if Raj changes his mind, too? Alex and I were totally in love once, and now he's using the word *fond* like I'm his great aunt or something. What if Raj decides he's only fond of me— without any warning? Without any clues? I can't go through that again. I just can't.

I can't control other people, I think. Then I climb inside the window, and get to work on the tub. But why am I so easy to reject and walk away from? What if I'm not special enough to make an impression on anyone? Reed was all about my great energy, and then he just changed his mind. Okay, no. That was different, I tell myself as I scrub the porcelain until it literally turns a different shade of white. Reed was just a stupid one-night stand. But he and Tamera are still together. He and Tamera have become a thing. Why didn't he want to become a thing with me? What's wrong with me? *Stop it, stop it, Becca,* I tell myself.

You're being totally crazy and irrational. I sacrifice my toothbrush to clean the grout.

As I start to clean up the main room, I put my collage in the closet. Of course, I can't help but focus on my last goal, "become a star," which I'd checked off like a total idiot. I scribble it out like a madwoman, then tear the page off the collage, and throw it on the ground.

"Oh fucky!" I say to myself. "Fucky, fucky, fucky!" And then I gasp. Did that weird phrase actually just come out of my mouth? I have to get out of here. NOW.

I fill my suitcase on wheels with dirty laundry from our hamper and roll it to the Laundromat next to the Mayfair. After I put in the second load of whites I pop over to a coffee shop for a decaf cappuccino. I'm so hyped up that I'm afraid the real thing will send me into cardiac arrest. A guy seated near the window with a laptop is looking at me. He's familiar, but I can't quite place him.

"Do I know you?" he asks.

"I'm in a Volkswagen commercial?"

"No, that's not it." Then he snaps his finger and points at me. "You were in Company One. You were great."

"Oh, thanks."

"You were at the party at Kingman's place, right?"

"Yes," I say.

"And I know your roommate, Anna."

"Sorry?"

"Yeah, from high school in Miami."

"You mean Marisol."

"I guess she goes by Marisol now. As her acting name? I guess it is more memorable than Anna."

"Are you sure you have the right person?" I ask. It's weird to me that Marisol hadn't mentioned that she'd seen an old high school friend that night. Or that Marisol isn't her real name. Aren't we best friends?

"I'm positive. I was a senior when she was a freshman. Anna Mercado."

"No, no. She's Marisol *Alvarez*."

"Right. Anna Marisol Alvarez Mercado. It's not like you forget the name Mercado, you know, because of the rum."

"Mercado rum? Like the biggest rum company in the world?"

"That's the one," he says, laughing.

"No, no. That's not her. She's totally broke. Like me."

"Um . . . no. She's from the *Mercado* family. I mean, I didn't know her very well. But she's kind of a legend. Everyone knew that she was going to inherit like two hundred million bucks on her twenty-first birthday. My mom was always trying to get me to ask her out." He laughs at the thought.

"It can't be," I say. "That makes no sense at all. Like, *at all* at all. Her car was almost repo'ed. I just paid her electricity bill. We share a studio apartment in a building right down the street, which my cousin calls a hovel."

"She was always a really good actress," he says in this way that makes me hate him.

"There's no way she lied to me," I say. My voice is quavering, and I can feel my cheeks flush with anger even though I have the feeling that this guy, this total rando in cargo pants, is the one telling me the truth.

He inches his chair away from me, like he's scared of what I might do next. "Hey, maybe you're right. Enjoy your cappuccino."

I run into the bathroom and splash water on my hot, teary face.

Later that evening, I wait for Marisol. I haven't been able to reach Raj today, but I bet he'll come over later. Around 9:30, the door flies open. Marisol enters in a red shirtdress and new ballet flats, not her usual vintage duds. Something about her is different. Her hair?

"I'm home," she says. "Now, tell me the news before I burst."

"Marisol, are you a millionaire? Are you some kind of heiress?"

She drops her bags and covers her face with her hands.

THIRTY-SIX

"YOU LIED TO ME?" I ask, standing up, feeling as though the walls of this tiny apartment have just closed in another few inches on each side. "You're some kind of undercover rich girl?"

"I didn't outright lie."

"Because I didn't ask you directly if you were a millionaire? What else is there? I mean, do you have a baboon heart?" A headache grips my forehead. I massage my temples.

"Becca, why does it matter?"

"Because I trusted you! Because I gave you almost the last of my money to pay your bills!" I cross my arms. "If it didn't matter, you would've told me."

I turn my back on her and storm into the bathroom, shaking.

"I thought if you knew who I was you would hold it against me—just like everyone else." Marisol follows me, standing in the door frame. "My whole life, this money defined me. Money I had nothing to do with. I was always just the rich girl."

"It's really hard to feel bad for you." With my makeup bag under my arm and my overpriced shampoo in my hand, I squeeze past her, back into the main room.

"I never knew who was my friend and who just wanted a glimpse at our house and the maids and my weird parents. The only people I could trust were my cousins, and they completely suck. I wanted to see if I could make it on my own. I wanted to see what I was like without the money. And I met you." She inhales roughly, her voice catching. "Becca, you're my first real friend."

"That's right. Your friend. I told you everything." I pull my suitcase out from under the bed. I remove my clothes from my one drawer and throw them in. "That was all real to me, but it was some kind of game to you, some kind of social experiment. You were just making shit up."

"It was real. I was broke. I just got the money this week."

"The *money*? Oh, you mean the two hundred *million* dollars?" I look around, panting, for whatever else is mine.

"And you wanted to do those things—pay for things. You said so. You made me believe it was your pleasure. Where are you going?"

"I don't know." I spot my overdue library book (a biography

of Zelda Fitzgerald), my mug, and my sneakers, and stuff them in my bag.

"Becca, can't you see? I'm jealous of what you have."

"You want to have fifty dollars to your name? You want to have to move back to freezing cold Boston and go to some community college? I doubt it. I mean, that's such complete and utter bullshit." I sit on my suitcase, twisting my body to zip it shut. She puts her hand on mine, stopping the zipper. "And by the way, that's something only a rich person would say," I add.

"People love you because of who you are. When you do things, when you get things, no one can say you didn't earn it. It's yours."

"This is my real life, Marisol." I shake her hand off of mine and zip shut the suitcase. "And I have nothing."

"But what about MTV?"

"They backed out. It's all over. Hal is in Palm Springs or something."

"Oh my God. I'm so sorry. Are you okay?" She steps toward me as if she's getting ready to hug me, but I put my hands up, stopping her. She retreats.

"You don't understand. It's so different for you. You can stay here and do whatever you want, whenever you want, for as long as you want. You can be an actress forever. I have to go deal with my life. Don't you think I want to stay out here with you?"

"Don't take your anger out on me." She stomps her foot like a little girl. Fat tears spill down her cheeks.

"You lied to me for our entire relationship. And the worst part"—my voice trembles wildly—"the worst thing is that I thought we were in it together, but this whole time I've been alone."

"We were. I mean, we *are* in it together."

I lose control of my voice. It has a life of its own. It's high and loud. "Then you should've told me the truth."

She pulls back, alarmed by my transformation.

I take a deep breath. "I need to get out of here." I strap on my backpack and bang out the door.

"Wait, don't leave! Where are you going?"

"To Raj's." I head out the door, leaving a pale, speechless Marisol in her doorway.

I knock on Raj's door, and he calls, "Come in."

I open the door and drag my stuff inside. He turns around and beams at me. Then he takes in my stuff, wrinkles his brow, and gives me the one-second signal. That's when I see he's on his computer, FaceTiming with Sierra.

"So we'll need to shoot tomorrow, if you're free," he says. "As early as possible."

"I'll be there at six a.m., camera ready," Sierra says.

"Perfect," Raj says. "I'll text you the directions. And thank you so much for doing this for me last minute. We should be able to get it done in one day, though if you could reserve Thursday in case we need to reshoot, that'd be great, too."

"You know I'd do anything for you, sweetie," Sierra says.

"Thanks, Sierra," Raj says.

"Call me Olivia," she says. "I'm going to start getting in character now."

"You cast her?" I ask, feeling as if this day couldn't possibly get any worse. My throat is as dry as paper.

"Okay, see you soon." Raj quickly signs off and turns to face me.

"Yeah," he says. "I know you said you wanted to play Olivia, but the part is so not right for you. Olivia is supposed to be this controlling, unemotional, unattainable—"

"Unattainable? Beautiful, you mean," I say.

"Oh my God, no. I mean, yes, but that's not why—"

"So you don't think I'm good enough. Is that it?" I ask.

I think it was Ms. Bishop who told me that the heart has muscle memory. Now I know it's true because the place where mine has been ripped in half is burning, tearing at the seams. Heartburn.

"Becca," he says, standing up and taking me by the shoulders. "It's about being right for the part. Just this one part. I have to nail this. The whole school is going to see this."

"Really?" I say, freeing myself from his grip. "So it's not about the fact that she looks like a model and has been on TV. You probably want to take her to the banquet, too, don't you? Because it will impress people."

"NO! Oh my God. I want to go to the banquet with you."

"You're just saying that because we slept together and you

feel bad for me," I say, tears streaming down my face. "Admit it."

"Becca, you're not listening to me." His eyes are wide and panicked.

"Oh no. I'm listening. The message is perfectly clear," I fume.

"You're overreacting!" he says. "Where is this coming from? And it's not like I wasn't going to cast you at all. I was thinking you would make the perfect hotel maid."

My jaw sets, and I can see from his face that he knows he's just made a huge mistake. "That's one of the best parts in the script."

"She doesn't even have a name, Raj," I say. My voice is so low that it's practically a rumble.

"If you'll just come and sit next to me and take a deep breath, I think I can explain this all in a way that makes sense to you."

"No way," I say. Whatever has come over me is strong and angry. "I'm getting out of here."

THIRTY-SEVEN

VIVIAN OPENS THE DOOR to her Pasadena condo, a cup of hot cocoa in hand. I called her from the Uber and told her what happened. She's made up the guest room with sheets, a blanket, and a pillow in a flower-print pillowcase. She's even laid a nice pair of pj's on the bed for me.

"I wasn't sure how you'd react to my call," I say after a hot bath in her sunken tub. I sit on her sofa and put my feet up on the matching ottoman.

"Becca, I'm your family," she says, and stands behind me to brush my hair, just like she used to do when we were little after we went to the beach.

"Thanks, Viv." My voice catches as she brushes my hair in a ponytail.

"You'd do the same thing for me," she says, and sits next to me on the sofa. "I have to say, I'm glad you're out of that place. I've had nightmares about that bathroom." She makes a face and shivers in disgust.

"Come on," I say. "It wasn't that bad."

"Yes it was," she says, and we both laugh.

"Marisol's place was a little nicer. There wasn't any peeling paint or weird bathroom stains."

"I should hope not! That girl is so lucky to have two hundred million dollars," Vivian says. She shakes her head and stares at the ceiling. "I can't even imagine."

My phone buzzes with a text. It's from Chase Quick Pay—Marisol Alvarez has sent you $600.00 and the following message: Here's what I owe you in cash. For what I owe you in friendship there is no sum. Call me.

"Speak of the devil," I say. "She's just paid me back."

"That's a start," Vivian says. "But I didn't trust her from the moment I met her. There was just something off about her that I couldn't put my finger on."

"I never felt that way, but I guess you were right," I say. It makes me feel sick. I wrap my hands around my coffee mug and take a deep breath. "I can't tell you how grateful I am to you for letting me stay until I figure out what I'm going to do. It won't be more than a week, I promise."

"Stay as long as you want." A sly grin crosses her lips. "Maybe you can help me figure out some wedding stuff."

"Wait, what? WHAT?!"

"I can't believe you didn't notice!" She extends her hand to me. A giant rock of a ring sits on her left ring finger.

"Oh my God! You're engaged? Who's the guy?"

"His name is Dan. He's a *lawyer*. An *esquire*. Gorgeous. Grew up in Pasadena. Mom's Chinese, dad's Jewish. Went to Yale and then Harvard Law. He's perfection!" She shows me a picture on her phone of the two of them walking on the beach in matching sweaters. He is pretty damn cute.

"Oooh!" I say, grabbing the phone and giggling. I'm happy for Vivian and desperate to change the subject from my troubles. "Where'd you meet him? Looks like he has a nice body."

"Becca!" she says, snatching her phone back. "I met him right here in this complex. He lives upstairs from me. Can you believe it? All that online dating torture and meanwhile the love of my life was right on top of me."

"Literally!" I say. "And under you, too, I bet!" She laughs and smacks me with a needlepoint pillow.

I laugh with her, but of course this makes me think of Raj, and I have to hold my breath for a second to keep from sliding into tears. "So, when do I get to meet Mr. Foxy, Esquire?"

"He's actually in DC for a few weeks working on a case, but as soon as he comes back we'll have dinner together."

"I'm so happy for you," I say, but as I do, I find myself curling up into a tighter ball.

"Aw, Becca. Don't worry. You'll get back on track." She places one of my feet in her hands and rubs it. "In the meantime, you can hang out here. How about this weekend we go shopping in Old Town? You can help me start my registry. What do you think, Williams-Sonoma, Sur La Table, or Crate and Barrel?"

"I have no idea," I say. "Is there a difference?"

"Oh my God, YES! But I can't do all three or I'll look greedy. You'll help me scope it out this weekend. Maybe while I'm at work you can compare their cookware options. I'd like a matching set, but something really high quality."

"Sure," I say, feeling like this is a task I can succeed at, even though it's pretty much the last thing I want to do. "I can do that."

"You know that you have to tell your mom about not applying to college, right?"

Actually, *that*'s the last thing I want to do.

"I can't believe you lied to me," Mom says when I call her first thing in the morning. Vivian has gone to work and I'm sitting at her kitchen table, drinking from one of her designer mugs. Chantal has texted me to tell me she'll cover another shift for me, but I'd better be back soon because "despite what you might think, I do have a life!"

"I'll pay you back for the application fees," I tell her.

"I know you will," Mom said. "But honestly, Becca, I'm not upset about the money. I just don't understand what happened. You've never lied to me before. Why didn't you come to me to talk? I could've helped you. We could have gone through this together. You wouldn't be in this situation right now. In fact, if you'd let me—"

"Mom, Mom, Mom, stop. Please." I can feel her revving up for a lecture. "I'm really scared right now. I'm really lonely."

"I know." She takes a breath. "I know. Do you have enough money to come home?"

"I have about eight hundred dollars total. But I'm not sure if coming home is what I want."

"I'll book you a ticket home as soon as possible. Then we can start over. Get you enrolled in some classes this summer. Hire that college specialist that Mr. Walker told me about—"

"You're not listening, Mom. I'm not sure if that's the best decision for me."

There are a few seconds of silence before Mom sighs and says, "I guess if there's one thing I've learned from this situation, it's that I can't make you do something you don't want to do. So what do you want?"

"I'm not sure yet," I say.

"Okay. We did say you'd give it a year. You're never alone in this world, Becca. You always have me. Why don't you just take a little time, see if you can get some perspective, and let me know. I'll come out there and get you if you want. You know that, right?"

"Yeah, I do." My mom really is the only one I have in this world. For sure and no matter what. "I love you to the sky."

"And back," she says.

That weekend, while Vivian and I are strolling from Williams-Sonoma to Sur La Table in Old Town, I look up and see a billboard that takes my breath away. "Time for Girls' Night Out . . . at the Olive Garden!" is written at the top in loopy purple script. Below is a picture of four girls drinking wine, sitting around a table with a checkered tablecloth and a centerpiece of breadsticks, bowls piled high with pasta steaming before them. The group is focused on the well-dressed girl in the center who's laughing with her mouth open, whose eyes are crinkling at the corners, whose hand is open, midair, mid-gesture, as if to catch the night by the necktie and take it for a spin on a nearby dance floor. It's Marisol. I feel like I've been struck by a blunt object.

There's no place I want to be more than at that table at the Olive Garden with that girl, whispering something ridiculous, recounting a childhood memory over a piece of mass-produced cheesecake—the story at hand told with the color and action of a tentpole movie—our laughter tilting the world in our direction, giddy on free soda refills. I fish my phone out of my purse.

"Marisol, I'm looking at your face in Old Town. You look great."

"Becca!" Her voice is full of relief.

"But I have to ask, what kind of heiress does a print ad for Olive Garden?"

"A very sorry one?"

"I miss you," I gasp into the phone. "I miss you so much."

"Come home, then," she says. "Please, come on home."

THIRTY-EIGHT

THE NEXT DAY Marisol picks me up in her Jeep, and we go whale watching in Dana Point.

We're sitting on a boat with a bunch of German tourists. The sky is damp and gray. She wraps her shawl around both of us. She talks about how lonely she's been this week, too. I don't bring up the money. I don't ask the questions I really want to. Like, do you get it all at once? Are there bricks of money piled in some vault, or is it in stocks and bonds? Have you spent it on anything yet? Even with Marisol, there's a dome of privacy around the subject of money. I'm not allowed to ask; I can just feel it. I need to have something private, too. So I don't tell her what I need to tell her most, that I slept with Raj and am confused as hell about my feelings. Instead, I tell her about how I'm going back to Boston.

"Wait, why are you going back to Boston?"

"Because I'm broke? Because everything fell through? Because . . . oh, I don't know . . . I don't have a secret stash of millions of dollars that allows me to do whatever I want."

Marisol grabs my arm, forcing me to look at her.

"This is the reason why I didn't want to tell you. I knew you'd push me away."

"What are you talking about?"

"If we're fortunate today, we may get a glimpse of a blue whale," a tour guide booms over a loudspeaker. "Lucky for us, there have been sightings in the area in the past few weeks. A hundred feet in length, two hundred and ten tons, with a heart the size of a Volkswagen Bug, blue whales are thought to be the heaviest creatures to have ever existed."

"You're the one who thinks you're not as good as people who have money, or people who get into college, or people who book commercials."

"That's so not true," I say, my arms crossed, my hands curled in fists.

"Listen to me. All these college rejections have really messed with you. You think the world is a club that you can't get into. But it's bullshit. You're looking for proof against yourself."

"Aren't you the psychologist."

"No, I'm your friend. And friends tell the truth." She blushes as she says this, realizing the irony. "You taught me that. I want my friend back, but that's not going to happen until you let go of this stupid, fucked-up idea that you don't deserve things." I tear up. I do feel alone. I do feel deprived. She takes my hand. "You deserve everything, Becca. You're incredible. A star." I bow my head as tears streak down my face. "And you don't have to feel alone ever again," she says, wiping away her own tears. "Not if I can help it."

She hugs me and I hug her back, clutching her sweater. She pulls out an antique handkerchief and dabs her eyes.

"I slept with Raj," I blurt, "and then I just freaked out."

"What?" She shakes me, smiling. "It's about time. When?"

"Over to the port, or left side of the boat, you can see a friendly pod of dolphins frolicking," the tour guide says. People rush to the left side of the boat, pulling out their cameras and binoculars. Marisol and I stay put.

"The night before I saw you. But then the very next day he cast that girl Sierra in his movie. Have you talked to him?"

"Of course I have. Since you haven't been picking up your phone, he's been knocking on my door asking if I've heard anything from you. I think you two just had a misunderstanding. It's possible to not be right for a part, you know. I think that's all that happened."

"I freaked," I say. "I just totally freaked out."

The sun is out and even though seconds ago it was freezing, suddenly it's hot.

"Folks, we have a blue whale!" the tour guide says. "She's approaching from the starboard, or the right of the boat. The captain is going to turn off the motor and see if she'll come to us."

"You need to talk to him," Marisol says. "Now, come on, let's go see this whale." We link arms and join the tourists. "Come back home. Please."

"I'm trying to get my shit in order."

Marisol doesn't respond. She just takes my hand. Moments later, I see a spray of water. Then a massive gray back rises from the water, taking our collective and international breaths away. A giant tail appears, raining ocean water. We gasp, and Marisol kisses my hand.

"Look, look," Marisol says, squealing.

"I know," I say, as the whale breaches. "She's like a miracle."

"She is," Marisol says, and rests her head on my shoulder.

THIRTY-NINE

I'M COUNTING MY TIPS at the counter—over two hundred and fifty bucks, not bad for brunch—when my phone buzzes with a text. It's a group text from Kingman. He's testing out some funky old plays tonight, public domain stuff, to see if any of them would be suitable for productions this spring. He's looking for actors to come and do read-throughs. No pay, of course, but he's going to bring some pizza and beer. Casting is not in any way guaranteed, he writes, but the people who show up get first crack at the material. I feel a buzzing in my chest at the thought of being back at Company One. It might not pay the rent, but it's real acting in a legit theater with like-minded people.

Peanut emerges from the kitchen with a salmon salad and places it in front of me.

"For me?" I ask. It's the priciest thing on our menu.

"Kitchen mistake." He winks and puts some change in a jukebox.

"Thanks," I say. Moments later, a Frank Sinatra standard fills the empty restaurant. Peanut sings along. To my surprise, he has a pretty voice.

"You sound good, Peanut," I say.

"I have dreams, too, you know," he says, and he smiles as he returns to the kitchen.

"I think you can make it," I call after him.

As I pour myself a Coke to go with my salad, I decide that Company One is like my college. Kingman is just as respected and knowledgeable as anyone teaching at Juilliard, I'm sure. But I didn't really get to learn from him the way that the rest of the cast did because I was a late addition. If I got in at the beginning of the process, I bet I'd grow a lot as an actress. I'm totally embarrassed about not having written that letter, but there are worse things in life than being embarrassed. Nothing could have been more humiliating than the Amelia gaffe, and that actually led to something good—or almost good. Which reminds me that I need to send her something for hooking me up with Hal.

Flowers, I decide as I take a bite of the finest food Rocky's Café has to offer, and the crooning voice of Frank Sinatra puts me in a sentimental mood. Flowers are classic.

When I show up at Company One that night, most of the old cast is there along with a handful of other people I don't recognize but who I gather are from previous shows. Tamera and Reed are holding hands.

"What's up, bud?" Reed asks me.

"Not much, chief," I say. "What's up with you?"

He smiles bashfully and Tamera leans into him. They have that look of love about them. That glow. I guess Tamera is the one to end his player ways. I'll never know why, and he probably won't either. Love is weird like that. Kingman gestures for us to sit around the table, which is set up in the middle of the stage.

"Okay," he says. "So tonight we'll be reading a play from the nineteenth century called *Billy the Kid*. This is some weird shit. I think we could have some fun with it. Or maybe it'll be a total dud. Who the fuck knows? Let's read it and see what happens. Who'd like to read for Billy, iconic bad boy of the West?"

Reed, the quintessential handsome cowboy, raises his hand. Kingman is about to toss him a script when I shoot my hand in the air.

"I'd like to try," I say. Kingman raises his eyebrows. He smiles and hands the script to me instead. "Go for it."

"I will," I say, and smile back.

❀

Despite Marisol's request, I'm not quite ready to return to the Chateau. After the Company One meeting, which was some of the most fun I've had since I've moved to LA, I go back to

Vivian's condo and spend another quiet night in her guest room. After she leaves for work, I decide to call Alex. Not because I want him back, but because I have something to say to him, regardless of how he feels about it. After I have a cup of coffee, I dial his number. This time I'm not sweating or panicking. I have no expectations.

He answers right away.

"Hey, Becca," Alex says. "What's up? Did you get the package?"

"Yes," I say. "Thanks for sending those. And also, Alex, I just want to tell you something." I'm about to tell him how much he hurt me, but I stop myself. I know he knows this all too well. "I wish you'd found a kinder way of treating me."

"I just felt like you wanted something I couldn't give," he says.

"Come on, Alex," I say. "You're better than that."

He's quiet for a moment. I can hear in this pause that he knows I've nailed him. Alex, smartest boy in our class, wordsmith extraordinaire, is speechless. "I'm sorry."

"Thank you," I say. And we both sigh.

"So, what are you thinking for next year?" he asks.

"I'm not totally sure," I say. "I'm working on it."

"I just want to put it out there that I think you're too smart to be an actress. And you're definitely way too smart for LA."

"Thanks," I say quietly, because I know he means this as some kind of compliment. People don't respect actors unless they're famous. Until then, we're just wasting our time. People think that we're selfish, reality-avoiding, self-obsessed, vain, insecure, immature dreamers. It's probably true for some of the actors out there, but I don't agree with this generalization at all. It's certainly not true for me or Marisol. As for LA, there's nothing about this place that's stupid. It's complex and contradictory and gorgeous and smoggy and too hot. But it's not stupid. "But I don't agree with you."

"That's fair," he says. "You always did have your own opinions."

Duh, I think.

"I got a new car," he says. "One I can take to go to Tahoe in the winter."

"That's great," I say, realizing with a little kick of elation that I don't care. "I hope you take some awesome trips in it."

After I hang up, I'm ready to go back to the Chateau. Maybe not for good, but for a little while, or at least until I figure out what I'm doing next. I pack my suitcase and take an Uber back to Hollywood. Marisol is waiting for me in her kimono.

"This came for you this morning," she says, and hands me an envelope from Raj. "Open it."

I do, and inside is the ticket to the banquet and a note.

I know you're mad, but I really want you to be with me tonight. Please come. You're so much a part of this, it won't feel right to not have you beside me. I love you. Raj.

"That is so sweet I think I'm going to puke," Marisol says.

"Marisol!" I say. "That's private."

"Shut up. You have to go."

"I don't know if I can face him after my freak-out."

"He told you he loves you, fool!"

I can't suppress my smile.

"But what if Sierra is there, too? What if I see her and panic?"

"First of all, I really doubt she's going. And secondly, do you really think that's going to happen? Do you really think you have so little control over yourself that you're going to spaz at a formal banquet at California Film School?"

"I honestly don't know," I say. "I scared the shit out of myself the other day."

"You need to get your head on right." She takes another look at the ticket. "Okay, this thing starts in two hours. I'm sending you for a walk around the block to clear your mind. When you come back I'm going to have an outfit laid out for you."

"If Sierra goes, she's probably going to look gorgeous," I say.

"Go for your walk and get perspective," Marisol says.

"I, like, invented Olivia," I say, as she's pushing me out the door.

"You're taking this whole situation the wrong way. Get out there and take some deep breaths."

I head out of the Chateau for a walk around the block. I blink against the bright light, wishing I'd brought sunglasses. It hurts to lift my gaze above the sidewalk. I walk past the house with the sofa on the front porch that Marisol and I think is a halfway house. I continue beyond the apartment complex with a dark red rock garden that looks like it's from Mars. I pass the house with the overgrown lawn, odd assortment of potted cacti, and the lemon tree. I pick up a fallen lemon that's escaped the chain-link fence. It's nestled under a tree whose roots are bursting through the cement and climbing with bougainvillea vines, the papery hot-pink leaves rustling in the breeze. It's hard to believe it's January. I'm about to turn onto Franklin, when who do I see running right toward me in his skimpy workout gear, dripping with sweat, a stone-cold look of determination in his eyes? Oh Fucky.

I can't, I think. I can't handle seeing him right now. I do an about-face, but before I can turn all the way around, he taps me on the shoulder. I can smell his sweat and feel the heat radiating off of his body.

"Hi," I say.

"Long time no see," he says, taking a microfiber towel from the waist of his shorts and wiping off his face. "So, I need to ask. Is that guy I've seen you driving around with your boyfriend?"

"Yes," I say without even thinking about it.

"Damn," he says. "You're so cute. I could just . . ." He sucks air through his teeth.

"Thank you, but please don't elaborate."

"You can probably tell that I'm always trying to improve myself."

"I can see that," I say.

"So I'd just like to know, why did you choose him over me?"

he asks. As ridiculous as he is, there's sadness in his eyes that I can't ignore.

"It's hard to say," I say. As I try to formulate an answer, I think of Alex. Yes, he could've been kinder to me, without a doubt. He could've treated me in a way that acknowledged everything we shared. But ultimately if he didn't love me anymore, there's not much he could do about it. He could've done better—a *lot* better—but he wasn't trying to be mean. Love can't be manufactured just because someone else wants it from you. "I guess we can't really explain our feelings, right?"

"I have no regrets," he says, staring into the distance. "The greatest risk is the one not taken."

"I believe that," I say.

"Do you? I have that quote in a very tasteful frame in my apartment, which you would know if you'd even given me a chance," he says.

"It's good advice," I say.

"And especially true when it comes to love. What's the worst thing that can happen?"

"A broken heart, I guess," I say, thinking to myself, I cannot believe I'm having this conversation with Oh Fucky, whose shorts are way too tight, and who I swear is standing in such a way that he wants me to check him out.

"Eh, there are worse things," he says. "Besides, in order for the heart to really open, it needs to break at least a little."

"Wow," I say, stunned by this unexpected wisdom.

"Booyah!" he shouts, making me jump a bit. "You didn't

know I was so deep, did you? Hey, are you going to use that lemon?"

"Take it," I say, and hand it to him.

"Did you know a lemon has more antioxidants than a pomegranate?"

"No, I didn't."

"See how much you could've learned from me," he says.

"My loss," I say.

"True dat. Now, if you'll step out of the way, I'm going to bring it home hard, like I always do, baby."

I step aside. With the lemon in one hand, he sprints toward the Chateau like a man on fire.

FORTY

EVEN THOUGH MARISOL gave me a ride in her Jeep, I feel like a star as I enter the Palace Theatre, a recently restored movie theater from the 1940s. California Film School went all out when they rented this space for their Winter Banquet. It's downtown, on a street mostly lined with dollar stores, food stands, and sketchy motels. But inside, the theater has been returned to the glory of the golden age of film. The lobby is flat-out gorgeous with a red carpet, grand staircase, sparkling chandeliers, gilded ceilings, and ornate murals.

I barely make it past the entrance when I spot Juice Man, taking a glass of champagne from a server's tray. *Okay, universe,* I think. *Message received.*

"I think it's time we meet," I say. "I'm Becca Harrington."

"I know," he replies.

I blink.

"You do?" I ask.

He nods.

"Who are you?"

"Sam Hallgren." We shake hands.

"Hello, Sam. So, what are you doing here and how do you know who I am?"

"I'm a CFS alum and this is a great event not only for the free food and booze, but also for finding new talent. I know who you are because I was an agent with the Talent Commune for the past few years."

He's an agent?

"I met with them," I say.

"I know," he says. "When we ran into each other in the building lobby, I saw on the sign-in sheet that you met with Athena."

"Yeah, we weren't a match," I say.

"But I've been keeping an eye on you."

"You have?" Is this why I've been seeing him everywhere? Because he was looking for me?

"Yeah, you were genuinely funny in that bear play. I was actually laughing during that chase scene. And I thought you nailed it in the Company One production. I mean, even *Variety* noticed. Plus everyone's talking about the girl in the Volkswagen commercial."

"Really?" Everyone? Who the hell is everyone? "Why?"

"Casting directors want *authentic*. And you have that in spades. It's very appealing—and rare."

"Wow," I say, standing a little taller. "I guess I do have that."

"Yes." He smiles. "Anyway, I'm actually starting my own agency. I'll only have a few clients. But if you'd be willing to take a chance on me, I'd like to take a chance on you. You want to come in to my office for a meeting next week?"

Are you freaking kidding me?

"I'd love to!" I say.

"Let's get it on the books." He whips out his iPhone and says, "How's Monday?"

"It's perfect," I say. I give him my number, and he texts me the information.

"See you next week," he says.

An agent! An actual agent who wants to work with me! I feel color fill my cheeks, and I can't stop smiling. I feel like I'm weightless, like my veins are flowing with champagne, as I maneuver through the crowd to look for Raj. I'm glad that I borrowed Marisol's floor-length emerald-green silk dress—a vintage piece that was a hand-me-down from Agnes. It fits me perfectly, and as I catch a glimpse of myself in one of the gilded mirrors, I realize I've never looked better.

Then I see him. Raj. He's in a tuxedo, looking as handsome as I've ever seen him. He's talking to an older couple, also dressed to the nines. In fact, I don't want to let him see me yet. I just want to admire him for a few more seconds. I definitely don't have to worry about manufacturing feelings for Raj. My love for him is clear and as palpable as the pounding of my heart. I can feel my cheeks flush as I approach him.

"Hi," I say. Without thinking about it, I slip my hand into his.

"Becca," he says, and smiles at me. "You're here." He squeezes my hand and looks at me with such sweetness and hunger that I have to look away or risk bursting into flames. He leans in to kiss my cheek.

"I'm sorry," I whisper.

"Me too," he whispers back. "It's okay." He pulls away and gestures to the older couple. "Your timing is perfect. There's someone I want you to meet. Becca Harrington, this is Bill and Margo Rushfield. Bill is my teacher and the head of the new media department."

"And a big fan of *Talk to Me*," Bill says.

"Really?" I ask. "Oh, right! Raj mentioned he showed it to you."

"He did, and I was really impressed. Your voice is so fresh. I think you have a lot to offer. You can imagine how pleased I was to pass on your application to Jonah Kaplowitz, our director of admissions."

"My . . . application?" I ask.

"That's right," Raj says, and squeezes my hand again. "The complete application."

"Isn't it too late?" I ask.

"Deadlines are more like strong suggestions," Bill says, and chuckles.

"At least when it comes to exceptional applicants," Margo says. "So don't quote him on that."

"Jonah will be contacting you for an interview soon," Bill says. "I'm making sure of it because I want you in my class."

"Thank you," I say. I'm breathless, bowled over by the joy that has been this day.

"You're welcome," he says. "Raj, good luck to you today."

"We'd better go mingle," Margo says. "See you two at the reception." Bill and Margo disappear into the crowd.

"Oh my God, how did you do that?" I ask Raj.

"Your application was done. Marisol found it. All we needed to do was to turn it in with your collage."

"But I didn't have a second recommendation letter," I say.

"Marisol wrote it," Raj says.

"As Kingman?" I ask, horrified for a moment by thoughts of a forged signature.

"No, just as herself. She wrote about your talent, your spirit, your courage, your ambition. You've got to read it. It's a work of art. She loves you. And so do I."

"I love you, too," I say as tears prick my eyes. "Thank you."

The lobby lights blink. An announcer says that the screenings will begin in five minutes.

"Let's go find our seats," Raj says. "The show's about to start."

Together we go inside.

☆☆☆☆☆ ☆

1. Get an (agent!) — Met with Athena at Talent Commune. — SAM HALLGREN!!!!!
      Follow up on SAG.
      — Carson Smith, ACE Agency, remembered me and got me an audition!.
✓ 2. Get curtains.
✓ 3. Get a pillow.
✓ 4. Buy pots and pans.
✓ 5. Get a kitchen table, bed, and a dresser.
✓ 6. Go to the grocery store and get ingredients for healthy meals.
✓ 7. Learn how to apply subtle yet effective eye makeup.
✓ 8. Get a job to make $ $ $!
✓ 9. Get a friend. (Friends?)
✓ 10. Get a new style, new wardrobe, etc.
✓ 11. Become a working actress! — Just call me Baby Bear!
   12. ~~Get a boyfriend~~   YAY VOLKSWAGEN!
✓ 13. BECOME A STAR!!! ☆
         — Actually... I'm gonna keep working on this one.

ACKNOWLEDGMENTS

A HUGE THANK-YOU—always—to Emily Meehan, life-changer and visionary. Endless gratitude to Kieran Viola, editor extraordinaire, who helped shape this book with her pitch-perfect ear, amazing storytelling skills, and patience. Working with you has been an absolute gift and an author's dream. Thanks also to Heather Crowley, Cassie McGinty, Marci Senders, and the whole talented bunch at Hyperion. You rock! Sara Crowe, my super agent, you make everything possible. Thank you. I could not have finished this book without the love and support of Kayla Cagan and Vanessa Napolitano, dear friends and fellow writers; Penny Hill, library buddy and life support; and my beloved friends and family. Most of all I'd like to thank Henry, the sunshine of my life.